A DREAM
TO CALL MY OWN

A DREAM TO CALL MY OWN

Brides of Gallatin County

BOOK THREE

TRACIE PETERSON

BETHANY HOUSE PUBLISHERS

Minneapolis, Minnesota

A Dream to Call My Own
Copyright © 2009
Tracie Peterson

Cover design by Andrea Gjeldum

Scripture quotations are from the King James Version of the Bible.

Published by Bethany House Publishers
11400 Hampshire Avenue South
Bloomington, Minnesota 55438

Bethany House Publishers is a division of
Baker Publishing Group, Grand Rapids, Michigan.

Printed in the United States of America

Library of Congress Cataloging-in-Publication Data

Peterson, Tracie.
   A dream to call my own / Tracie Peterson.
      p.   cm. — (Brides of Gallatin County ; 3)
   ISBN 978-0-7642-0682-5 (alk. paper) — ISBN 978-0-7642-0150-9 (pbk.)
— ISBN 978-0-7642-0683-2 (large-print pbk.) 1. Sisters—Fiction. 2. Frontier and pioneer life—Fiction. 3. Montana—Fiction. I. Title.
   PS3566.E7717D74   2009
   813'.54—dc22

                                    2009005412

To those in Belgrade, Montana,
who bless me daily.
You know who you are.

Books by Tracie Peterson

www.traciepeterson.com

A Slender Thread • *What She Left For Me*
Where My Heart Belongs

SONG OF ALASKA
Dawn's Prelude

ALASKAN QUEST
Summer of the Midnight Sun
Under the Northern Lights • *Whispers of Winter*

Alaskan Quest (3 in 1)

BRIDES OF GALLATIN COUNTY
A Promise to Believe In • *A Love to Last Forever*
A Dream to Call My Own

THE BROADMOOR LEGACY*
A Daughter's Inheritance • *An Unexpected Love*
A Surrendered Heart

BELLS OF LOWELL*
Daughter of the Loom • *A Fragile Design* • *These Tangled Threads*

Bells of Lowell (3 in 1)

LIGHTS OF LOWELL*
A Tapestry of Hope • *A Love Woven True* • *The Pattern of Her Heart*

DESERT ROSES
Shadows of the Canyon • *Across the Years* • *Beneath a Harvest Sky*

HEIRS OF MONTANA
Land of My Heart • *The Coming Storm*
To Dream Anew • *The Hope Within*

LADIES OF LIBERTY
A Lady of High Regard • *A Lady of Hidden Intent*
A Lady of Secret Devotion

RIBBONS OF STEEL**
Distant Dreams • *A Hope Beyond*

WESTWARD CHRONICLES
A Shelter of Hope • *Hidden in a Whisper* • *A Veiled Reflection*

YUKON QUEST
Treasures of the North • *Ashes and Ice* • *Rivers of Gold*

*with Judith Miller   **with Judith Pella

TRACIE PETERSON is the author of over seventy novels, both historical and contemporary. Her avid research resonates in her stories, as seen in her bestselling HEIRS OF MONTANA and ALASKAN QUEST series. Tracie and her family make their home in Montana.

Visit Tracie's Web site at *www.traciepeterson.com*.

CHAPTER ONE

LATE JANUARY 1881

Maybe it was cabin fever as well as the announcement from Beth that she was expecting. It might even have been the anxiety of waiting for Gwen's baby to finally arrive. Whatever the reason, Lacy Gallatin awoke an hour earlier than usual with only one thought on her mind: *I have to get out of here for a time.*

She got up and dressed quickly, layering warm flannel trousers over thick wool stockings. Next she put on her heaviest split wool skirt and warmest blouse and sweater. Lacy then tied her hair back in a single braid and completed her outfit with her heavy winter boots.

Taking up her saddlebag, Lacy packed several articles of clothing. She penned a quick note to her sisters, doing her best to explain that the gloomy weather had taken its toll on her.

She read the last lines aloud, as much to strengthen her conviction as to assure herself she'd said the right thing. " 'I will be all right. Please don't send anyone after me. I'm not certain where I'm headed, but I assure you I can take care of myself.' "

And she could. Lacy had a little money and a lot of know-how. She was a good horsewoman and a crack shot with the rifle. There had been no reports of highwaymen since the weather had turned so bad the past month. There would always be the threat of wolves, but Lacy could contend with them if she had to. That left only battling the elements.

Hurrying downstairs, Lacy grabbed a few items of food and stuffed them into her bags along with her clothes. If a blizzard came up before she figured out where to go, she'd be able to wait it out. She pulled on her heavy coat and scarf and secured her flannel hat. Her last act was to grab matches, a small tin pot, and a canteen from the back porch.

Blackness engulfed Lacy as she slipped from the house. Within another half hour or so her family would wake up to start their day. The long hours of darkness didn't stop or even slow life when it came to caring for livestock and seeing that the community had access to the store. Lacy was glad there wasn't a stage due in or out. The weather had reduced the number of trips being made to Gallatin Crossing, and given Gwen's condition, that had been a very good thing. There would be no big breakfast to prepare and serve. No abundance of laundry to wash.

Lacy sighed. She felt she fell short even when it came to doing her part at Gallatin House, the roadhouse she and her sisters operated. She had done minor repairs and some of the heavier work after their father was killed, but now that Gwen and Beth had married and Hank and Nick were in residence, she was relegated to household chores. That left Lacy with very little purpose. She simply didn't belong anymore.

The cold air bit at her face and hands but did little to deter Lacy from her task. She pulled on her gloves—heavy woolen ones that she used for outdoor work—and set out across the yard. Her boots made a crunching sound in the snow and left a very obvious trail from the house to the store.

Hank had helped Nick to build a rather large corral behind the store where he could keep the stage horses ready and waiting. To Lacy's benefit, the store hid the corral and her activities. She could only pray that everyone would remain asleep or otherwise busy with their own chores while she got away.

The horses had taken shelter together in the loafing shed and seemed somewhat curious as Lacy interrupted their morning. "It's all right, boys," she told the gathered geldings. Her own mount nudged her for a treat, but Lacy shook her head. "Not this time, fella." She saddled him quickly and tied on her saddlebag. She climbed into the saddle and wrapped the canteen strap and tin pot's handle around the horn.

"Come on, boy," she urged as they moved across to the gate. Lacy easily managed the gate on horseback. She'd done this a number of times before, and the gelding seemed to understand now what was expected of him. With a quick glance at Gallatin House, Lacy could see that lamps were lit in the upstairs windows. Her family was awakening to face a new day. It was time to leave.

A whine caught her attention. She glanced down to see that Major had followed her. "Not this time, boy. Go home." The dog looked at her sadly. "Go on, now. Go!" she commanded with as much harshness as she could manage. Major dropped his head and turned back toward the house. Lacy felt terrible for putting him from her, but she had no idea of where she might go. She had odd images of just riding around in circles for days.

"I should have thought this through better." The horse nickered as if in agreement. "Oh, what do you know?" She nudged the horse's flanks and put him in motion.

Lacy was glad it had stopped snowing. The roadway was much traveled, leaving the previous snow beaten down by stage and freight wagons, as well as local ranchers and riders coming and going. With no more than a new inch or so, the horse would have a fairly easy time of it.

In the coming light of morning, Lacy could just make out her way. She hadn't really considered her path but knew almost instinctively that she was headed for Patience and Jerry Shepard's ranch, four miles out of town. Patience had been like a mother to her, and Lacy desperately needed that right now. Perhaps she would just ask Patience to sit for a time and talk; then Lacy could head out to . . . to where?

The winds were surprisingly calm and as the light dawned over the southern reaches of the mountains, Lacy could see that the clouds had cleared. Maybe they would have a bright sunny day after all.

An orange-yellow sun rose in full, streaking the skies in red and pink hues. It wasn't a good sign; even the Bible warned about such things as an omen for bad weather. Lacy tried to put it from her mind. At least the temperature seemed to warm a bit as the sun climbed higher. She knew that by now her family would be preparing to face the day. They wouldn't worry about where she was for a time, but when breakfast was on the table, someone would go to fetch her and find a note instead.

"They'll probably be mad," she told the horse. "Dave will

be madder than the others. As the law in this area he'll take it upon himself to hunt me down." The thought of Dave Shepard, Patience and Jerry's son, brought unexpected warmth to her cheeks. As deputy, Lacy knew he had plenty to keep him occupied today. He'd spoken the night before of going to Bozeman if the weather was good.

"Hopefully, he'll just do as he planned and leave me alone. He might even think I've gone to Bozeman."

The horse bobbed his head as if agreeing. Lacy patted his neck. "I'm sorry for bringing you out in the cold without so much as a few oats to start your day. I'll make it up to you, though. The Shepards will see you well cared for."

"Well, at least we know now why she wasn't downstairs to help," Beth said, waving the note at her sister. "She's decided to take herself on a little journey."

"What do you mean?" Gwen asked.

"She says the winter has gotten to her, and we're not to worry about her or her whereabouts." Beth handed Gwen the letter. "Honestly, sometimes that girl doesn't make any sense to me."

Gwen shook her head. "I wonder when she left. It must have been sometime in the night."

"What must have been sometime in the night?" Hank asked his wife as he entered the kitchen. He went to take up a coffee mug and stepped to the stove. He looked up at Gwen. "Well?"

"Lacy decided to go off by herself."

Hank poured coffee into his cup. "Off by herself where?"

"We don't know," Beth admitted. "She just said winter was getting to her. She also said she'd be all right and that we weren't to send anyone after her."

"Has she done this before?"

Gwen nodded. "Yes, but it's been a while. You know how unpredictable she can be."

"You must be talking about Lacy," Dave said as he came in behind Hank. "Ah, I see you had the same idea I did." He grabbed a mug and poured himself some coffee. "Nick is stoking up the fire in the front room, Beth. He said he'd get Justin down to breakfast in just a minute."

"Lacy's gone," Beth announced matter-of-factly.

Dave looked at her as if she'd gone mad. "What do you mean, 'gone'?"

"Gone. She took off. She left a note saying she wanted some time away."

Gwen nodded in confirmation. "She says she can take care of herself, but . . ." Her words trailed off as she clenched her eyes shut and clutched her stomach. Then she opened her eyes and smiled softly at her husband. "Hank . . . I think it's my time."

"Are you sure?" Beth asked.

"I've been having some back pain since last night, but now it's starting to intensify and spread to the front. I think the baby is coming."

"What should we do?" Hank asked, turning rather pale.

"I suppose send for the doctor. If Gwen's been having pain all night," Beth surmised, "the baby could be nearly here. I'll help her to bed."

"But what about breakfast?" Gwen asked as if they'd all suddenly gone mad.

Dave laughed. "We can manage it for ourselves. You let Hank and Beth get you settled in. I'll go for the doc."

Dave was just happy to be out of the house. Women giving birth made him nervous. He could still remember when his younger sisters had been born. He'd been quite young, and his mother's screams of pain were terrifying.

Thankfully, there was a new doctor in Hamilton. It wouldn't take long at all to reach him and get help. Dave urged the horse to pick up speed, glad that the latest snow had been only a light dusting. He noticed fresh hoofprints leading out of town and wondered if they belonged to Lacy's mount. It wasn't that she was the only one who could have passed this way. He considered the direction and depth of each print. The rider was lightweight, so it might be her. Beth seemed to think Lacy might have gone out the night before, but if that were the case, the new snow would have covered any tracks.

He was still thinking about this when he finally made the turn toward Hamilton. The tracks continued on the main road to the north. He wondered if they'd still be there when he came back. The skies to the west were darkening with clouds, and the whole line seemed to be moving their way. It'd be just his luck to lose the prints in another snowstorm.

Dave made his way into Hamilton, trying to put the worrisome thoughts from his mind. The little town was already up and running, with local merchants sweeping off the dry white offering from the night before. Several people waved as he passed down the street.

Dave knew the new doctor's office and home was not far.

He quickly covered the distance and was rewarded to see the doctor's wife whisking snow from the steps of their house.

"Morning, Mrs. DuPont. Is the doctor in?" Dave asked without bothering to dismount.

"Oh, goodness, he is, but he's terribly sick. He's run a fever all night and is coughing something horrible."

"Guess he's not up to making any house calls then." Dave scratched his chin. "Mrs. Bishop is set to deliver her baby. She's been having pains all night."

The woman nodded. "I'm sorry. Your best bet would be to get a midwife. I'd go myself if I didn't have to take care of my husband."

"I understand." Dave thought for a moment. "I hope Doc gets to feeling better."

"Physicians never make good patients," she mused. "They're always trying to second-guess their illness and oftentimes make less of it than they should." Her face brightened. "Say, your mother would be quite capable of delivering a baby. She's helped with that before."

"I hadn't thought of that, but you're right." Dave tipped his hat. "I'll go there straightaway."

"Give her my regards, and we'll be praying that all goes well."

He turned the horse and headed out of Hamilton. He picked up the tracks again and followed them, surprised as they turned toward the Shepard ranch. His hopes rose as he felt more confident that the prints had been made by Lacy's horse.

It was nearly nine when Dave reached the ranch. His father was forking hay onto a wagon when Dave led his mount into the barn.

"Well, we seem to be blessed with visitors today. I sure didn't expect to see you this morning. What brings you out here?" Jerry leaned on the pitchfork and waited for his son's reply.

"Gwen Bishop is having her baby. Dr. DuPont is too sick to attend her, so I thought maybe Ma would come." Dave glanced at the stall and spotted Lacy's horse. "I take it Lacy is here."

"Yup, rode in just after dawn." He came and took hold of Dave's mount. "I'll put your horse away and then I'll hitch the carriage. Tell your ma I'll be waiting for her," his father said. "Could you maybe stay behind and get this hay out to the west field?"

"Sure," Dave said. "Let me go explain things to Ma, and I'll get right to it."

Dave bounded across the yard and leaped up on the porch, easily clearing the three steps as he had when he was a boy.

He entered the house, calling, "Ma!" Making his way through the rooms, Dave headed for the kitchen, where he knew he'd find her at this time of the day.

What he hadn't expected was to find Lacy Gallatin standing in the kitchen. He'd figured, knowing his mother, Lacy would be tucked into bed somewhere, being pampered and cared for. Lacy looked at him with such wide eyes that Dave knew she was equally surprised to find him there.

"I told them not to send anyone after me," she muttered and went back to kneading bread dough.

"I didn't come for you, although I will say it was pretty inconsiderate of you to just ride out like that and worry everyone."

She looked up and met his gaze. "I left a letter."

"Yeah, I know. But it certainly didn't say you were coming to my folks' place."

"I didn't know that I was."

His mother came in from the porch. "It's starting to snow

again." She spotted her son and broke into a big smile. "What a nice surprise."

"Gwen is having her baby and Dr. DuPont is sick. Pa's hitching the carriage. Can you come and help?"

"Absolutely. Let me get my things," his mother said. She stopped in midstep, however, and turned back to Lacy. "Can you handle the baking? We can't let all these loaves of bread go to waste. Oh, but you probably want to be there, too." Patience looked upset by the dilemma, but Lacy quickly put the matter to rest.

"I'll finish them, don't you worry. Tell my sister I'm praying for her safe delivery. There's nothing much I could do to help there, so it's best I make myself useful here."

Dave didn't miss the look of worry on her face. She bit her lower lip and ducked her head as if to hide it from him, but he'd seen it nevertheless.

"I'll stay here and see Lacy safely back to Gallatin House after the baking is finished. I know she'll be anxious to be with her family at a time like this."

Lacy said nothing, her expression unreadable.

Lacy couldn't believe this turn of events. She'd come to get away from all her troubles, yet the biggest one of all followed her like a hound to the fox.

She put the last of the bread pans in the oven and checked the fire. Everything looked perfect. Stretching to ease the pull of her back muscles, Lacy felt a bit of relief knowing that Dave was occupied elsewhere. His father had given him the task of feeding stock in the west field. This area didn't usually have so much snow, so Jerry hadn't taken the animals to a different pasture. Instead, he'd brought them all closer to home to keep them contained within easy distance of the house. But this winter had been devastating. The temperatures had dropped so rapidly that large geese had actually frozen fast in the pond and died. Jerry had mentioned losing several pregnant cows, as well as a number of steers. It wasn't a good season to be a rancher.

A glance out Patience's kitchen window startled Lacy. It was snowing quite heavily. In fact, it was very nearly a whiteout. She hadn't even noticed the wind blowing but could hear evidence of it now. The sound was mournful, almost like a cry. It was typical of the unpredictable mountain weather.

Dave came stomping in from the back porch. "It's blown up a bad one." He shook the snow from his coat onto the porch floor. "We're gonna have to wait this one out."

"What do you mean?" Lacy asked. She began placing already baked loaves of bread onto the table.

"I mean we're not going to be able to head out to Gallatin House until this clears up."

She looked at him and could see how red his face was from the cold wind. She took pity on him. "Want some coffee?"

He grinned. "That would be good. Maybe a slice of fresh bread, too?"

She nodded. "I'm sure your mother wouldn't mind."

Lacy hurried to pour him a cup of coffee. She put it in front of him as he took a seat at the far end of the table. "The bread's still warm. It might not cut well."

"I don't mind. If you get me a knife, I'll do it myself."

She went to the cupboard and got a plate, then fetched a knife from the counter. "There's fresh butter, too."

Lacy brought the butter to the table, then hurried back to check the oven. She felt odd. It wasn't that she was doing anything she hadn't done at Gallatin House in serving Dave food, but somehow here it seemed much more intimate.

"Where are the ranch hands?" she asked. "Will they need lunch?"

"They're off in the far west field waiting for calves to be born. Knowing Ma, she sent them with everything they'd need. They'll probably set a tent up by the creek. No doubt with the temperature dropping, they'll need to hack the ice open from time to time in order to allow the cattle to drink."

"They'll stay out in this?" Lacy asked, glancing at the window. The wind was now clearly audible.

"They'll rotate in and out. We've got too many heifers birthing this year to leave them alone for long. The hands will be fine." Dave took a big bite of the bread and smiled. "Mmm."

Lacy didn't know why, but his delight in the impromptu meal rather unnerved her. She went to the wash pan and began cleaning up the empty bread pans. "I'm sure I can get back on my own. There's no need for me to stay here after I get the baking done."

"Are you afraid of staying here with me?" he asked softly.

Lacy turned and met his gaze. She made the mistake of looking at his lips for a moment, then turned away. "That would be silly," she said in a voice that didn't sound at all convincing.

"It would be," Dave agreed, "but that doesn't mean you aren't afraid."

"I simply want to get home and do what I can to help. Gwen's having her baby, after all. I'm going to be an aunt. I only stayed here to relieve your mother's mind." Her hands were shaking so badly she had to plunge them into the water and hope Dave wouldn't see.

"Look, the storm is bad," Dave said. "We'll just have to

make the best of it. If the weather clears soon enough, I'll get you home. If not, we'll stay here."

Lacy turned around so quickly that she flung water across the room. "You mean spend the night?"

"Well, you were already going to do that, weren't you?"

"Yes, but . . . not with you here."

He laughed and tossed back the last of his coffee. "I stay at Gallatin House all the time, and it doesn't seem to bother you."

It bothered her a great deal, but Lacy wasn't about to admit it. "Yes, but there are other people there. Not only that, but you live in the annex. That's a whole different building. But your folks won't be here, and neither will anyone else."

Dave leaned back with a lazy grin spreading across his face. "I know. Kind of intriguing, don't you think?"

Lacy felt her cheeks grow hot. "Don't you care that it will ruin my reputation?"

He laughed and folded his hands behind his head as he let the chair tip back against the wall. "Lacy Gallatin, you've never cared what people thought about you or your reputation."

"Yes, well, I've never done this before." She eyed the doorway, wanting only to run for the haven of the room Patience had given her.

"Done what?" he asked. It was clear he was enjoying her discomfort.

"Oh, bother. I'm not going to stand here and argue with you." She turned her attention to the stove and felt the warm blast of air against her face as she opened the door. The bread wasn't done, so she couldn't even occupy herself with pulling the loaves out.

She straightened once the stove door was back in place. This wasn't the deliverance from problems and emotions that she had hoped for. In fact, this was very much like a fascinating nightmare—one that she clearly wanted to escape but at the same time couldn't help but be intrigued by.

Turning, she found Dave watching her closely. He wasn't smiling anymore, and that was almost more worrisome. Lacy could take his teasing, but she wasn't sure what to do with his serious side.

CHAPTER TWO

Gwen gasped for air. "But . . . what . . . what if . . . something goes wrong? We need . . . a doctor."

"Nothing's going wrong," Patience reassured her. "The baby is nearly here, so there's no time to send for anyone else. Besides, I've done this many times before. You're doing just fine."

"I don't . . . feel . . . fine." Gwen panted and looked out the window into the darkness, trying not to focus on the pain. Sweat trickled down her neck. "You know my . . . our . . . mother died giving birth."

"Yes, but you aren't your mother." Patience wiped Gwen's forehead with a cool damp cloth, then handed it to Beth. "Please get this wet and continue wiping her forehead."

Beth nodded and hurried to the bowl and pitcher on the

nightstand. "I hope my little one doesn't give me this much trouble."

Patience smiled. "Every baby is different in some way, but there's always pain and suffering. You barely remember it afterward, though. The joy of the child just takes away the memory of the misery."

Gwen, however, felt as if she were being torn in two. There was no possible way that she would ever forget exactly how bad this felt. She didn't care if she ever had another child. Then Gwen was seized by the strangest urgency to expel the baby from her body. Almost against her will, she bore down. "I think it's coming."

Patience checked. "Yes, you're very close. Keep pushing. Beth, forget the cloth. Come help your sister. Lift her shoulders so she can push down harder."

Gwen couldn't get away from the pain. It radiated throughout her entire body and emerged as a scream and desperate plea. "Make it stop!"

Hank heard Gwen scream from downstairs and looked up as he clenched his teeth and gripped the arm of the chair. *Things must be bad*, he surmised. "Is it always like this?" he asked Jerry. Major came to his side to offer comfort, but Hank ignored the dog.

Jerry looked up from where he was playing checkers with Justin, Nick's nine-year-old son, by the fire. "Always. The first one's the worst, though. You don't know what to expect, and it all seems so overwhelming."

Hank paced back and forth while Nick whittled. Nick seemed almost as upset as Hank and had nearly carved the piece of wood out of existence. Hank shook his head as their eyes met. "Next time, it'll be you."

"Don't remind me."

Jerry laughed. "You two need to settle down. There's nothing to be gained by worrying."

"I'm not just worrying," Hank countered. "I'm praying, too."

"Don't you think the one kind of cancels out the other?"

Hank shook his head. "Why should it? God knows I trust Him, but this situation is more than I'm used to."

"So trust Him all the more. I remember when Dave was born. I was all by myself with Patience."

Hank thought he must have misunderstood. "You were alone? But I thought Dave was born back East, in the city."

Jerry grinned as Justin jumped over his last two pieces. "Looks like you win." The boy beamed. Jerry got to his feet and yawned and stretched.

"Dave was born during a yellow fever epidemic. There wasn't an available doctor or nurse anywhere in the city. The hospitals were full of the dying. Even the midwives were either sick or off helping someone else. I sent for my mother, but she lived a good distance away, and I'd waited too long."

Nick looked at the man as if he were crazy. "And you actually delivered Dave?"

"Yeah, I sure did. I was so naïve and wet behind the ears. Goodness, but we were just children having children. Leastwise, that's how it felt."

"What did you do?"

"I did what I could. I didn't know a whole lot about birthing, but I learned fast. Dave was born easy as could be, but I wasn't at all sure what to do about that umbilical cord and afterbirth. Patience had passed out cold, and I stood there looking at the baby and the cord and knew I probably needed to free him up. After all, I'd never seen an infant with all of that other attached."

Hank laughed. "I can't even imagine. I would have been the one passing out cold if I'd been left to deliver our child."

Jerry shrugged. "You do what you have to. Patience came to, and I yelled at her." He laughed. "I told her not to ever faint again, and you know, I don't think she has. Even birthing the girls. Anyway, she was the one who told me what to do. She told me how to tie off the cord and cut it." He gave a slight shudder. "Never want to do that again."

Nick shook his head. "I hope that doesn't happen to me."

"I suppose a fella just has to be ready for anything." Jerry warmed his hands at the fire, then turned and gave his backside equal time.

Hank thought of how horrible it all might have been had Patience not been able to come. He didn't know what they would have done, especially since it had started snowing again.

"My mother showed up just after I'd finished cleaning things up, including Dave. She looked him over, declared him fit, and then congratulated Patience on delivering a beautiful baby. I was indignant. I cleared my throat and said, 'I'll have you know I did the delivering. She just pushed and screamed.' "

Hank couldn't help but laugh. "And what did your mother have to say to that?"

"She told me I had the easier of the two jobs and needed to never forget that. I tell you, I felt mighty deflated after that."

Nick chuckled and put away his knife. He held up the piece of wood, now hardly more than a stick. "Guess I've worried this enough." He bent down and scooped up the shavings and tossed them, along with the remaining piece, into the fire. He was dusting off his hands when another scream split the air.

Hank reached for the banister but held fast. Patience had told him not to come upstairs until he heard the baby cry. He looked at Jerry and shook his head. "Why doesn't the baby come?"

"Don't worry. Babies have their own schedule."

Hank blew out a hard breath and plopped onto the chair. "This is killing me."

"I'm sure it isn't doing Gwen all that much good, either," Jerry said.

Hank grew a bit light-headed. "Gwen's ma died giving birth."

"Justin's ma, too," Nick added. "I keep trying to forget about that." Justin came to his side and put his arm around Nick's shoulders.

"You two are worse than a couple of old women at a Sunday social. Stop expecting problems. Some women do die, but more of them come through just fine."

"But something could go wrong." Hank leaned forward, his head in his hands. "I know she wanted . . . counted on a doctor being here. I let her down. If we were in Boston, I'd have the best of doctors at her side—no offense to Patience and her skills. I'm just not any good at life on the frontier."

"Bah, this has nothing to do with that. Like I said, Hank, I lived in the heart of the city and couldn't get a doctor to attend Patience when her time came. Things still worked out. And you've got my gal up there, and she's had a lot of experience with birthing. Both having and delivering."

Just then, they heard a cry. Hank wasted no time. He bounded up the stairs, hardly touching them as he went.

Without bothering to knock, he crashed open the door to his bedroom and looked to the bed, where his wife had collapsed back against the pillows. Beth was wiping her forehead.

"Is she . . . are they . . ."

Patience looked up and smiled. "Mama is just fine. So is your baby daughter." She held up the squalling infant.

Gwen opened her eyes. "Hank."

Nothing sounded more beautiful to him than his name on her lips. He came to her side and sat down. Taking her hand, he kissed it gently. "I'm here."

"I'm sorry I didn't give you a son," she said with a weak smile.

"Good grief, woman, I don't care about that. She's a beautiful baby. I'm happy to have a daughter. I'm even happier to see you. How do you feel?"

She chuckled. "I've been better, but I've certainly been worse."

"You've never been more beautiful," he said, brushing back errant strands of hair from her face.

"I think I'll go let everyone know about the baby," Beth announced.

"Good idea. Let them know they're both doing fine. Then maybe bring Gwen a piece of toasted bread and some of that nettle leaf tea I had you brew. That will help her milk to come in strong."

Hank watched Beth go, then turned his attention to where Patience was cleaning his daughter. The tiny infant looked hardly bigger than a toy doll. "Is she extra small?" he asked without thinking that such a question might worry Gwen.

Patience laughed. "Hardly. She's a fine size, and her lungs

are good and strong. I'll have her dressed and wrapped in just a minute, then you can hold her for yourself."

Hank looked at Patience and then to Gwen. "I don't think I should. I'd probably just drop her."

Gwen patted his hand lovingly. "You'll get used to holding her, and then you won't think twice about it." She drew a long breath and closed her eyes. "Goodness, but I don't think I could move if I had to."

Hank leaned over and kissed her lightly on the lips. "Thank you for my beautiful daughter."

She smiled without even opening her eyes. "Might I say the same." It was more statement than question.

"What are you going to call this little girl?" Patience asked, crossing the room with the baby. She placed the infant in Hank's arms without waiting for his approval.

Hank stared down in wonder at the tiny bundle. The baby looked back at him with an expression that suggested she was trying to figure out who he might be. He smiled and suddenly didn't feel all that awkward at all. The infant's eyes opened wide. It was as if she wanted him to take special note—they were the same piercing blue as his.

"Julianne," he said, reaching up to touch his daughter's hair. She had an abundance of light brown hair with just a hint of curl.

He looked up to find Gwen watching him. "You seem pleased."

"I am pleased," he assured. Hank placed the baby in Gwen's arms. "She's absolutely perfect—just like her mother."

Gwen gave a chuckle. "I'm glad you think so, but we both know I'm far from that." She ran her finger along Julianne's face. "She's so soft."

Hank wasn't a man given to tears, but he couldn't fight against the dampness that clouded his vision. He had a daughter. Flesh of his flesh and bone of his bone.

"Is the baby ugly?" Justin asked, sounding almost hopeful.

Beth laughed and poured Gwen some tea into a cup. "Of course she's not ugly. She's beautiful. I'll bet you were beautiful when you were born."

Justin shrugged. "I've seen a whole lot of new babies, and they're ugly. They smell bad, too."

"Oh, Justin, you are just being silly." Beth picked up the tray and headed toward the front room with Justin right behind her.

"There you are. I'll take it on up. You deserve to rest," Patience said as she descended the stairs.

"What's our Mr. Bishop think of his new daughter?" Jerry asked his wife.

She smiled. "I think he heartily approves. They're calling her Julianne."

Beth made her way to where Nick stood. "I think it's well past time for Justin to go to bed. I know I'll be headed there in a few minutes myself. We were supposed to have a noon stage tomorrow, and while I can't see them getting through this blizzard, I need to be up and ready. After all, I won't have Lacy's help."

She frowned and turned to Jerry. "You don't suppose they got stuck out in this on their way back to Gallatin House, do you?"

"Nah. Dave knows better than to risk it. Patience told me they couldn't possibly have headed out before noon, and the snows started in well before then. Dave would have seen the problem right away and made sure they stayed at the ranch."

"Poor Lacy," Beth said. "I thought she looked upset when I told everyone that I was expecting a baby, but she said she was fine."

"Why should she be upset?" Nick asked. "Babies are good news, not bad."

"Yes, but I think she's feeling . . . well . . . maybe out of sorts. You know, we're married, and Gwen and Hank are married, and we both have children now. Lacy probably wonders what's going to happen to her in the middle of all this."

"Hopefully she'll find someone and settle down," Nick said with a shrug. "Nothing all that hard about it."

Beth rolled her eyes. "Of course not. Maybe she could just order a husband from back East."

Nick looked at her oddly. "Why would she have to do that? Dave's already crazy about her."

Jerry yawned and nodded. "It's true. That boy has been gone over her for a long while now."

"But Lacy doesn't see it. She doesn't know that he cares; she just thinks he likes to find fault with her." Beth motioned Justin to come to her. "Look, you can read for ten minutes in bed. All right?"

"Do I have to go to bed now?"

Beth leaned down and gave her stepson a kiss on the forehead. "Yes. I'm going to call a school holiday tomorrow, but you'll have to help me in the morning. And if the stage does manage to make it through, I'll need your help then, as well."

"But no school?"

"No."

Justin headed for the stairs and let out a joyous cry. "No school!"

The adults laughed as the nine-year-old bounded up to his room. Beth smiled at Nick. "I'm going to get the guest room upstairs ready for Jerry and Patience, and then I'm heading to bed."

"I'll go warm it up for you," Nick said with a wink.

Beth's mouth dropped open, and she felt her cheeks grow hot. He hadn't really said anything inappropriate, but the suggestion that they would share a bed seemed uncalled for. She started to say something, then decided against it. Jerry knew full well they shared a bed—they were married after all. *I'm just being silly*, she told herself.

"You two are embarrassing me something fierce," Jerry said, feigning disgust. "You'd think you were still courting."

"Never got to court," Nick replied. "Beth was in too much of a hurry. Did I ever tell you that she proposed to me?" He ducked just as a book sailed by his head.

Beth hoped her expression made it clear that if he wanted her help to ward off the night chill, he'd better be quiet and go about his business. Nick grinned and headed for the stairs.

"I think I'll just go on up."

Jerry laughed. "Sounds wise."

CHAPTER THREE

"It's getting late," Dave said.

The clock chimed nine and startled Lacy. She looked at the rather domestic scene before her. Dave sat reading the Bible by the fire while she busied herself mending some shirts she'd seen Patience working on earlier. She'd picked up the work out of desperation to keep her hands busy. Now, however, it only served to remind her of what life might be like married to Dave Shepard.

"Did you hear me?" he asked.

Lacy nodded. "I heard you and the clock."

All evening, Lacy had wanted to make an excuse to leave Dave. She'd wanted the safety of her bedroom, for fear of saying or doing the wrong thing. Just being around him made her so nervous that she couldn't think straight. When had this happened? When had he made her anything but frustrated and angry?

She cast a quick glance at him. "I don't think the storm is letting up."

He put his Bible aside and went to the window. "No. I think if anything, it's worse. We'll probably hear it blowing all night. I'll stoke up the fire, but the rooms will probably be chilly. If you need extra quilts, Ma keeps a stack of them in the cedar chest in her room."

Tucking the sewing back into the basket beside her chair, Lacy got to her feet. "Good night, then."

She didn't even look at Dave for fear of what he might do. The day had been so very taxing, and Lacy found her mind overwhelmed with thoughts. Confusion held her cornered like an animal trapped by hunters.

Making her way to the upstairs room, Lacy closed the door behind her and set the latch. She leaned against the door and wrapped her arms around her body. What was happening to her? She felt weak and strange. *Maybe I'm sick*, she thought. She reached up to feel her own forehead.

She'd first noticed the sensations at supper, a touch of restlessness that she had accounted to the weather. Worse still, there was a tightness in her stomach and her heart seemed to race, leaving her rather breathless. She had cooked a meal for her and Dave to share, and when they'd sat down together, Lacy had found it all so uncomfortably intimate. The table was set for two and the lamp cast a golden glow around the room. Dave's features didn't look nearly so gruff and stern—in fact, he was more than a little bit handsome.

The wind howled and rattled the windows across the room. Lacy startled and felt herself almost cowering.

I'm not at all myself. It takes more than this to upset me.

Lacy straightened and relaxed her arms. This was completely silly. She was a strong woman—capable of enduring a winter storm. She drew a deep breath. So what if it trapped her at the Shepard ranch? So what if she and Dave were forced to endure each other's company for several days?

"I'm quite able to suffer his presence, no matter how long it takes. I simply need to be sensible about it."

Lacy knew that even if the storm abated in the night, they would be hard-pressed to leave tomorrow. After all, even if she and Dave could manage to get to Gallatin House on horseback, Jerry and Patience would find it nearly impossible to get a wagon through the typical drifts that blocked the roads after such blizzards. Someone would need to stay at the ranch and care for the horses and milk cows if they couldn't make it back.

Lacy crossed the room to the small dressing table and sat down. She looked at her reflection in the mirror and wondered why the woman who stared back looked so terrified.

"It's just a storm," she said and began taking down her hair.

But she knew it was more than the storm. Her thoughts were betraying her. She had feelings for Dave she couldn't explain—feelings she was terrified to explore. When had he become something more than an irritation in her life? When had he changed from the roadblock to finding her father's killer to a man who made her heart race and knees grow weak?

Her sisters had often suggested that he cared for her, and Gwen had commented more than once that they made a nice couple. But Lacy had always put aside such thoughts.

She touched her lips and thought of the times Dave had kissed her. She'd enjoyed it more than she cared to admit. Picking up the hairbrush, Lacy studied her face as she began to stroke through the cinnamon-colored mass.

"Exactly what do I feel for him?" she begged the woman reflected there.

Rafe Reynolds threw a broken beer mug into the crate of trash. The storm was keeping his business to a nonexistent state. He hadn't had a single customer all night, so they'd used the time to spruce things up. Now, however, there wasn't much left to be done.

Cubby crossed the saloon, and Rafe couldn't help but notice his son had grown up practically overnight. He was at least six feet tall, his hair the color of his mother's. Rafe grimaced. Maryland. He hadn't thought about her in years. She had been a feisty girl, six years his junior and named for her prostitute mother's home state. Pretty and blond, she had used her looks to make her way in life, and Rafe had fallen hard for her.

At nineteen, she had waltzed into town as if she owned the place. Men were immediately drawn to her—Rafe included. She had a way about her that held everyone captive. Rafe had wanted her from the start. But not for the brothel or other men. He wanted Maryland for himself. And he thought she'd felt the same.

He had suggested they marry almost before she'd settled in. Maryland had laughed and instead told Rafe that she had no intention of chaining herself down to one man or place. This surprised Rafe greatly. Most single women were actively pursuing a husband. Maryland had suggested, instead, that they simply have a good time together and see where it took them. Rafe was captivated.

"I'm going to bed, Pa," Cubby announced.

"We got enough wood?" Rafe asked in a gruff manner.

"Yeah. I brought in enough to last a couple of days. We'll be warm enough. The girls have plenty, too."

Rafe nodded and said nothing more. He watched his son leave the room and let out a long, heavy breath. Why had things gone so wrong? Rafe had loved Maryland. He was happy when she announced that she was pregnant with his child. Even then, however, she hadn't wanted to marry him. Rafe had argued the point with her, desperately wanting to give her his undying love and his child a name. She thought him old-fashioned and silly.

"The boy can have your name," she had told Rafe, "but I like my own well enough to keep it for myself."

Rafe poured himself a whiskey and tossed it back. She hadn't known how her statement had hurt him. Maryland hadn't cared about anyone but herself, as was evident in her desertion of Rafe and Cubby when the latter had only been eight weeks old. She'd left nothing behind but the baby and had even taken all of the money Rafe had put aside to purchase a house for his little family.

The prostitutes in the brothel helped him care for the boy, but they could do nothing to ease Rafe's misery. Finally one of the women suggested he go after Maryland while they took care of Cubby. Rafe had jumped at the opportunity. For some stupid reason, he had been convinced that he would win her back. Instead, he showed up two days later in a town some fifty miles away, only to learn that she'd gotten herself killed in a saloon fight. Rafe had paid for her burial, but the matter had forever hardened his heart against women. Maryland had used him, and he couldn't forgive her.

The roar of the winter winds outside only served to chill Rafe to the bone. He poured another glass of whiskey. This time he nursed it slowly, feeling the burning liquid slide down his throat.

Cubby was all he had in this world for family. Yet the boy caused him pain and grief every time Rafe looked at him. Many had been the time he'd wanted to abandon Cubby, but something always held him back. Maybe it was the need to hold on to that little piece of Maryland. Maybe it was the desire to leave something of himself behind and have a say in how the boy became a man.

"Well, that ain't exactly worked out the way I'd hoped, neither." Rafe drank the remaining liquor and got to his feet. There was no sense in remembering the past or even contemplating the future.

Lacy awoke with a start. Her dreams had turned to nightmares, marked by the storm outside, as well as the one within. She'd dreamed that Gwen had died giving birth to her baby because Lacy couldn't find the doctor. Then Beth had gone into labor and died, as well. Throwing back the covers, Lacy shivered at the chill of the room. She hurried into a robe Patience had lent her and paced the drafty room. The room seemed to suffocate her, and Lacy longed only for the warmth of the fire and the light of day. She could do nothing about the latter but knew that the fire could still offer her comfort. Of course, leaving her room might force her to encounter Dave.

She contemplated that for several minutes and felt a moment of disgust as she realized she would love to have his comfort. Pulling back the latch, Lacy paused. She wanted him to be awake. She wanted him to hear her and come to her.

Without concern about the noise she made, Lacy hurried downstairs and into the front room. She paused at the sight of a man silhouetted against the fire. Dave. She watched him for a moment as he stirred up the flames and put another log on the fire. It was as if she'd known he would be there. He replaced the poker then turned to find her watching him. He didn't seem any more surprised at her appearance than she had been at his. In fact, when he crossed the distance between them and took her in his arms, it felt like the most natural thing in the world.

"You're trembling. Are you cold?"

She nodded, and he led her to the fire. Without completely letting go of her, Dave positioned Lacy close enough to regain her warmth. She looked up at him. Her fingers ached to touch his face, but Lacy refrained from showing any emotion.

"You're still shaking," he murmured.

Lacy knew it wasn't from the cold this time. Time seemed to stand still. Dave's gaze pierced Lacy's guarded heart. It was like he could read her thoughts and knew exactly what her feelings were.

He reached out and put his hand against her cheek. "Lacy, why do you have to make it so tough on yourself? On us?"

She shook her head, barely able to think rationally. "I don't know what you're talking about."

"I think you do." He pulled her into his arms and covered her mouth with his lips.

Lacy felt the wind go out from her. She fought against her desire to wrap her arms around Dave's neck, and lost. His kiss deepened, and Lacy felt him bend her backward ever so slightly. She was lost. Lost to her emotions and his will. She wanted the moment to go on forever.

Dave's mouth left her lips and trailed along her cheek and neck. Lacy couldn't suppress a moan. Something in the back of her mind told her things were out of control—warned her to stop.

And then with unexpected swiftness, Dave pushed her away and turned. "I'm sorry. I should never have done that." He crossed the room in long determined strides and was gone. Lacy crumpled to the ground and put her hands to her head.

"What have I done?"

Her wanton response caused her cheeks to blaze in embarrassment. Dave would surely hate her now. She'd acted no differently than one of Rafe's girls. She buried her face against her bent knees.

"Oh, forgive me, Lord," she whispered. "Forgive me . . . Dave."

Dave Shepard paced his room, uncertain what to do. He certainly couldn't just go to sleep, as he should have done hours ago. He could still feel Lacy warm and soft in his arms. He could still feel her lips against his.

Shaking his head, he walked to the window. He could only pray the storm would let up, and that God would help him to keep his longings in check. Lacy would surely think even worse of him now.

He had done them both a disservice. He had come much too close to compromising everything he believed in.

"But I love her so much," he whispered. "I want her to be with me forever. I only wanted to convince her that my feelings for her are real."

He looked back at the closed and locked door of his bedroom. She was just on the other side. Maybe locked in her own room now. Maybe still standing by the fire. Either way, she was out there, and he wanted her more than he wanted his next breath.

"Help me, Lord. I never meant to dishonor you or her. Forgive me."

It was very nearly a sunless morning that Beth awoke to. She found Nick already dressing for the day and hurried to match his efforts.

"Is it still snowing?"

"Yup. I figure I need to tend the horses, though. They were set well enough for yesterday, but I need to get over there and make sure they have water and feed."

"Can I help?"

"No. I want you and Justin to stay inside. I'll tie a line to the house so I can find my way from the barn if the snow blinds my way." He looked at her and smiled. "I like your hair down like that."

Beth touched her hand to her long tresses. "It must look frightful right now."

He came to her and reached out to still her hand. "No, it's beautiful."

She wrapped her arms around his neck. "You are such a flirt, Mr. Lassiter." She kissed him lightly on the lips, then turned to get her hairbrush. "I shall have to prepare something special for your breakfast."

He chuckled and moved toward the door. "I'll get Justin up."

Beth finished dressing her hair, then made her way downstairs. She was surprised to find Patience already busy in the kitchen. "You're a guest in our house," Beth declared. "I won't have you working."

Patience laughed. "I feel like you gals are family. Besides, I would lose my mind without something to keep me busy. I checked on Gwen and the baby already, and they're both doing fine—although I'm not entirely convinced that Hank will survive. I thought seeing the baby born safe and sound would reassure him, but he seems more nervous than ever."

"Nick told me he was fit to be tied last night. Poor brother-in-law of mine. I have half a mind to make him some special oatmeal."

"How kind," Patience said, turning back to check the coffee.

Beth grinned. It wasn't a kindness she was thinking about but rather a prank. She'd made some nearly unpalatable oatmeal for Hank on another occasion, and even to this day, he always looked at anything Beth prepared with an eye to caution.

"Do you suppose Dave and Lacy made it through the night without trouble?" Beth asked.

"Where those two are concerned, there's always trouble. I'll be fortunate if the house is still standing when we return."

Beth gave an unladylike snort. "And if Dave's still alive, it will only be because he managed to outwit my sister."

Patience began making hotcakes. "I don't know why those two can't see how perfect they are for each other."

"I was just thinking that last night," Beth admitted. "Maybe we need to help them along. You know—help them see the attributes of the other. Put them in situations where they will see that they can do more than argue and bicker with each other."

"It's a thought, though it will probably take a good knock on the head to get any sense into those two when it comes to matters of the heart. Neither one seems inclined to give the other even an inch of space."

Beth shook her head in agreement.

"We'll pray for them," Patience declared. "In time, maybe the good Lord will help them see that they really care for each other."

"That'll probably be the only way," Beth said. "An act of God."

CHAPTER FOUR

Hank finished buttoning his starched white shirt just as Julianne began to cry. He peered into the cradle and marveled once again that God had done such an incredible work. The baby seemed oblivious to his presence. Her tiny eyes were squinted closed and face reddened from her effort to get attention. Even so, he thought her the most beautiful creation in the world. It humbled him greatly to know he'd had even the smallest part to do with her existence.

Gwen stretched in bed. "Would you bring her to me? She's hungry, no doubt."

Looking at the small squirming bundle and then to his

wife, Hank smiled. "She's demanding, that's for sure. I heard her cry several times last night."

"I think she's absolutely perfect."

Baby Julianne began to cry all the more. Hank reached down and drew her into his arms. She hardly weighed anything at all. He couldn't remember a time when he'd ever held such a tiny infant.

The baby began to nuzzle against him, and Hank laughed. "Sorry, little one, but I can't do you any good." He looked up at Gwen. "But I know who can."

Hank took a step to cross to the bed and caught his boot on the rocker of the cradle. In the flash of a moment, he clutched Julianne tight to his chest while he fell to one knee.

Gwen gasped and threw back the covers as if to come to their rescue. "Are you all right?"

"I'm fine," Hank said in disgust. He got to his feet and handed her the baby. "She's fine, too."

"What happened?" Gwen took the crying baby and immediately put Julianne to her breast to calm her.

His temper got the best of him. "What do you suppose? I tripped."

Hank felt stupid. He could have fallen on the child and killed her. "I shouldn't even have picked her up." He crossed the room and got his coat. "From now on, I won't."

"Oh, Hank, it was an accident."

He looked at his wife. Despite her hair mussed from sleep, she had never been more beautiful. Hank calmed just a bit. "Sometimes I feel like I'm really failing you, Gwen."

"But why?"

He shook his head. "I can't explain it."

Gwen's expression softened. "Please try. Come sit with me."

With a sigh, Hank put his coat aside. He came to the bed and sat down beside her. Gwen reached out her hand. "Tell me what's bothering you, Hank."

"I just feel ill-equipped to do what needs to be done. I thought I'd done a good thing by buying Mr. Vanhouten's land, but now with things going as they are, I don't think it was a good investment. If we wanted to start ranching it would be different, but I know even less about that than about running a frontier mercantile. Business at the store goes well enough, but not as smoothly as I would like. Now this. If I'd harmed her . . ." His voice trailed off.

Gwen squeezed his hand. "You are a good man, Hank. And you will be a great father."

"But there's so much I don't know. Montana, fatherhood, even being a Christian. I feel like I completely make a mess of things on a daily basis."

Nodding, Gwen reached up to touch his face. Their eyes met. "Everyone feels like that from time to time. I'm terrified of motherhood, yet I want it more than anything. Julianne means more to me than I can say, but I worry that I, too, will do something to harm her. And if that happened, I don't think I could live with myself."

Hank shook his head. "You mustn't say such things. You are going to be a wonderful mother." He drew a deep breath. "I'm sorry I sounded harsh. I was angry at myself—not you."

She smiled. "I know. But, Hank, even if something had happened to cause her harm, I wouldn't blame you. Julianne is in God's hands. We have to believe that. Children die all the time. I can scarcely bear to think of it, but they do. Throughout my pregnancy, I thought of such things, and Patience was good to help calm me. Even when I was delivering Julianne, I kept remembering my mother's death."

"I worried that you would." He took hold of her hand and held it close. "I feared for you, as well."

"All we can do is put our trust in the Lord. Death and sickness are a part of life; we cannot escape from it. I pray God will give us long years with our daughter and any other children He blesses us with, but if not, I know He's already made provision."

Her words were like a balm on Hank's soul. "I know you're right." He glanced at the clock and let go of her hand. "I have to get the store opened. I'll be back to see you at lunch. Send someone if you need me sooner." He kissed her forehead, then gently touched his fingers to the baby's head. "I love you."

"I love you, too, my darling."

Hank crossed the room and turned at the door. He was so very blessed to have Gwen in his life. A niggling doubt crossed his mind, however. He should be the one to comfort her with words of faith—not the other way around.

Will I ever be the godly man she needs me to be?

It was still snowing when Lacy awoke. She stood at the window of her bedroom for a long time and contemplated how to handle the day. She would have to face Dave, after all that had happened the night before, and it made her feel very uncomfortable. How could she possibly look him in the eye after having responded to him in such a wanton fashion?

She leaned her cheek against the icy windowpane. "What's wrong with me?"

The silent room offered no answer. Lacy straightened and looked to her clothes. She knew she would have to dress and face the day, but the thought of it was almost terrifying.

What must he think of me? What will he expect? Should I apologize immediately or pretend that nothing happened?

Lacy considered these things even as she pulled on her skirt. She didn't understand her feelings. There was something about Dave Shepard that seemed to draw out all of her emotions at once. She could find herself so angry with him—frustrated because he treated her like a child. Then she could turn around and kiss him with more passion than she knew she possessed.

The buttons on her blouse were tiny and troubled her shaking fingers. None of this made sense. Every time Dave touched her—goodness, every time she thought of him touching her, Lacy felt her knees go weak.

"Do I love him?"

How could a person even be sure about such things? She'd listened to her sisters talk about their feelings for Hank and Nick, but she couldn't honestly say she'd ever explored the depths of her own heart when it came to Dave.

"I've not even considered getting married," she murmured. Why, even when Cubby declared his desire to court her, Lacy hadn't taken the matter seriously. She'd not given it a second thought.

She sat down to comb out her hair and thought about the situation until her head throbbed. Lacy finally determined that falling in love wasn't something she could allow herself. It would steal her focus away from getting justice for her father.

But just as quickly as she settled on that thought, Lacy reminded herself that her very trip to the Shepard ranch had come about because of her discomfort when Beth announced her pregnancy. Lacy wanted a husband and family of her own; there was no denying that. It was as if there were two warring parties inside Lacy's body—the logical reasoning of her brain and the emotions of her heart.

With her hair finally braided into a single plait, Lacy knew she couldn't put off the inevitable. She smoothed her brown wool skirt, drew a deep breath, and opened the bedroom door.

She could hear someone in the kitchen humming. No doubt Dave probably wondered why she wasn't up yet. Then again, maybe he was just as glad she wasn't. Lacy could smell the undeniable aroma of coffee and bacon and felt her stomach clench in hunger. With her failure to show up, Dave had apparently started the morning meal.

Dave stood at the stove pouring a cup of coffee when Lacy finally braved the room. "Morning."

The humming stopped as he turned. "Morning." He looked as uncomfortable as she felt. "It's still snowing."

Lacy nodded. "I see that." She forced herself to walk confidently across the room. "I see also that you have the bacon cooking. Sorry I'm late."

"It's not a problem. I've cooked for myself plenty of times."

Lacy's fingers trembled as she took up her apron. "Well, I can see to it now. Have you already taken care of the livestock?"

He moved to the kitchen table and took a seat before replying. "I did. Fed and watered the horses. Milked the cows. Chickens aren't laying much."

"Ours weren't, either," Lacy said, forcing her thoughts on anything but the longing she had to throw herself into Dave's arms. "We had them on the back porch, but it wasn't helping all that much with the temperatures being so low."

Lacy took up some of the bread she'd helped to bake and began to slice it. "I'll toast this to go with the bacon. There's plenty of applesauce and cheese, too." She sawed at the loaf as if it were a log, smashing the soft center until the piece looked something like a U. Drawing a deep breath, Lacy forced her touch to go lighter with the next piece. She would have to say something about the previous night. She couldn't just keep mutilating the bread.

She dropped the knife on the counter and turned to face Dave. He was watching her intently, completely disregarding his coffee.

"Look, I . . . well . . . I'm sorry. I can't imagine what you must think of me. My behavior last night was completely uncalled for and entirely out of character for me." She began to twist her hands and found she couldn't keep herself from pacing.

"I don't know why I acted that way, and I know you must think very badly of me." She paused, almost hoping Dave would say something, but he didn't, and that only served to make her feel all the more uncomfortable.

"The past few weeks have had me fit to be tied. I suppose a lot of it has to do with the weather," she continued. "But that doesn't mean I should . . . act . . . well, you know how I acted."

The silence was about to kill her. Pausing at the far end of the kitchen, Lacy finally braved a glance at Dave. He got up slowly, never letting his focus stray from her face. With determined steps he crossed the room to where she stood.

Lacy knew he was going to take her in his arms. She

stiffened against any hold he might take, but he didn't even try to touch her.

"You did nothing wrong, Lacy." His words were soft and alluring.

Her mind whirled with a hundred things to say, but nothing seemed to make much sense. She lowered her head and stammered to explain herself. "I . . . well . . . when you kissed me . . . I . . ." Oh, why couldn't she speak reasonably?

He lifted her chin and Lacy met his blue-eyed gaze once again. There was something in his expression that pushed away all possible hope of reason. Lacy felt as if she were melting right into the floorboards.

"You did nothing wrong. When I kissed you, you responded exactly as I'd hoped you would."

"Only a loose woman would carry on so," Lacy said, trying hard to keep her wits.

"Or a woman in love," Dave said softly. "Why are you fighting this?"

She shook her head and tried to back up, but she had nowhere to go. Her back was against the wall already. "I don't know what you're talking about."

He smiled ever so slightly. "Let me remind you, then."

Lacy's eyes widened as he pulled her into his arms. She felt the strength of his well-muscled arms as they tightened around her.

"Are you starting to remember?" he asked, almost teasingly.

She started to reply but was instantly silenced when Dave kissed her. Lacy knew she was in trouble. Dave Shepard had some sort of power over her that she could not explain. Was he right? Was she in love with him? As much as they fought, how could that possibly be?

Dave's kiss deepened, and Lacy had no will to fight him. She wanted his kiss. She wanted it very much. Her heart hammered, and everything but Dave faded from her mind.

Without warning, he pulled back. He didn't release her, but Lacy felt as though she were about to fall into a void. She tightened her hold on him.

"We're meant to be together, Lacy. I've known it for a long time. I was just waiting for you to figure it out for yourself. I can't wait anymore. I don't want to play games."

"I . . . don't know. . . . I can't think."

"Good." He grinned. "That'll make it easier for me to say what I need to say."

He kissed her again, only this time it was brief and less intrusive. "Marry me, Lacy."

Those three words seemed to set off an alarm in her brain. Lacy's eyes flew open, and she pulled back hard only to slam up against the wall. "What?"

"You heard me." He moved closer and watched her intently.

A brief flurry of sense came rushing back, and Lacy thought of a hundred reasons they weren't right for each other. "But we hate each other. Think of all the times you've yelled at me. I never do anything right by you."

He chuckled. "We don't hate each other. At least, I could never hate you. The times I've yelled at you were purely due to my fear of losing you."

"Losing me?"

"Of course. When you don those boy's britches and go scouting around for highwaymen and killers, or climb up on roofs to repair shingles, I'm terrified you'll get hurt—even die." He touched her cheek and stroked back wisps of hair. "I was afraid I'd never get a chance to tell you how much I love you."

She shook her head rapidly, dislodging his touch. "No. You don't love me. You can't."

"And I suppose you don't love me." He grinned. "Oh, that's right, you hate me."

She shook her head even more fervently. "I don't . . . I . . ." She stopped and looked at him. "I don't know what I feel."

"Let me remind you again." His mouth covered hers without giving her so much as a chance to protest.

Lacy knew her fight was lost. She couldn't fight her own desires, much less his. Dave lifted his head and whispered against her lips. "Marry me."

"It will never work. We'd just hurt each other." Her thoughts were blurring and all she could think of was the way his lips felt against her own.

"We'll make it work," Dave whispered. "If we put our minds to it, we'll do just fine." He kissed her cheek and then trailed kisses along her jawline to her ear. "Now say yes, and marry me."

"No," she murmured.

"You know it's what you want—you know it's right."

She closed her eyes and gave in to the power of her emotions. "Yes." She barely breathed the word.

Dave let her go. "Yes, what?"

She sighed. "I'll marry you."

"Do you promise?"

Lacy opened her eyes and nodded. Before she could take it back she answered, "Yes."

His eyes were dark with passion, and Lacy knew in that

moment there was no possibility of telling him no. She wanted him to kiss her again—to hold her in his arms forever. She might regret her decision tomorrow, but for the moment, Lacy would have rather died than move from Dave's arms.

CHAPTER FIVE

The snowstorm finally let up the following night, leaving everything covered in a white blanket that reflected the moon's light, making it as bright as day. Lacy stared out the bedroom window and thought of all that had happened. She and Dave had said very little about marriage after she'd agreed to his proposal. Each had found ways to keep busy elsewhere throughout the day, as if realizing they needed the time apart to sort through any misgivings.

Lacy was full of doubts and questions. She couldn't believe she'd agreed to marry Dave. It was a mistake. A big mistake. She would have to find some way to convince Dave that it just couldn't work. If he agreed, then it wouldn't be like she was breaking her promise.

"Why did I ever promise to marry him?" she murmured.

It wasn't like she couldn't take it back, but breaking a pledge was something she couldn't easily do. She'd always struggled with such things. It was the reason she hadn't wanted to promise Gwen that she'd give up looking for their father's murderer.

"But you did break that promise, and you can surely break this one," she told herself.

Yet she couldn't bring herself to figure out if she honestly wanted to break the engagement. Dave was right about one thing—something happened when they were together. He said he loved her.

"He loves me?" she questioned. Lacy still couldn't understand how that could be possible.

She thought of her sisters and the life they'd known together. They had always been so close. It had been necessary to work together to keep the household running. Their father had worked hard, too, but now that Lacy was grown, it was easy to see where his incompetence had nearly cost them everything. George Gallatin had been a good soul—well-liked by his neighbors and friends, beloved of his daughters—but the man had little ability for earning a living or keeping to a budget.

Lacy hadn't realized until that moment that much of her hesitation to unite her life to that of another had to do with her fears of what that might mean. If her husband were like her father, it could prove to be more work and sorrow than she knew even now. She had once accused Dave of being lazy and not doing his job properly, but Lacy knew that wasn't the truth. So why worry about whether or not he could support a wife and family?

It would be dawn soon, Lacy figured. She couldn't bear to

face another conversation with Dave—not until she could think through everything and decide what needed to be done.

She gathered her things and decided to go home. It wouldn't be easy with the deep snowdrifts, but her horse was a good one, and Lacy knew they could find their way. For a moment, she thought about leaving Dave a note, then decided against it.

What can I say? What could I possibly put on paper that would explain the fears and anxiety I have?

Her chest felt tight, as if an iron band had wrapped itself around her. Lacy swallowed hard, feeling close to tears. "I'm not going to cry," she admonished herself aloud. "It would be silly to cry."

She took up her saddlebags and gave a quick glance around the room. The single candle didn't afford her much light, but Lacy could see well enough to know she'd left nothing behind. Opening the door, Lacy listened to hear if there was any sound coming from downstairs. With any luck, Dave would still be asleep.

The hallway floor creaked as Lacy tiptoed to the stairs. She grimaced, hoping that Dave wouldn't be awakened by her departure. She felt marginally guilty for making this hasty retreat. What would he think of her? Would he realize just how silly she was and take back his proposal? Would he hate her?

"I could never hate you," he had told her.

Lacy felt her eyes blur with tears. Why couldn't he just despise her, or at least feel indifferent? This wouldn't have to be so hard if he didn't care about her so much.

She hurried down the stairs and out the back door. To her surprise, it wasn't nearly as cold as it had been. Perhaps a Chinook wind would blow through to warm everything up and melt away their blanket of white. It wasn't unusual to see heavy snow one day and have it gone the next.

Dave had kept a nice path shoveled to the barn. Instead of walking through a foot or more of snow, Lacy found the last of the storm had deposited only a matter of inches. She easily traversed the icy path and pushed open the barn door.

She found the lantern and hurried to strike a match. But in the dim light it was difficult to see what she was doing. The gelding whinnied softly and danced nervously as Lacy attempted to secure the saddle. Her mind flooded with memories of another desperate horse ride.

"You ride better than any of us," seven-year-old Beth had told her. *"You have to go find Pa."*

Gwen had nodded solemnly. *"We'll care for Mother, but you must hurry. She's bleeding."*

A sob broke from Lacy's throat. She leaned her face against the cold leather saddle.

Mother had smiled weakly at her from the bed. *"Don't be afraid,"* she had told her five-year-old daughter. *"Everything will be just fine."*

"But it wasn't, Mama," Lacy whispered. "And it's not now, either."

Lacy couldn't have stopped the tears that now flowed down her cheeks any more than she could have forced yesterday's storm to abate. She clung to the saddle horn and cried.

How can I marry you, Dave?

She asked the question over and over in her mind. *How can I marry him when I am such a wretched mess? He doesn't know about me—about this. It's not fair to burden him with my guilt and sorrow. I've failed so many people throughout my life. How can I possibly marry and risk failing him, as well?*

And it wasn't just Dave. What if there were children? And why shouldn't there be? What if she gave birth and raised sons and daughters, only to fail them? Lacy couldn't even bear the thought.

What can I do to make this right?

She stiffened as someone embraced her from behind. Lacy had no doubt it was Dave. She fit too well in his arms. She turned and buried her face against his chest, feeling her felt hat fall by the wayside as she pressed against him. Her arms wrapped around his waist as best they could, and Lacy held fast.

Dave hadn't known what to expect when he found Lacy's prints in the snow. He'd feared that perhaps she'd left in the night, but then he realized she had to still be there. There were no horse tracks coming from the barn. There wasn't even another set of boot prints to reveal that Lacy had returned to the house.

The soft glow of lantern light had easily guided him, but more so it was the sound of crying that drew Dave to the stall where Lacy stood against her mount. His heart nearly broke for the vulnerable young woman. She seemed years—even a decade—his junior as she cried.

Taking hold of her had been the most natural thing in the world. Dave had worried she would fight him off, but instead, she had welcomed his touch. With her face buried tightly against his coat, she clung to him as if she were drowning and he were her only hope of rescue.

Dave stroked Lacy's hair and tried to think of something soothing to say. He didn't know why she'd fallen apart like this. He suspected she was running away from him—from the feelings she had for him. Had those emotions caused her to break down?

"It's . . . it's . . . not fair," she murmured, her voice ragged.

"What's not fair?" Dave asked.

"You. This." She shook her head against him. "Not fair."

"I don't understand, Lacy." He loosened his hold and raised her face gently. "Look at me and tell me what this is all about."

She opened her reddened eyes. "I'm so confused. I didn't ask for this. I didn't want this." She shook her head again. "No, I did, but . . . oh, I can't explain it."

He stroked her cheek with his thumb. "What are you afraid of?"

She laughed, but it was anything but an expression of glee. "You. Marriage. Failing yet another person."

Dave smiled. "Is that all?"

Lacy pushed away from him. "Is that all?" She wiped her eyes on her coat sleeve. "Isn't that enough?"

"I don't know." He crossed his arms and leaned back against the wall. "Should it be?"

"Oh, Dave, you have no idea of who I am." She looked at the rafters. "I'm a mess. I'm more trouble than even you want to deal with."

"Let me be the judge of that."

When her eyes found his again, Dave wanted only to take her in his arms again. Mercy, but the woman could stir his blood. He held fast, however, sensing that it was more than a little important that Lacy air her fears and thoughts.

"It's not fair." She waved her arms and the gelding shied away. "It's not fair. I don't want to feel like this."

"Like what, Lacy?"

"I don't want to care about you. I don't want to melt away every time you touch me."

He shrugged with a grin. "I kind of like that part."

"Of course you do," she railed. "Men!" Lacy kicked her saddlebags.

"All right, calm down."

"If I could do that," she countered, "I wouldn't be out here trying to sneak off."

This caused Dave to laugh. "Lacy, let's go in the house and talk this out. It's freezing out here." He crossed to where she stood. "Go on. I'll unsaddle your horse."

"No. I have to go home."

"You can go home after we talk." Dave uncinched the saddle and pulled it from the gelding's back. Lacy stood watching him but said nothing more. When he'd accomplished the task, he took her by the arm. "Come on."

She didn't resist as Dave led the way to the house. Once inside, she didn't bother to take her coat off or even move from the chair where he deposited her. Apparently she was resigned to letting him have his way, and for this, Dave was grateful.

He stoked the fire in the stove, then came to sit down beside her. "Now tell me what's not fair and why you were crying as if you'd lost your last friend."

Lacy picked at the buttons of her coat, refusing to look up. "I don't want to love you."

"So you admit that you do," Dave replied, rather pleased with himself.

Her head snapped up at this. "I didn't say that."

"Then what are you saying?"

She put her hands to her face and rubbed her temples. She looked like someone trying very hard to figure out a great mystery. "I don't know what I'm saying or thinking. That's the problem. I just know that you weren't in my plans."

"And just what plans did you have?"

Lowering her hands, she looked him in the eye. "I want to find my father's killer."

"As do I. We both want the same thing, as far as I can see."

"But *I* want to find him."

"What does it matter who finds him, as long as he's found?" Dave asked. "Honestly, Lacy, why can't you be content to know that I care about the matter as much as you do and trust me to see the job done?"

"Because I need to help." She got up and walked to the stove. Holding her hands out to the warmth, she continued. "All of my life, I've made a mess of things. I've failed people—people who suffered because of my inability to do what was required of me." She turned and looked at him with an expression that nearly sent Dave into her arms. "I don't want to fail anyone else."

"You haven't failed nearly as much as you think. We all make mistakes, and we all have tasks too big to handle. That doesn't make you a failure. You did your best, didn't you?"

"But it wasn't enough."

"Lacy, doing your best is all that's required. God expects no more. Ma always said that with human beings, most everything is impossible at one time or another. But with God, all things are possible."

"I want to believe that."

Dave got up, but Lacy held her hands out. "Don't. Please don't touch me. Something happens to me when you touch me."

He grinned. "I know. Something happens to me when I touch you. It's the passion that's between us that makes me certain we're meant to marry—to be together always." He came to a stop at the point where her fingers touched his chest. "Lacy, I love you. I love your fire and passion."

"I can't let passion rule my life," she said, her voice softening to a bare whisper.

"Passion is the stuff of life," he replied, never taking his gaze from hers.

"I'll only fail you," she said, shaking her head slowly as she let her arms relax back at her sides.

Dave reached out and touched her face. "We'll fail at something, no matter whether we're together or alone. We'll even fail each other, but I'm figuring our successes will outnumber those times. Our love will see us through, and together, we'll find a dream to call our own."

"But I just know I won't be any good at this," she said, looking hopelessly at him.

Dave chuckled and let his hand trail behind her neck to pull her closer. "Would you care to place a bet on that? I think you'll be very good at being my wife."

"Gambling is a sin," she whispered, stepping into his arms. She put her arms around him and sighed.

"So is lying."

She looked at him with a puzzled expression. "Lying? What have I lied about?"

"You're trying to lie to yourself. You're trying to convince your heart that you don't want this—that you don't want me."

Her cheeks reddened, and Dave knew he'd very nearly read her mind. "Ah, Lacy," he sighed against her ear. "I promise you, you won't regret marrying me."

CHAPTER SIX

"She's the most beautiful baby in the world," Lacy declared, taking Julianne in her arms. "And so very tiny."

Gwen beamed with pride. "I think her quite perfect, myself."

"As do I," Beth said, "but I'll probably think my own even better." They all laughed at this.

Lacy sat down on the bed beside Gwen and marveled at the infant. "She looks like you, Gwen."

"I can also see something of her father," Gwen said. "Especially around the eyes."

Beth nodded. "I agree."

Lacy gently touched the baby's cheek and laughed when Julianne turned her face as if to feed. "Is she hungry?"

"I doubt it, but anytime there's the hope of sucking," Gwen replied, "Julianne seems more than happy to comply."

"I wish I could have been here for you. Was it awful . . . having her, I mean?"

"It was quite painful, but as Patience told me, the memory of that is fading in the wake of the child given me." Gwen smiled. "I would definitely do it again—just not too soon."

Lacy couldn't begin to imagine what it was like to be a mother. She thought of Dave and his proposal, and all that it would mean. Would she be like Beth and get pregnant right away? What if she couldn't have children?

"So are you ready to talk to us?" Gwen asked.

Lacy looked up. "What do you mean?"

Beth placed a blue-and-white quilt over the rocking chair and took a seat. "Are you ready to tell us why you ran away?"

"And what happened while you were gone?"

Lacy frowned. "Why do you suppose something had to happen while I was gone?"

"Because there is something in your expression that makes us believe it did," Gwen replied before Beth could. "You were out there an awful long time with Dave."

"Some would say more than long enough to ruin your reputation," Beth added with a grin.

Lacy shook her head. "We couldn't help it that a blizzard came up. People can just think bad of me—they do anyway. They judge me on what I wear or do all of the time. I didn't do anything wrong."

Gwen's expression softened. "No one thinks you did. But something obviously happened. You and Dave look at each other differently."

"It's true," Beth said. "So you might as well tell us everything."

Lacy focused on Julianne, knowing it would be easier to confess to her niece than to her sisters. "Dave asked me to marry him."

Beth laughed and clapped her hands. "I knew it!"

"It does explain an awful lot," Gwen said. "It's about time he proposed."

Lacy looked up at the joyous faces. "What do you mean?"

"Well, it was clear that he was completely gone over you. Beth and I talked about it just the other day with Patience. She felt the same way."

Lacy handed Julianne back to Gwen and got up. "I don't know why any of you would even think such things. I don't mean to sound shocking, but as far as I can figure out, the attraction we hold for each other is purely physical."

Beth looked at Gwen and back to Lacy. "That's a very good place to start, don't you think?"

"I don't know what to think," Lacy said, turning to pace in her routine fashion. "Just because I like the way he looks and how he makes me feel when he kisses me doesn't mean we ought to marry." She stopped and looked hard at her sisters. "Does it?"

"Well, if you had no physical attraction, then I would be worried about that. So many women find it necessary to settle for a man or marriage that they do not want," Gwen replied.

"Sure, imagine if you were forced to marry, say, Rafe." Beth giggled. "You wouldn't even have a physical attraction."

"I'd shoot myself first," Lacy told them. "Or maybe I'd just shoot *him*."

Gwen laughed. "You don't mean that."

"Maybe not, but I'd never agree to marry him."

"Did you agree to marry Dave?" Beth asked.

Lacy drew a deep breath and nodded. "I did. I don't know why I did, and frankly the entire matter is causing me a great deal of distress."

"But why?" Gwen questioned. "It's so evident that you two belong together."

Lacy considered this for a moment and came back to the bed to sit. "Why do you say that? Tell me, please—because I'm desperate to know and understand."

Gwen looked at Beth as if for help. "Well, I suppose there's the way you listen to each other and talk things out."

"You mean argue and bicker?" Lacy crossed her arms. "That hardly seems like a beneficial thing."

"But you don't just fight over things. You respect each other enough to consider what's being said. I've seen it happen over and over. You might not like what Dave has to say, but you consider it."

"Yes, and then usually do exactly as I please," Lacy admitted.

"You are very headstrong," Beth agreed. "But I think you two find comfort even in your disputes. You see eye-to-eye on more than you might think."

Lacy considered Beth's words. "It just seems there ought to be something that is . . . well, more in common."

"You both love Montana and adventure," Gwen offered.

"You're both very practical, and when a job has to be done, no matter how messy or troublesome, you just dig in and do it," Beth said.

"And you both have great inner strength and faith in God,"

Gwen said as if going down a mental list. "Oh, and you are both incredible with horses."

Beth nodded. "Yes, and you have deep compassion on those who are treated unjustly."

Gwen thought for a moment. "You neither one care for strong drink or gambling."

"But you both like elk steak and berry cobbler." Beth looked at Gwen. "I swear Dave Shepard could eat his weight in berry cobbler."

Lacy couldn't help but laugh at this. "I could have those things in common with just about anyone out here."

"But can you add that to the physical attraction?" Gwen asked in a most serious tone. "Is there anyone else who makes your legs feel like they're no stronger than egg noodles?"

"Or leaves you breathless when they do nothing more than throw you a certain look from across the room?" Beth added.

Lacy couldn't deny the truth of either comment. No one but Dave made her feel that way. She drew a deep breath and let it out in a long sigh. Maybe there was enough to merit marriage between them.

"But I don't know if I love him."

Her sisters once again exchanged a glance and Gwen asked, "Can you imagine living life without him?"

"And still be happy?" Beth supplied.

Gwen nodded and continued. "If he decided to break off the engagement and moved away tomorrow, could you easily let him go?"

"Or would you feel as though you'd lost a part of yourself—of your heart?" Beth questioned softly.

Lacy was terrified to even know the answers to those

questions. She wasn't yet ready to know the truth of it. "I can't . . . I can't even begin to ask myself those things."

Beth smiled. "When you can and you're willing to acknowledge the truth of the answers, then you'll know for sure if you love him."

The stage finally made it through the snow the following day. There were enough passengers to keep Gallatin House filled to overflowing, so Rafe wasn't all that surprised when one man sought the saloon out for refuge.

"Do you have a room for an old friend?" the stranger asked.

Rafe studied the man for a moment. There was something vaguely familiar about his stance. His reddish brown beard and mustache seemed hastily grown and perhaps foreign to the man, but his brown eyes held a hard glint that Rafe recognized. This was the look of a man hardened by life.

"Don't tell me you don't recognize me, Rafe. Why, my feelings will be hurt all to pieces if you do that."

It was the voice . . . that gentle drawl . . . that brought back the memory. "Jefferson?"

"Of course it's me!" The man stepped forward, dropped his saddlebags, and gave Rafe a big bear hug. "How in the world are you?"

"Well, I'll be," Rafe said, shaking his head. "Jefferson Mulholland."

They'd known each other in St. Louis, and Rafe had even written a letter to Jefferson when he was searching for new girls. Rafe stepped back from the man's embrace and shook his head. "What brings you to this part of the country?"

"You do," Jefferson replied.

"Me? But why?"

Jefferson laughed and headed to the bar. "Serve me up a drink, and I'll explain."

Rafe followed behind and tried to imagine what his old friend might want. Suspicion was Rafe's approach to life, and just because he and Mulholland had looked after each other's interests at one time didn't mean the man wasn't trouble now.

"Whiskey or beer?" Rafe asked.

"A beer is fine. We can save the rest for celebrating later. That is, if you decide you want to consider my proposition."

So he had come with an agenda. Rafe grabbed a glass and filled it. What could his old friend want? He looked up with a lopsided smile and put the beer on the bar. "And what proposition would that be?"

Mulholland drank down half the glass before answering. "I've been studying this area. It hasn't been all that easy to get information, but as it worked out, I made the acquaintance of a man who once worked some ranches in these parts."

"If you've been studying on it, then you probably know the decision the railroad made to go in to the north instead of coming through here."

Jefferson smiled in a smug, confident way that left Rafe uneasy. "That's what they say, but I have a feeling we can convince them to quickly attach a spur line to this area."

"But there would have to be something mighty valuable to the railroad to do such a thing," Rafe countered. "I'm afraid this area doesn't have much in that way to offer."

"Not yet, but maybe in time."

Rafe watched Jefferson as he downed the rest of the beer in one drink. The man wiped the foam from his mustache and grinned. "I have a foolproof scheme to see this little community double in size overnight."

Shaking his head, Rafe refilled his friend's glass as Jefferson pulled a bag from his pocket. He plopped the drawstring pouch onto the bar with a thud.

"What's that?"

"The answer to our problems."

"I didn't say I had any problems," Rafe replied in a skeptical tone. He eyed Mulholland warily.

Jefferson Mulholland laughed. "While I was in Bozeman, I heard about robberies, highwaymen, and murders from this area. It seemed the perfect place to create a gambling hall. Men of such reputations need a place to spend their ill-gotten gains."

"You want to set up a rival saloon?"

"Not at all, my friend. I want to come in as a partner and expand this town to become a place of pleasure and diverse entertainment. The property will be cheap, because people are already looking to sell and move, are they not?"

"Some are. Some are less inclined to go."

"And once we convince the quiet and conservative folks of the neighborhood that the area is about to take a turn for the, shall we say, more wild side of life, they will be eager to leave."

"But how do you propose doing this?" Rafe asked. He leaned against the bar and looked hard at Mulholland.

"With this." Jefferson picked up the pouch and opened it.

He spread his handkerchief on the bar and spilled a tiny portion of gold dust from the bag.

"Gold? But there isn't any gold here."

"None that has been found so far," Jefferson said, smiling. "I propose we help things along."

Rafe narrowed his eyes. "In what way?"

"How much land can we get our hands on—I mean right away? Can we get a good portion of land along the river?"

"I have some, but as for the rest, I don't know. Hank Bishop owns a good stretch to the north, and then there are other families who own portions to the south. I know of a couple of folks ready to sell out and move north because of the railroad, and one family moved to Bozeman when their business burned down."

"Good. I think it's time we act on the circumstances at hand. Between the two of us, we can surely come up with enough money to get things started."

"But I still don't understand. Get what started?"

Jefferson smiled. "A gold rush." He patted the bag.

"But I already told you, there hasn't been any gold found in this area."

"There will be. I have another bag just like this, and a few of fool's gold. It would be simple enough to hire some fellows to pose as panners who have found a fortune in gold on the Gallatin. I'll simply have them use my gold in order to get things started, then we even plant a little here and there."

"You'd give your gold away?"

"Not exactly." Mulholland carefully wadded up the handkerchief and stuffed it and the gold back in the pouch. "My investment will be minimal compared to what we'll demand of those who come to get rich. If we own the land, we can issue leases and work out arrangements with others to share a percentage of what they pan out of the river. Of course, you and I know that there really won't be anything to be had, except by those lucky few who are on our payroll."

Rafe grinned. "I'm starting to like this idea. We can sell them supplies and liquor at well over our cost."

"Exactly. Folks have to have a place to live, as well. I can get an order of tents shipped in, and we can charge rent. By the time folks get discouraged and move on, we will have made a small fortune."

Doubt niggled at the back of Rafe's mind. "But why come here and bring me in on it?"

Jefferson sobered. "You once helped me when I was down on my luck. I owe you a debt, and I'm not the kind to let it go unpaid."

To Rafe's way of thinking, that debt had been settled long ago. He and Jefferson had helped each other out of more than one mess, but if the man felt duty bound, who was Rafe to suggest otherwise?

Just then Cubby came in from the back room. "When's the next shipment of whiskey due in, Pa?"

Jefferson laughed. "This can't be little Cubby."

Rafe nodded. "In the flesh. The boy's sixteen now."

"A good age to be useful," Mulholland said with a smile. "Do you remember me, son?"

Cubby shook his head. "Should I?"

"No, of course not. You weren't much more than two or three the last time I saw you. I'm an old friend of your father's and soon to be his business partner."

"Partner?" Cubby looked at his father. "What about Wyman?"

"Wyman's hired help, nothing more," Rafe declared. "Jefferson is a visionary."

"What's that?" Cubby asked.

Rafe laughed and eyed Mulholland with great interest. "The means to a better life."

CHAPTER SEVEN

As the first week of February slipped away, Dave Shepard's proposal seemed more like a dream than a reality. Whenever Lacy would think back on her time at the Shepard ranch, she wondered if she'd somehow made more of the situation than it merited. Maybe Dave wasn't serious at all. Maybe the passion of the moment had caused him to speak first and think later, and now he regretted having asked her to marry him.

Lacy thought it was entirely possible. After all, she had responded out of the intensity of the moment. Why couldn't Dave have done likewise? She was just starting to relax a bit when Dave brought up the topic at breakfast one morning. The fact that he lived in the Gallatin House addition put him at their table for almost every meal, much to her chagrin.

"I'm sure by now Lacy has told you our news," Dave announced.

Gwen nodded. "We were very happy to hear of your engagement."

Lacy focused her attention on the last of her pancakes. So much for thinking she'd made too much of the situation. Still, how dare he bring this matter up now—without having discussed it with her first? She pushed the food around and waited for someone to speak further on the matter.

Nick slapped Dave on the back. "Yes, I wanted to say something but wasn't sure if I was allowed to."

Dave laughed. "Usually this family is no good at keeping secrets, but it seemed like this issue was being tiptoed around, so I thought I'd just throw it out on the table."

"I'm glad you did," Gwen said. She picked up the coffee pot. "Anyone need a refill?"

Dave and Hank held out their cups while Lacy wanted to crawl under the table. She still hadn't come to terms with how to deal with her engagement to Dave.

"So, Lacy, have you set a date?" Beth asked.

Lacy wanted to kick her sister under the table. She looked up reluctantly and shook her head. "No, there have been far too many other things to focus on."

"Truly?" Gwen asked. "Such as?"

Lacy silently wished she could find the laudanum Hank had taken away and dose them all. "Well, we . . . we . . . have to decide about the land and where we're going to live." It was as good an excuse as any.

"I suppose that does merit consideration," Hank said. He cut a piece of sausage in two and ate in silence.

"It's very important to know such things," Lacy said, believing it was better to push on with the conversation than to let anyone else bring it back to setting a date. "Have we heard any more about the railroad land that Adrian said would be offered?"

"Not a word," Hank said. "I do have plans to get on it, however. I was thinking when Dave rode over to Bozeman, I just might join him. Maybe you could watch the store for me, Lacy."

She nodded in a most enthusiastic manner. "I'm sure I could. There haven't been any problems in the area for some time. When I was picking up cheese from Rachel the other day, she credited it to the fact that Dave is now in the area all the time." She wanted to kick herself. There would be no getting Dave to leave with comments like that.

Beth spread butter on a muffin. "I'm sure Dave's presence has a great deal to do with it. Sometimes just having a representative of the law reminds folks to keep order. With the highwaymen knowing that Dave is out there, tracking their every move, they are bound to be less inclined to attempt robberies."

"Not to mention that it's been minus twenty degrees a good portion of the winter," Dave said with a chuckle.

Nick and Hank laughed, too. "Nah," Hank said, shaking his head, "they're scared of you, Dave."

"If you and Dave are heading to Bozeman, maybe Lacy should go, too," Gwen suggested. "She needs to pick out material for her wedding dress."

Lacy nearly choked on her pancake. Just when she had

81

begun to think the conversation might steer away from her and Dave, Gwen found a way to bring it front and center.

"She's welcome to come along," Hank said. "I could probably get Cubby to watch the store. We could take the wagon and pick up anything else that's needed."

Lacy shook her head vehemently. "I figured I'd just have Hank order in some material when the time came."

"Well, the time has come," Beth said in a teasing voice. "You don't want to let this get away from you. We should get the gown started right away. After all, I'll be having the baby in June and—"

"I don't imagine Dave intends to wait that long to tie the knot," Nick interjected.

Lacy pushed back from the table in frustration. "Just stop. We haven't set a date, and frankly, I don't even know what kind of dress I want. I do know that I wish you would all stop trying to plan out my life."

She left everyone gape-mouthed at the table and hurried into the kitchen. Grabbing her coat and hat, Lacy decided some fresh air would do her good. Chopping wood had always been an effective way to spend her anger.

Pulling on her gloves, Lacy drew a deep breath and let it out again. She picked up the axe and went to work as if it were her personal job to provide firewood for the entire valley. After splitting about ten logs, she was startled to look up and find Cubby watching her.

"What do you want?"

"You looked pretty upset. I thought maybe you'd want to talk," he offered.

"Talking won't fix anything."

"Why not?"

She put the axe down and only then realized she'd worked herself into a sweat. She wiped her forehead and looked back at Cubby. "Talking got me into this mess to begin with. I'm tired of people trying to make me see and do things their way."

"I feel the same way. Pa's always trying to tell me what to do and what's best for my future. Like he's set a good example himself."

"Exactly!" Lacy's eyes were bright. "You are exactly right. People who can't figure out their own messes shouldn't be dictating to others how they can solve theirs. Sometimes I think I should just leave."

"Funny you should say that, Lacy. I've been thinkin' the same thing. I am sixteen now, you know."

"I remember."

He grinned. "I figured you would. Anyway, I've been ponderin' the idea of making my own way. You could come with me."

"Well . . . things are complicated right now," Lacy said.

Cubby closed the distance between them and took hold of Lacy's gloved hand. "I'd take good care of you. We could go anywhere you wanted to go."

Pulling her hand from his, Lacy shook her head. "It isn't that simple, Cubby."

"Call me Quennell. Cubby sounds like a boy's name. I'm a man now, and I want folks to respect me."

"But I like Cubby. Cubby sounds friendly and comfortable. Still, if you really aren't happy with it, I suppose I can learn to call you Quennell."

The young man pushed back his dirty blond hair and smiled. "You can call me Cubby if it's that important."

"It isn't that." She heaved a sigh. "I really can't explain. I should probably just gather some of this wood and get back to my chores."

"I hate seeing you sad, Lacy. I know things are hard, but I want to take you away from here. I want to get us a place of our own. I want to marry you."

Lacy couldn't keep from rolling her eyes. "So you're just one more person who wants to dictate my life to me."

"No, it's not that. I love you. I care about you."

"So does everyone else, apparently. And because of that, they believe they have the right to impose their will upon me. No, Cubby, I'm not leaving with you, and I'm not marrying you."

He frowned and then his expression turned hard. "It's because of Dave Shepard, isn't it?"

"If it were, it wouldn't be any of your business." She turned to leave, but he grabbed her by the shoulders and forced her to face him. "Let me go, Cubby."

"No. You're no better than my father's women. You talk nice to a fella and make him think he's got a chance, then you go off and allow some other man to take liberties with you. Don't think I didn't see you and Dave Shepard that day in the cemetery."

"What are you talking about?"

"You let him kiss you!"

Lacy knocked his hands away. "What if I did? I've never pretended to be anything other than friends with you, Cubby. I told you long ago I'm not interested in marrying you or having anything but friendship between us."

He slapped her hard across the face, leaving Lacy breathless. The sting against her cold skin sent a burning sensation across her cheek. "How dare you? You're no better than your father.

He treats women like animals, and apparently you've learned well. Go home, Cubby. Go home and leave me alone."

He looked torn between apologizing and hitting her again. Lacy stood her ground and put her hands on her hips. Finally he muttered something she couldn't make out and turned back for the saloon. Only after he'd gone inside did Lacy allow herself to wince. She put her hand to her face and touched the spot gently.

"I didn't realize you were out here," Dave said, coming from the back porch.

After having battled Cubby, Lacy was in no mood to deal with Dave. She bent to pick up firewood. "I'm trying to get my work done."

"Let me help."

"No, that's all right." She straightened and forced a smile. "I have it."

"What happened?" Dave asked, eyes narrowing. He reached out and turned her cheek to better view it.

"I don't know what you're talking about."

"Someone hit you. I can see a clear handprint on your face." His voice lowered. "Lacy, who did this?"

"It's not important, Dave. It was just a misunderstanding."

"It looks like more than that. People don't just go hitting each other and have it be a mere misunderstanding. You're going to be my wife, and it's my place to take care of you. I demand you tell me who did this."

"Everyone seems to be demanding something of me." She threw the wood down. "Frankly, I'm sick of it. I said it wasn't important, and it's not."

It was nearly the end of February, and the citizens of Gallatin Crossing had been enjoying milder temperatures. After a winter of sub-zero weather, temperatures in the twenties and thirties felt almost balmy.

The nicer weather left everyone more than ready for spring, even though they knew it was still a long way off. Hank figured it was a good time to plan for the future. With Nick and Dave gathered in his office, he shared a letter that had come that day.

"It's a mixed blessing," Hank said. "The bad news is that the stage company refuses to renew our yearly contract. The good news? Well, they've agreed to keep us on month-by-month until something better comes along."

"That doesn't sound all that good," Nick said, taking a seat opposite Hank. "I need a steady income—now more than ever."

Hank nodded. "As do I. I tried to point out that the railroad can't possibly be complete for at least two years, so surely they could at least renew for that long."

Nick raised a brow. "And?"

"And they wouldn't budge. Told me they didn't feel it was in their best interest."

"Never mind that we've been loyal workers, upholding their contracts and schedules," Nick said bitterly.

"So what do you suggest, Hank?" Dave asked.

Hank reached under his desk and pulled out a rolled-up map. "Adrian Murphy sent this. It's the rail line plans. He's marked out a potential town site that would serve the railroad well. It's just ten miles or so northwest of Bozeman."

Nick and Dave leaned forward to look at the map as Hank unrolled the paper. "This is the location Adrian told me about."

Hank put his finger on the map. "The railroad will go through Bozeman here. Then it will follow along this line." Hank drew his finger along a faint marking.

"Where are we currently from that line?" Dave asked.

"Here." Hank pinpointed the spot south of the planned railroad.

The three men considered the distance between locations. Hank knew they'd be thinking the same thing he was. It would be cheaper to sell out and rebuild than to try to move any of their buildings to the new site.

"It would mean starting from bare ground," Hank said. He left the map out and took his seat. "I've been asking about the land prices. The railroad has a certain easement, as well as land given by the government that they can use as incentives to get people to build towns. I think we can benefit by this quite nicely."

"But what of our land here?" Nick asked. "I would need to sell it, and I won't get a very good price for a piece of land alone, since the fire burned all the buildings."

"We could arrange to build a cabin. With our friends in the area, we could surely put up a small log structure. That would help a little bit."

Nick nodded. "I suppose it would, at that. Of course, Rafe still wants to buy it."

Dave frowned. "I can't find any way to prove his involvement in your fire, but I feel sure he was at the start of it. Someone threw a lit lantern into the hay. It didn't get there by itself."

"But why do you think Rafe's behind it?" Hank asked.

"He's the one clamoring to buy the land. Nobody else has stepped forward asking for it. Have they?"

"No," Nick admitted. "Still, he hasn't been pestering me at all. Seems like he'd be pressing to see the matter resolved if it was important enough to set fire to my barn. I just don't want to falsely judge him on this."

"Yes, but on the other hand," Hank said thoughtfully, "as Dave said, he's the only one who really stood to gain from it."

"He couldn't be sure I'd sell." Nick shook his head. "Rafe is a selfish man, I'll give you that, but I can't believe he'd want to destroy me like that—even risk killing me and my family."

"Hey, where is everybody?"

Hank recognized Cubby's voice. "We're in the office, Cubby. Come on back."

Cubby bounded into the room, his face clearly showing the excitement his voice betrayed. "Gold!" He was rather breathless. "They found gold on the Gallatin."

"What? Who found it?" Nick asked.

"Some men . . . my pa. . . ." He panted to regain his breath. "They're over at the saloon."

"No one has ever found gold in this area before," Dave said. "Are you sure it's not fool's gold?"

"My pa's friend Mr. Mulholland knows about such things, and he says it's gold for sure."

"This could change everything," Nick said, looking at Hank. "It might very well mean new life for this town. If there's a gold rush, the railroad may be willing to build a side line down from the main road. I could rebuild the livery."

"And the stage would definitely make stops here for the miners," Hank said, grinning. "You're right. This changes everything."

CHAPTER EIGHT

"We can't possibly keep up with this crowd," Gwen said, wiping her brow with the edge of her apron. "How many men have we fed lunch to today?"

"At my last count, it was fifty-two," Beth replied.

"Feels like one hundred and two," Lacy interjected. "I've never seen men eat so much. We're out of nearly everything."

Beth brought an empty pot to the counter. "At least they like beans and corn bread."

"But we're even out of beans now," Lacy said, shaking her head.

Gwen put on a fresh pot of coffee. "Hank put in a triple order for most of our regular supplies. He said it should be delivered today, if the weather holds."

Lacy went to the kitchen window and gazed out at the brilliant March skies. "Doesn't look like rain or snow is threatening. There isn't a cloud anywhere." She turned and surveyed the stack of dishes to be washed. "Guess I'd better get to work."

"I can't bake too much until we get more flour," Beth said, lifting the lid off the flour barrel Hank had brought them just three days earlier. "This is nearly empty."

Julianne began to fuss from the corner where Gwen had her set up in a small makeshift bed. "I guess the men aren't the only ones who are hungry." She went to pick up her daughter, and the baby instantly calmed.

"Maybe we should charge more," Lacy suggested. "That would surely discourage some of the miners from coming here. In fact, I don't see why we need their business anyway. They just make it more difficult to deal with the stage folks."

"Lacy's right," Beth said. "Maybe we should figure out a way to schedule things so that we only deal with the miners after the stage folks have departed."

"I'd like that," Gwen agreed. "Still, with you expecting and Lacy trying to plan a wedding, we have more to do than we can keep up with. We'll make ourselves sick if we keep trying to go at this pace."

Hank was having no better time of it at the store. He'd sold out his fifth shipment of gold pans, picks, and shovels. The new arrivals were none too happy to hear they'd have to wait for the afternoon freight delivery before they could set out to work.

"I understand you own a lot of the land around here," one

man said, approaching Hank. "I wonder if you'd lease me a claim."

"No," Hank replied. He'd already been approached at least two dozen times about the same thing.

"The saloonkeep said you should be willing to. We could split any of the profits I made. Just give it a chance, mister."

Hank shook his head. "I'm already dealing with squatters and men tramping through to get to other claims. The answer is no."

The man grumbled and stepped away from the counter. He was quickly replaced by two other men who had a list of supplies they hoped to secure.

Raising his arms, Hank tried to calm the throng. "Look, if you would all quiet down for just a minute and listen, we could save some time." Little by little, the room went silent.

"Thank you. As you can see we're out of most everything. I have three freight wagons due in this afternoon. If they keep to their schedule, they'll be here within the hour. I'll need time to secure the shipment, but then I can deal with each of you. For now, I'd like you to form a line here at the counter. We'll write down what you need and your name. Then come back this afternoon around five, and we'll divvy up and you can pay."

"Are you taking any credit, mister?" one man called out from the back.

"No. There's too great a risk with panning for gold. If you haven't got the money to buy what you need, you shouldn't even be here."

"But we are here," another threw out.

Hank looked at the ragtag collection of men. Some were young, while others were quite grizzled with age. They all had a look of expectation and confidence in their expression. They had come here to make their fortunes—no matter the cost. Hank could have told them they might do better to open a store than to try and pan for gold, but he wasn't entirely sure he wanted the competition. He'd been so busy and so prosperous that he'd taken Nick on as a full-time employee. Besides, who could tell when the bottom would give out and everyone would move on to the next gold discovery?

A few of the men left the store, while most of the others lined up and gave their information to Hank. By the time the last fellow had gone, Hank had twenty-seven slips of paper, detailing the men's various needs.

"Looks like you've gone out of business," Dave said as he stepped up to the register. He glanced around at the empty shelves and then looked at Hank. "They've stripped you clean."

Hank nodded. "You ought to see the list I have for what they want once the freighters get in. It'll be all I can do to pull out the supplies for Gallatin House and Rafe first. I've had to send out requests for supplies from every direction."

"I don't doubt it," Dave said. "I think we were wise to have me start sleeping over here nights. Smart, too, to turn that loafing shed into a jail of sorts. Not that it's going to hold any truly determined soul."

"Something's going to have to be done about that," Hank said, shaking his head. "Those men get awfully mean out there—especially after drinking."

"I heard that Mulholland has brought in an assay man. I have to say, I'm still stumped at there being gold in the river. You'd think someone would have found something before now."

"I know what you're saying, but Nick mentioned some

dynamiting being done upstream as they're trying to build a road. Maybe it's opened a vein and washed it down this way."

"I suppose that's entirely possible. It's the first speculation that makes sense." At the sound of wagons, Dave went to the door. "Looks like the freight is in. Guess I'd better go out there and control the men before they get carried away."

"I'd appreciate that, Dave. I'll get Nick. He's been working with the horses out back."

As the second anniversary of their father's death drew near, Lacy found herself facing increased pressure to marry. She was grateful for the constant work required by the gold rush; it allowed her to avoid committing to a wedding date, given that she and Dave had very little time together alone. The madness that consumed their little community was the perfect excuse to keep things exactly as they were.

Beth was growing quite large in her pregnancy and constantly reminded Lacy that it would only be another six weeks or so until she would deliver her child. She hoped Lacy would have the wedding right away or else wait until well after the birth. That had been the best thing anyone could have said. Lacy used the excuse when Dave came to her that evening after supper.

"I don't want to set a wedding date until after Beth gives birth and recovers. She'll work much too hard to see that I have a nice wedding otherwise."

Dave frowned. "Are you sure you aren't just delaying this because you're trying to back out?"

Lacy thought about it for a moment. "If you want to end our engagement, I won't fight you."

"You won't, eh?" He crossed to where she stood and pulled her into his arms. "Somehow, I don't believe you."

Lacy trembled but fought to keep her wits. It seemed the only time she wasn't overcome by his touch was when they were fighting. "You know my father has been dead now for two years."

He frowned. "Not quite, but I know the date is fast approaching."

"We're no closer to catching the killer than we were two years ago," Lacy protested. "Cubby swears his father knows what happened, yet I don't see you dragging Rafe into Bozeman to be questioned."

Dave dropped his hold. "I can't just force the man to go with me to Bozeman. I don't have any evidence against him."

Lacy went to the fireplace and warmed her hands. The chill of the night air made the fire a welcome sight. She drew a deep breath and turned back to face Dave. "I really can't marry you until this is resolved."

"What?"

"You heard me. I want my father's killer caught. I want justice for him. I can't have a wedding and enjoy the idea of sharing my life with someone while that is yet undone."

"That's just an excuse."

She shook her head. "You know it isn't." She took a seat in the rocker next to the fireplace. "I've wanted this since the night our father died."

"That may be, but you're using it as an excuse for delaying our wedding."

She shrugged. "Think what you will. It's not that way at

all." She looked at the floor and studied the pattern of the new rag rug to avoid Dave's intense stare.

"You're deliberately trying to make me mad so that I won't pester you with planning our wedding. Maybe you even hope I'll break the engagement. I think this has very little to do with your father's killer being caught, however."

Lacy crossed her arms and began to rock. "Then tell me, Mr. Shepard, what you think it has to do with."

"You're afraid. You're just scared, and that's all there is to it."

She didn't like him pinpointing the truth. "Maybe you're scared, too. Scared to find Pa's killer."

"That's ridiculous."

She met his gaze. "It's no more ridiculous than you saying I'm too scared to marry you." She hoped he wouldn't notice the slight tremor to her voice.

Dave shook his head. "You are the most irritating and aggravating woman I've ever known."

"Then why do you want to marry me?" Lacy asked with a sweet smile.

"Sometimes I wonder," he muttered and stalked out of the room without another word.

Lacy felt a strange urge to go after him but held herself in place. She wasn't about to give him the satisfaction of believing himself to be right about her fears.

"What are you and Dave fighting about now?" Beth asked as she entered the room and carefully lowered herself onto a chair. "He looked madder than a wet hen."

"He's just angry that I won't set the wedding date."

Beth smoothed out her oversized white blouse. "And why won't you?"

"I'd rather wait until after the baby comes and you are fully recovered. I think we need to focus on one event at a time. Besides, everything is in such an uproar right now. The town is overflowing with riffraff. It's not exactly the kind of setting I want for my wedding."

"I suppose I can understand that." Beth rubbed her stomach. "This little one is in an uproar, as well. I sometimes wonder what in the world must be going on in there."

Lacy came to kneel beside her sister. Putting her hand on Beth's belly, she smiled. "Goodness, he's strong."

"So you're convinced it's a boy, are you?"

"I think so. You're carrying this baby completely different from the way Gwen carried Julianne. I'm thinking it must be a boy."

"Or a herd of cattle," Beth said, smiling. This quickly gave way to a yawn. "I'm so exhausted all the time, and my back is always strained from this load."

Lacy felt the baby kick hard against her hand. "It's no wonder. But see, it completely justifies my decision to postpone the wedding." She looked up and met Beth's tired expression. "We have to be certain that you and the baby are strong and healthy. I want you and Gwen to stand up with me, after all."

Beth touched Lacy's cheek. "I would get off of my sickbed to be there for you. You know that."

"I know, but I don't want it to happen that way." Lacy sighed and got to her feet. "Come on, little mama. I'll help you upstairs and draw you a nice hot bath. That will soothe your aching back."

Beth allowed Lacy to help her up. The sisters embraced. "Little sister, whatever your reasons for putting off your wedding," Beth began, "I hope you won't let it come between you and Dave and the love you share. It would be a pity to see you two at odds over something so trivial. Dave really does love you. . . . Don't make him wait too long."

"If he loves me so much, he won't mind. After all, I think this is important. Besides, he can use the time to find Pa's killer. He knows how important that is to me."

Beth looked at her for a moment as if trying to figure out how to phrase her words, then nodded. "I'm sure he does."

That night as Lacy sat brushing out her hair, she thought of what Dave had said about being afraid. She couldn't deny that his comment held merit, but it wasn't the reason in full.

"How do I make sure I'm doing the right thing? How do I know for certain that our love is real—that it will last?"

She abandoned the brush and went to check the lock on her door. Hank had told them all that despite having locked doors for the private section of the house, it would be wise to keep their bedrooms secured, as well. Lacy had to agree. The number of rowdies had increased drastically with the finding of gold.

There were robberies on a regular basis, as well as assaults and barroom brawls. Lacy leaned against the door and thought of Dave. His work had become so overwhelming that some residents had suggested he get an additional deputy or two to work with him.

Things have certainly changed overnight, Lacy thought. She made her way to bed and turned down the lamp until the room went dark. The silence of the night was only temporary, however. A rifle was fired off several times and multiple voices filled the air.

Lacy rushed to the window, remembering with dread the night her father had been killed. Had someone else been murdered? She opened her window and looked out on the street below. A crowd had gathered over to the far end of the road near the trees. Several of the people held lanterns in order to better survey the situation. Lacy stiffened at the sight of a mound lying lifeless on the road.

"You killed him, sure thing!" someone declared.

"Good thing, too. He needed killin'."

"Yeah, he's been nothing but a nuisance."

Lacy saw a light go on at the store next door and watched as Dave emerged. Her heart began to pound.

"What's going on?" he demanded as he crossed the distance. Lacy could see he had his rifle in hand.

"Old Blaylock killed a bear," a man announced.

"It's that old black that's been bothering the miners," someone else added.

Lacy relaxed a bit and drew a deep breath. It was just a bear. No other man had died in the melee of this sinful town.

"But they might have," Lacy whispered. "It could just as easily have been someone else's pa."

CHAPTER NINE

"I'm glad you could stay and talk with me a bit while Dave helps his dad," Patience told Lacy. She poured more tea into Lacy's cup and smiled. "Tell me all about the wedding plans." She sat opposite Lacy and looked at her in expectation.

Lacy feigned interest in the tea and sampled it. "This is very good. Thank you." She tasted the steaming liquid again and added, "Gwen will expect me to get back before four with the milk and eggs. The stage is due in at six."

"I completely understand." Patience poured cream into her tea and beamed at Lacy. "I can hardly believe you're to become my daughter. What a blessing that will be. A mother always worries about the wife her son will take, but in your case, I haven't a single concern."

"Maybe you should have," Lacy replied. She frowned and reached for a cookie.

"Why do you say that?" Patience asked softly.

"I suppose because I've never been good at anything in my life, and I certainly have no reason to believe marriage will be any different. I fail at most everything, and . . . and I think that's something you should know."

Patience laughed. "Oh, my dear, we all feel that we fail at one time or another."

Lacy shook her head vehemently. "I fail all the time. I didn't even do well in school. Any success has been nothing more than pure luck."

"I don't believe in luck, Lacy."

"To be honest, neither do I." She shrugged. "If I did, I'd have to confess that I possess absolutely none."

Patience put down her cup and eyed Lacy with a compassionate yet firm look. "You might as well continue your confession. I have a feeling there is a great deal more to be said that you are keeping hidden inside."

"What good is confession? It won't change anything."

"Maybe not, but on the other hand, it might." Patience smiled. "Lacy, I've come to care for you as a daughter even before you agreed to marry Dave. I want us to be close—to feel free to discuss anything that is on our hearts."

Lacy swallowed the cookie without even tasting it, then chased it down with a liberal gulp of the tea. What could she possibly say to Patience Shepard that would make sense? She couldn't even sort through the matter herself. How could she hope that others could reason through the mire?

Lacy put down the cup and saucer and squared her shoulders. "I'm a misfit."

Patience's eyes lit up in delight. "Aren't we all?"

"No, you don't understand. All of my life, I've been the outcast. I've tried to do the right thing—be the perfect young lady as my sisters were—but I can't be that person. I'm not like them."

"But that doesn't mean you aren't acceptable and lovely in your own way."

Lacy thought back on all the reprimands from teachers and relatives to sit up straight, walk like a lady instead of a horse, speak softly, and hold her temper in check. When other girls wanted to play with their dolls, Lacy had wanted to ride horses, and when those same young ladies delighted in getting their first grown-up gown, Lacy shamed her sisters by wearing boys' trousers.

But not only had she been a misfit, she often made the wrong choices. If she didn't fail outright at a task, she often made such a mess of it that someone else had to help straighten out the situation.

"When I was a young girl," Lacy began, "I remember my mother saying that I was the son my father had always wanted. I was such a tomboy and didn't like the same things my sisters enjoyed."

Patience nodded. "I can well imagine."

"The reason I was such a good rider was that I was always pestering my father to teach me about the horses. He would take me riding with him and show me all sorts of things—how to track, how to shoot, how to clean game. My mother and sisters were mortified when I'd come home bloody and caked in dirt, but I loved it. I didn't even care that the other children made fun of me."

"You certainly wouldn't have been made fun of here,"

Patience assured her. "Out here, you have to be able to fend for yourself whether you are a girl or a boy. Jerry taught our girls how to work right alongside their brother. He said it was important that they be able to defend their home or provide for it, should the need arise."

"That's how it was when we finally moved to Texas," Lacy admitted. "I thought I would finally be able to live the life I enjoyed. We were so isolated that no one cared that I dressed like a boy. My mother was greatly relieved that she could send her five-year-old daughter out to kill a chicken for supper. It was a job no one else wanted."

"But then she died," Patience offered, as if knowing the subject would be hard for Lacy to bring up.

Lacy met the woman's eyes. "Yes. She died and we moved yet again, and my grandmother was appalled that I was such a wild creature. She immediately set to work trying to change me, and all the while, I lived with the growing guilt that I had failed my mother. And because of that, she died."

Lacy got up and walked to the fireplace. She stared into the hearth as if a fire were blazing there. "When my grandmother would point out my flaws and faults, I felt that she really wanted to tell me that I'd killed my mother."

"That would have been not only cruel but wrong," Patience said with such tenderness in her voice that Lacy couldn't help but turn. "You weren't to blame, Lacy."

"I can reason that now, but I don't believe it. I failed to find our father, and our mother died because she didn't have adequate help."

"As I understand it, your mother bled to death while trying to give birth. When that happens, there is very little anyone can do. Even a doctor would tell you it would take a miracle to save a woman in such a situation."

Lacy considered this a moment, believing in her heart that Patience wouldn't knowingly lie to her. Then Lacy looked away again.

"I don't think I can marry Dave."

"But why?"

She didn't bother to look at Patience. Lacy knew she'd see a grief-stricken expression that would pierce her heart and remind her again of failure. "He deserves someone better."

Patience laughed, but it sounded forced. "Lacy, you silly goose. Do you love my son?"

Lacy pondered the question for a moment. "Oh, Patience, I don't honestly know. I've asked myself that question over and over. I'm not sure what it really means to love someone that way." She stepped back to where they'd been sitting and gripped the back of the chair she'd once occupied. "I do know that I care enough about him to not wish someone like me on him."

Dave's mother lowered her face and shook her head. "Lacy, I know that Dave loves you with all of his heart, and he's never wished to marry anyone else."

"Patience, he doesn't really know me. No one does. I'm not like Beth or Gwen. I'm driven to do things my sisters would never consider. I want a life that is nothing like the one they've dreamed of."

"And what would that life look like?" Patience asked.

Lacy shrugged. "It wouldn't look like this," she said, waving her arm across the room. "I hardly see myself having tea parties and crocheting doilies for the backs of my chairs. Do you know I actually envy the men out there, panning for gold in my backyard? I love the wilderness and animals—horses, in particular. I'm not at all conventional. I'd just as soon drive a stage as bake in the kitchen. I hate household chores and would much rather be mucking a stall."

Patience laughed. "But a good farm or ranch wife needs to be able to do that, as well."

"I suppose, but . . ." Lacy paused and felt her cheeks grow hot. "Dave wants a wife he can be . . . well, loved by. He'll want children and a home. I just don't know if I'm cut out to be that woman. If I'm not better at being a wife and mother than I've been as a daughter and sister, then we'll be doomed before we even get started."

Patience got to her feet and came to where Lacy stood. She took hold of Lacy's shoulders. "Do you not want to be a wife and mother?"

Lacy sighed. "I want it, but at the same time I'm terrified of it."

Patience nodded. "I think most everything you've said here today speaks of your deep fears of disappointing someone—of not being all that they need. But, Lacy, marriage can't work that way. People put expectations on one another, and they are always disappointed. It's best to go into a marriage not expecting anything but honesty and love. Build the rest together, and trust God to show you the way."

"But I don't even know if God hears me anymore. I think He was probably the first one I failed."

"We all fail God," Patience replied. "Remember, the Bible says we've all sinned and fallen short. There is no perfect person walking the earth, so stop trying to suggest that you need to be without fault. So you've failed at various things; so have I. I feel like I failed with my daughters. They would much rather live back East with their grandparents than endure another moment here. I can't help but feel that it has as much to do with me as with Montana."

"I seriously doubt that," Lacy said. "You've always seemed like such a good mother to me."

"And you seem like a good sister and a fine young woman. Yet you stand here telling me you are neither." She reached up and brushed back some loose strands of hair. "Lacy, you are much too hard on yourself. Not even God judges you as harshly as you judge yourself. He certainly doesn't expect the perfection you've come to expect of yourself. He only asks for you to seek and trust Him. He's the only perfect one in this world."

"I try to turn to Him, but I never seem to get things quite right. Gwen and Beth are both such admirable women of God. They never seem to question Him."

Patience smiled. "I know for a fact they have both questioned God at various times. What's important is that you fix your eyes on Him and not them. You have your own path and they have theirs."

"But what if I'm not enough . . . for Dave?" Lacy felt tears well in her eyes. "I don't want to make him miserable, and I certainly don't want him to hate me."

"I don't think that's even possible," Patience declared, "but my advice to you is to be honest and talk to him. He's a good man, Lacy. He won't take advantage of your doubts."

"It's not merely doubt," Lacy argued. "I have failed too many people to mark it off to doubt alone."

"You may have convinced yourself that you've failed everyone, but that doesn't mean you have."

Lacy shook her head. "I don't understand."

"Saying a thing doesn't make it so." Patience smiled and added, "No matter how many times you say it. On the other hand, if you choose to believe something for long enough, it has a way of altering your life. Consider Gwen and how she believed herself cursed. Do you see what I'm saying?"

The room closed in around them. Lacy felt a sense of confusion that only seemed to complicate her long-felt beliefs. "I don't know."

Patience put her arm around Lacy and led her back to the chair. "Sit. You look as though you might faint."

Lacy did as she was told. She closed her eyes and settled back into the chair. "I used to think that Gwen was silly for her beliefs. Beth and I told her that such things were nonsense."

"And what did she say?"

Looking up, Lacy drew a deep breath. "She said we didn't understand. She said she'd made bad choices and that she was punished because of that."

"And after that did you believe her? Did you think she was cursed?"

"No, but I had to admit strange things did happen. A lot of folks did die around us."

Patience knelt beside Lacy. "That's not surprising. People die, you know." She gently took hold of Lacy's hands. "Lacy, do you blame Gwen for Harvey's death?"

"Of course not." Lacy straightened. "He had the measles."

"I know, but for a long time Gwen blamed herself and believed Harvey had died because of her curse."

"But it wasn't true."

"So was it true that she was to blame for your mother's death?"

Lacy stiffened and shook her head. "No, that was my fault."

"Your fault that your mother lost too much blood to live?"

"But if I'd been able to find Pa, he would have known what to do."

"No, Lacy. He wouldn't have. Sometimes these things happen. It's just like with Gwen looking for people to die around her, because some foolish woman told her that death would be her constant companion. You're looking to fail because you believe that's all you're capable of."

"But even you said we all fail."

A smile crossed Patience's lips. "And so we do. But when that is all we can think of—all that we focus on—we see failure in everything we do."

Lacy thought back through her life and all of the times she'd disappointed those around her. "But I've made so many mistakes. It wasn't just that I didn't find Pa in time to save my mother; I've never acted in the way folks wanted. I've never been a proper lady like my sisters. My grandmother used to rant at me all the time. She would berate my father for letting me wear britches and ride astride."

She closed her eyes and could see her grandmother's disapproving scowl as she waggled her finger at Lacy. *Mark my words, no man is going to want a hoyden for a wife,* she'd told Lacy on more than one occasion.

"And it wasn't just my grandmother. Every woman in my life disapproved. I disappointed them all." She opened her eyes and met Patience's observant gaze. "Dave doesn't approve of me, either. He lets me know all the time that I need to act more ladylike."

Patience laughed. "Dave realizes you are every inch a lady. That's why sparks fly between you! He knows that the things you do—the work and manner in which you dress—are all part and parcel to being a woman living on the frontier."

"I can't be a wife. I know nothing of how to be one. I can only cook moderately. I can mend things pretty well, but my sewing is otherwise atrocious. I don't dance very well at all, and I certainly can't sing."

Patience got to her feet and put her hands on her hips. "Lacy Gallatin, you have many talents that are far more useful to a man living in this territory. You ride and shoot, you can set up a camp and hunt down food if necessary. Your family will never go hungry, even if the meal is poorly prepared." She smiled. "A woman on the frontier has to be able to work hard at her husband's side. Dancing and singing are hardly important when there's a blizzard blowing in and your best breeders decide to start dropping their calves early."

"But that's all well and fine for a rancher's wife. I'll be a lawman's wife. Dave will probably become the sheriff or town marshal wherever we live, and I in turn will be expected to keep a tidy little house, maybe even cook for the prisoners in our jail." She frowned. "Of course, that might be a deterrent to breaking the law."

Laughing, Patience shook her head. "Lacy, you are perfectly capable of learning to do anything you need to. And you aren't alone in this. The Bible clearly shows that the older women are to teach the younger. I'm more than happy to help you in any way I can. I'm sure your sisters feel the same. Girls aren't just born knowing how to cook and sew. Believe me, you won't be the first bride who goes into her marriage burning the supper."

"You just don't understand," Lacy said, getting to her feet. "No one does. Dave doesn't deserve a wife like me."

Dave slipped away from his parents' house, having overheard most of his mother's discussion with Lacy. He felt a new tenderness in his heart for the woman he'd asked to be his wife. Lacy's fears were evident, but at least now he understood the reasoning behind them. He'd never considered her role as the wife of a lawman. If he did take on a position of town marshal or sheriff, he would be a community leader of sorts. Lacy was right—it would put them under public scrutiny. No wonder Lacy was afraid.

"You heading back to Gallatin Crossing?" his father asked as Dave walked into the barn.

"Yeah, as soon as Lacy is ready. I went to get her, but she and Ma were talking."

His father smiled, then bent to line up several milk cans. "Your mama is going to love having a daughter around. I think you couldn't have picked a better woman."

"Thank you," Dave said, leaning up against the stall. "I've loved her for a long time now."

"I know," his father said with a chuckle.

"How so? When did you first know that I loved her?"

His father shrugged. "Probably when her pa died and you made it your personal crusade to find his killer."

"But . . . that was just a part of doing my duty."

"Was it? Seemed a mite more personal than that."

There was no sense in denying his father's point. Dave knew deep in his heart that he had given George Gallatin's death more attention than any other crime in the area. It always bothered him that Lacy thought him slack on his duties when it came to finding the killer. She had no way of knowing how it consumed him.

"Can I ask you something?"

His father straightened. "You know you can."

"Well, I know that Lacy is worried about finding her father's killer. I want that, as well, but she's putting it between us like a dragon I need to slay before she'll marry me."

His father considered this and nodded. "And if you can't find the killer?"

"That's the thing. I think I can. The pieces are falling into place, and I'm hopeful it won't be long before the truth is known. But then what?"

"You afraid she'll come up with some other task for you to accomplish?"

Dave nodded. "I can't help but think that resolving this matter isn't really the point at all. Sure, she wants the guilty party to pay, but I think it's just an excuse because she's afraid of getting married. I overheard her telling Ma that she's afraid she'll fail at being a wife and mother."

"Can't be worse than you being afraid of failing at being a husband and father."

Dave thought on this for a moment. The truth was he hadn't thought much past getting Lacy to marry him. He knew he'd need to provide for her—to take care of her—but in all honesty, he hadn't feared it.

"But I don't really feel afraid of anything like that," Dave told him. "I love Lacy, and I know that I will go to whatever lengths necessary to care for her and see that she has what she needs. But if she puts this wall of fear between us . . . well, that's something I'm not sure I can tear down."

His father nodded. "But God can, son. He's not asking you to be Lacy's savior."

"But I want to be everything to her," Dave admitted.

"Then you'd better call it off here and now."

His father's stern expression took Dave aback. "What do you mean?"

"You can't be everything to her, Dave. God won't have His place usurped. You need to understand that. You can't be Lacy's heavenly Father or a replacement for her earthly one. You'll be a whole lot happier if you understand that from the start."

Dave knew his father was right, but it still bothered him that he couldn't give Lacy the strength and security she longed for. He wanted to make her fears cease in the overwhelming flood of his love. Why was that so wrong?

"Justin has been so difficult lately," Beth said as she struggled to get up from her chair. Her growing stomach was becoming more and more of a burden. "I think the influx of people to the area has caused more bad than good where he's concerned."

"The few children that have been added have definitely been less than a good influence," Gwen agreed.

"They're a rowdy bunch, to be sure," Lacy said. She put the final touches on polishing a brass spittoon. "There, that looks better."

"I just don't know what's gotten into him lately," Beth said. She moved to the far end of the dining room and stretched to measure one of the curtains.

Lacy jumped up. "You know you aren't supposed to put your hands above your head when you're pregnant."

"That's just an old wives' tale," Gwen chided. "But even so, I think we can get the measurements for you, Beth. Why don't you just sit and take it easy. It's just a few weeks before the baby will be here. No sense bringing your delivery on early."

Beth put her hand to the small of her back. "I suppose it

would be better if you measured. My stomach would just get in the way."

Lacy took up the task and easily calculated the dimensions of the curtain. "So how are your plans going for Justin's birthday party? He will be so surprised that you've arranged to throw him a grand celebration."

"I hope so," Beth said, shaking her head. "He seems so troubled. He hasn't been able to focus on his schoolwork or anything else. I finally gave up and called an end to school for the summer even though it's only the middle of May."

"With everything that's happened around here, that's probably for the best," Gwen said.

"He's a good boy, but he seems so . . . well . . . I don't know." Beth rubbed her stomach. "I thought he was happy to be a part of our family."

"Maybe he's just settling in," Gwen suggested. "You know. Everything was new to him before. Now the new is wearing off and everything has become routine."

"She's right," Lacy said, handing Beth the tape measure. "Maybe he's just bored."

They heard a commotion from the backyard. The sound of arguing poured in through the kitchen window. Beth frowned. "Whatever is that all about?"

"Whatever it is," Lacy said, striding toward the back door, "it doesn't sound good."

Gwen and Beth followed Lacy outside. Lacy quickly assessed the problem and stepped in between Justin and another boy just as the latter took a swing in Justin's direction.

"Whoa, now. Stop this fighting," Lacy demanded. She took hold of the stranger's collar and held him fast. "What's this all about?"

"He was stealing," Justin declared, trying to work around Lacy to hit the boy.

"Stop it, Justin," Beth said, stepping forward. "What was he stealing?"

"He tried to take my pocketknife. The one Pa gave me."

"Did not!" the boy yelled and fought against Lacy's hold. "I was just lookin' at it."

"You did, too," Justin said, reaching out again to take hold of his adversary.

Beth wrenched him back. "Justin! Stop at once." The next moment she abruptly dropped her hold of him.

Gwen stepped forward. "What's wrong, Beth?"

"A sharp pain," Beth gasped, her hand upon her stomach. "I think it's the baby."

"It's too early," Lacy said, forgetting the boy she held. "We'd better send for the doctor."

"Can you settle this matter?" Gwen asked her, nodding toward the boys.

"Of course. Get Beth inside, and I'll deal with them."

Lacy turned to the two boys. "Just look what your fighting has caused. Now aren't you ashamed?"

The stranger looked to the ground. "I didn't mean no harm. I just wanted to see the knife."

"Justin, did you falsely accuse this boy of trying to steal from you?"

"No. He told me I was too little to have a knife like that and that he was old enough and would just keep it."

Lacy looked back at the boy. "Is that true?"

"No."

It was clear the boy was lying, but Lacy had no way to prove it. "I think you'd best go now. Don't be coming back here if you plan to bicker and fight. Otherwise I'll have to go speak with your folks."

The boy made a mad dash toward the river community, while Lacy turned back to Justin. "I'm sorry he tried to take your knife."

Justin looked up in surprise. "I didn't think you believed me."

"Why shouldn't I? It was the truth, wasn't it?"

He nodded. "He really did say he was going to keep it."

Lacy put her arm around his shoulders. "I believe you, but now we need to think about your mama. You've been making it kind of hard on her."

The boy's eyes widened. "Is she gonna die?"

"I don't think so, but you really need to behave yourself and stop being naughty. You're a good boy, Justin. I don't know why you're acting up, but it's really hurting your mama's feelings."

Justin shook his head. "She only cares about the baby anyway. She never even talks to me anymore."

"Having a baby is sometimes hard, but I know my sister loves you very much. Now, come on. Let's go see if there's anything we can do to be helpful."

Justin moved away from her. "I don't want to." He took off running toward the front of the house, leaving Lacy to stare after him in surprise. Beth was right. The boy wasn't acting at all like himself. One minute he was worried about Beth dying, and the next he wanted no part of being around her.

"Apparently the children in our household can be just as confusing as the adults."

"You should remain in bed until the baby comes," the doctor advised as he gathered his instruments.

Beth frowned. "But there's so much to do around here. Especially now."

"We'll take care of it," Gwen assured. "If nothing else, we'll hire someone to help out."

"That's right," Lacy affirmed. She looked at the worried expression of her sister. "Honestly, Beth, everything will be all right."

"But what about Justin's party? He deserves to have a nice birthday, and I've been planning it for weeks now."

"I can take over the arrangements," Lacy said. "I'll come and sit with you, and you can tell me everything you wanted to do."

Gwen nodded. "We'll make sure Justin has a wonderful day."

Lacy saw movement at the door and realized Justin had been listening just outside. "If you'll excuse me, I need to tend to something."

She followed Justin to his room and even though he'd left the door wide open, she knocked. "May I come in?"

Justin looked up from where he sat on the floor in the corner of his room. He was surrounded by his toy soldiers. "I don't care."

Lacy crossed the room and surprised him by settling herself beside him. "I'm sorry your surprise was ruined."

He shrugged. "I don't care about my birthday."

"Well, I do," Lacy countered. "I want you to have a wonderful party. Your mother and father want that, too."

"Nobody cares about me now that the baby is nearly here,"

he said, picking up a lead soldier. "Pa's always busy, and Mama is always talking about the baby."

"The baby is important, but no more so than you are."

He looked back to his soldiers and with a single sweep of his hand, knocked them all over. "That's not true."

Lacy stiffened. "I have no reason to lie about this, Justin."

She got to her feet and looked down at the child. *It would be nice,* she thought, *if I could say the perfect thing to ease his misery.* "You can pretend no one cares," she finally said, "but that doesn't make it so."

Walking away, Lacy was reminded of her talk earlier with Patience. *"You may have convinced yourself that you've failed everyone,"* she remembered Patience saying, *"but that doesn't mean you have."*

Now I'm using the same words to convince Justin of his mistaken beliefs. She sighed. He was no more convinced than she had been with Patience's declaration.

"Saying a thing doesn't make it so," Lacy murmured.

She sought the refuge of her own room and closed the door. Was it possible Patience was right? Had Lacy convinced herself of something that wasn't true?

Grandmother Gallatin's harsh words came back to haunt her. *"You're hopeless, Lacene. Just hopeless."*

The words danced around Lacy's head in a taunting manner. She feared the years hadn't changed a thing.

CHAPTER TEN

Rafe studied the ledger in his hand and laughed. "I think we've hit our own vein of gold," he told Jefferson.

The man lifted his beer in salute. "I told you there was a fortune to be made."

"How long can we keep this up? Folks are bound to get discouraged when they don't actually find any gold."

Jefferson shrugged. "Whenever things seem to settle down, we can stir the pot with a new find. Not only that, but a lot of folks are stuck here now. That's the best thing about gold rush towns. Folks sell off everything in hopes of getting rich quick. Once they find out the dream is nothing but dust, they have to face the realization that they have nothing—not even enough money to move on. The responsible among them will come to us for work in order to support themselves and their families, and the slackers will be drinking or gambling themselves into debt."

"Either way, we benefit." Rafe smiled.

"Don't forget: There's money to be made simply with the creation of a gambling town. There are plenty of examples of it across the frontier. Not only that, but with this town growing, the outlying ranches will come to depend on us as a quick way to turn a profit when we purchase beef and such from them. Everyone will benefit. The railroad will have to recognize that fact and deal accordingly."

"I can see that you're right on that count."

Jefferson nodded. "Now if we can just get Bishop to give up on the place and sell out, so much the better."

"I've had my eye on Gallatin House for a long time," Rafe told him. "I was always after George Gallatin to sell it to me. Thought once he was gone, the girls would give it up, but I underestimated them."

Mulholland tossed back the last of his beer. "You can't count on anything where women are concerned." He examined his empty glass and shrugged. "Still, there might be other ways to motivate Bishop. Maybe we could stir up this nest of hornets and see what happens."

Rafe looked at his friend, not quite understanding. "What do you suggest?"

Jefferson smiled. "Well, perhaps we can double your previous efforts to encourage the prim and proper folks of the area to leave. After all, if there are constant fights, shootings, and unsavory characters milling about, the good folk are bound to pack up and seek peace elsewhere."

"That's true enough. We've already seen quite a few relocate to Bozeman."

"Then let's help the rest decide."

"But what about the law?"

Rafe's friend rubbed his chin thoughtfully. "Well, the way I see it, there is only one man fighting to keep law and order in this town. Compare that to the hundreds who have poured in to find gold, and I think the odds are in our favor."

"But if there are too many problems, he'll no doubt hire deputies to help him keep the peace," Rafe said. "I know Shepard. He won't sit idle."

Mulholland smiled. "He will if he has a bullet in his head."

"Whadd'ya mean, we can't come here for grub anymore?" The man was caked in dirt that had been streaked with sweat.

Hank and Nick stood their ground on the porch of Gallatin House. Hank had just posted a sign that announced they would no longer act as a restaurant for the area.

"We have a contract with the stage line to feed and lodge travelers," Hank said. "At this point, that's all we can keep up with. I'm sorry, but you'll have to get your meals elsewhere."

"And that, my friends, is not a problem," Jefferson Mulholland announced from behind the crowd.

Hank looked out to find the well-dressed man leaning casually against the fence post. He seemed rather pleased with the turn of events. In fact, Hank thought Mulholland looked as if he'd planned this very thing all along.

"We have a new tent café set up for you fellas. There are beautiful ladies to wait on you and the fare is as delectable as any you might secure here at Gallatin House. In fact, we have hired a popular chef all the way from Denver." He motioned behind him. "If you'll just make your way to the far side of the saloon, we can begin seating you right away."

The men began shuffling off in the direction of Rafe's place. Some were still muttering their displeasure, while a few were actually cursing the disturbance to their routine. When the last of the men had moved away, Mulholland came forward to the edge of the porch.

"Gentlemen, I hope this will help to ease the misery of your dear ladies."

Hank nodded although the sarcasm in the man's voice was evident. "I'm sure it will."

"We could handle the stage, as well," Mulholland offered. "After all, we have available beds. Nothing as elaborate as Gallatin House, but perhaps we could work on that."

Nick eyed the man suspiciously. "What are you saying?"

"I'm here to make you a good offer on the place. The store, too." He grinned. "Why, I'm sure we could even work out something for all of the property you own."

Hank shook his head. "Gallatin House belongs to my wife and her sisters. Any arrangements to sell will be up to them."

"But you two are the men of the family, are you not? Surely your women do not make such important decisions for you."

Mulholland's smirk wasn't lost on Hank. "I will let my wife know of your suggestions and get back to you on the matter." Hank turned to make sure the sign was secure and hoped that Mulholland would take this as an indication that the conversation was over. He didn't.

"You know, this town is turning into quite the place for

gambling and such," Mulholland continued. "Our businesses are thriving, and we are in a good place to help you out. Why, I've heard from several folks that you are considering a move north as it is."

Hank looked at Nick, then turned back to the smiling man. "It's common knowledge that the railroad is laying track to the north. We believe it might be in our best interest to relocate."

Mulholland sobered and nodded. "That's why I want you to take this as a serious offer, Bishop." He produced a fold of papers from his coat pocket. "I think if you read through this, you will see that we are giving you a legitimate and generous offer."

He stepped forward and extended the papers, and Hank took them out of curiosity as much as anything. He was rapidly coming to the point, however, where he would have to contemplate any offer in order to see to his family's well-being.

"I'll let you know," Hank told him.

An exchange of accusations and obscenities broke out across the distance from the saloon. Two men, each holding a knife, came bounding out of Rafe's place.

"Ah, apparently there has been some sort of disagreement," Mulholland observed. "I suppose it would be wise to see this brought to an amicable end. If you'll excuse me."

Hank and Nick watched Mulholland retreat back to the saloon. He signaled a couple of men from near the door, and after speaking to them, Hank watched as the men pulled out their revolvers and headed for the fight. One of the men lunged at the other, cutting a broad slice across the other man's face. The injured man let out a yell, then dove for the man.

One of Mulholland's men fired a shot into the air and waited for the men to react. He commanded them to put down their weapons, and Hank was rather surprised when the men did just that.

"I guess Rafe and his friend have their own system of justice," Nick said.

"What's happening?" Lacy questioned, coming through the front door. "Who's shooting?"

"There's been an argument next door." Nick pushed her back into the house. "Stay inside. There's no telling if that's the end of it."

Before Lacy could protest, Hank motioned to Nick. "We should probably get inside. I'd like to look this offer over and discuss it with Gwen and the others."

"I suppose if we are to get out of this den of iniquity," Gwen said, clutching Julianne to her shoulder, "we should consider the offer."

They were all gathered in Beth and Nick's room so that Beth might be able to join in the conversation. Lacy thought she seemed rather hesitant about selling out but knew that her sister was concerned about the dangers, as well.

"I'm not happy selling out to them," Beth said, "but I suppose given the situation, no one else is going to want to buy this place."

"It's true." Gwen nodded. "The good folks are leaving as fast as they can, and Rafe and his friends are taking over."

"They even seem to have formed their own law," Nick said, glancing to where Dave stood.

Lacy said nothing. She'd actually been relieved that the conflict and strife of the area had kept Dave too busy to pester her about marriage. She had nearly convinced herself that she should go to him and break the engagement completely.

"I've seen their brand of law," Dave finally answered. "It's not much on the side of justice. Still, Rafe has a right to have guards for his place. If there's going to be fighting and trouble on his property, he can throw out the offenders and deal with the situation instead of sending for me."

"That doesn't stop the fights down in the camps along the river and creeks," Lacy interjected. She suddenly felt it necessary to defend Dave. "Rafe's men seem only to irritate the situation and make more work for you."

He gave a halfhearted smile. "Well, at least I'm needed."

"You're too much in need," Hank interjected. "The very nature of this gold rush begs for law and order, yet rejects it as well. We've had laundry stolen right off our lines and chickens from our coops."

"Not to mention the threat of being accosted just trying to walk from here to the store," Gwen remarked.

"Or when fetching water from the hot springs," Lacy added.

Beth nodded. "And the bullies that have accompanied their elders to this gold rush are not the kind of children that make good playmates for Justin. He's always getting into fights."

"I think the time has come for us to make some decisions," Hank said, putting his arm around Gwen's shoulders. "Tomorrow, I'm going to head out to meet with the stage manager and see about securing a contract for the future."

"What kind of contract?" Lacy asked.

"Nick and I have been talking about it. We figure if the stage company will agree to give us a five-year contract, we in turn can immediately set out to recreate our businesses up north along the railroad."

"A five-year contract?" Beth asked. "Who would ever agree

to that? Why, there wouldn't be anything to base it on. There wouldn't be a hotel there or even the railroad at this point."

"I realize that," Hank said, "but I think the stage company owners will see the sense in doing this. We can even give them a say in how they'd like to see things set up. At first, we'd need to continue together as we have been doing. Nick can run the livery and blacksmithing, and you ladies and I can run the hotel and even a small store.

"I even plan to speak to the railroad officials. My thought is to pinpoint the exact place that will benefit all of us. We can build the hotel there and hope that others will come to expand the area and make a real town."

"Hank and I think it might even be possible to get the railroad to discount a piece of their easement property for the hotel and livery," Nick said. "Property that would be close to the depot and make it advantageous for their travelers to grab a meal or spend the night."

"Sounds like we would need to expand the business," Gwen said. "We're overworked as it is."

"Yes," Hank agreed. "However, if we can secure a commitment from both the stage and the railroad, we could hire additional folks to help."

"That makes sense," Lacy said, still wondering what part—if any—she and Dave would play in such a move.

Two days later, during Justin's birthday party, Lacy was still considering that thought. Her engagement to Dave filled her head with all sorts of thoughts regarding the situation. Did he plan to move north, as well? Maybe he planned to go back to working out of Bozeman. He might even want to go back to the ranch and work with his father. Patience had said they expected their operation to grow rapidly with the hope that they could provide the railroad with beef for its workers.

"I want to thank you for doing this, Lacy," Nick said, interrupting her thoughts.

She looked up and smiled. "I didn't want Justin to miss out on his party just because Beth has to be bedfast."

"He's been difficult lately," Nick said. "I think he's troubled by all the changes of late."

Lacy nodded. "I'm sure he is. Just look how it's affected the rest of us. There's never any peace and quiet anymore; everything has been in turmoil since gold was found. Hank told me the other day that the amount of mail has tripled, both going in and out of Gallatin Crossing."

"Yes, it's been a huge change for him to leave a peaceful farm life in Kansas to come here. And now the quiet of Montana has been stripped away in the wake of cries for gold." He looked to where Justin was opening a gift from Gwen.

"I'm sure he'll survive. Children are often better at navigating change than adults," she said, thinking back on her own life. "You've become the father—given Justin the family—he's always wanted."

Nick shook his head. "Sometimes I'm still amazed that he's here—that he's with me at all."

Looking to where Justin was already focused on yet another gift, Lacy couldn't help but smile. "He's a smart boy, and I think for the most part he's happy to be here."

She saw Dave squat down beside Justin and hand him a large box. The boy's face lit up, and Lacy moved just a bit closer to see what gift had delighted her nephew.

" 'Richter's Anchor Blocks,' " Justin read aloud. "What is it?"

"Why don't you look inside and see," Dave encouraged.

Justin opened the package and displayed some of the pieces of red brick, blue slate, and buff stone. She could see from the way he began to manipulate the pieces that he could easily put together buildings for his toy soldiers. Perhaps there were enough blocks there to create an entire city.

Dave looked up and caught her watching them. He smiled, and Lacy couldn't help but return it. Justin was obviously happier with this gift than any other, and she was touched by Dave's thoughtfulness.

"It looks like Dave's gift has met with Justin's approval," Nick said. Just then, Justin abandoned the blocks and came to his father.

"Come see my building blocks," he declared. "There's a special way to pack them in their box and instructions on how to make all kinds of things."

"I'll be right there." He turned to Lacy. "I just wanted you to know how grateful Beth and I are for how you've stepped in to befriend Justin and for all the party preparations. You'll make a good mother yourself someday."

She considered his statement even as she moved to the sanctuary of the kitchen. Everything was changing before her eyes. Her sisters had families of their own. Gallatin Crossing had become a nightmare of chaos and underhanded dealings. Hank was even planning to get them relocated before winter set in. She frowned as thoughts once again came to her about where she belonged in all of this.

Lacy longed to take a walk in the cemetery but shied away from that idea. The river was only a short distance away, and there were numerous tents and squatters there. Sadly, some of the graves had even been vandalized. She sighed. There was nowhere to go. No hope of refuge or quiet contemplation.

She heard Julianne begin to fuss and cry in the front room. It was only a moment before Gwen appeared with her daughter in her arms.

"Oh, I didn't know you were in here," her sister said, shifting the baby. "Julianne is overtired, and I'm going to put her to bed."

"Would you like me to take her up?" Lacy asked.

"That would be lovely. I'll stay down here and see that Beth doesn't overdo. I'm still not convinced she should have come downstairs."

"Well, Nick carried her, so it's not like she expended any energy doing so," Lacy said, taking Julianne in her arms. The baby seemed unhappy with the transfer, but Lacy only smiled. "You go ahead. We'll be just fine."

Cubby had never cared for the taste of whiskey, but tonight he allowed himself to forget that fact and tossed back his fourth drink. His father would be livid if he found out Cubby had wasted the best stock on himself.

"He'll just have to deal with it," the boy said, slurring his words and weaving on his feet.

The only reason Cubby was indulging in the fiery liquid was the memory of Lacy telling him he was just like his father. Those words still haunted him. Something inside had told him that this was what everyone thought of him so he might as well give in to it. After all, it might be true.

He thought of his father's ruthlessness—his lack of concern for anyone but himself. "I'm not like him," Cubby whispered, staggering to his feet.

The back door to the saloon had been left wide open to let in the cool night air, and Cubby made his way to the undulating portal. Gripping the wall, he tried to straighten. Why couldn't he focus?

He stumbled out the back door and barely caught himself before he kissed the ground. His head spun and his vision blurred. "I'm not like him!"

Cubby pressed upward and eased onto his knees. He pulled a revolver from his waistband. His father had insisted he carry it to guard the precious liquor stores from the gold rush rowdies. Now, without thinking of the problems it could cause, Cubby pulled back the hammer and pointed it toward Gallatin House.

"I'm not my father!" he shouted and fired a shot into the air. He heard the breaking of glass and fired twice more.

The noise was deafening and caused Cubby to reel back on his heels. "You don't understand. I'm not like him at all!"

He fired again, then felt the gun knocked from his hands. He looked up to see Wyman shaking his head.

Wyman bent over and picked up the pistol. "You idiot. What do you think you're doing? Get up."

Cubby shook his head.

Wyman laughed and yanked the boy to his feet. "You're drunk. I ought to leave you here to rot, but someone would probably steal your boots. Come on, I'll get you inside."

Cubby tried to bat away Wyman's hold, but his hands only sliced through empty air. "I'm not like him," Cubby told Wyman as the older man dragged him back into the saloon.

Wyman looked at Cubby in confusion. "Like who?"

Cubby tried hard to straighten and square his shoulders. "Like . . . him. Like . . . my father."

His father's right-hand man laughed and pushed Cubby past the storeroom to his own quarters. "You're exactly like him. Right down to the bone."

Cubby shook his head, but that only served to increase his dizziness. He lost his footing as Wyman pushed him toward his cot.

"Sleep it off, Cubby. You'll pay for this tomorrow, but right now you're no use to anyone."

"I'm no use to anyone," Cubby muttered and closed his eyes. "No use."

Lacy was face down on the floor of the bedroom when Hank and Dave rushed into the room. She had covered the baby with her body and could tell from Julianne's cry that she was still alive.

"Don't move, Lacy," Dave commanded. "You're covered in glass."

She felt her muscles automatically stiffen. When she had heard the gun shot and breaking glass from the room next door, Lacy had instinctively dropped to the floor, with Julianne tucked safely beneath her. Seconds later the window shattered behind her.

The men worked to clear the broken bits of window before Dave lifted Lacy and Julianne from the floor in one sweeping motion. Hank quickly retrieved his daughter and checked her for any cuts.

"She looks fine," he declared and handed her to Gwen, who stood at the door looking horrified.

"What happened?" Gwen asked, clutching Julianne tightly.

"Some idiot was out there shooting off his gun," Dave said. "Are you hurt, Lacy?"

Touched by his tenderness and concern, Lacy met his worried expression. "I don't think so."

He reluctantly set her on her feet. "Are you sure?"

Lacy watched as Hank crossed the room to look out the broken window. She could see now just how narrowly she had escaped danger. They'd been standing in front of the window only moments ago, and now . . . She shuddered.

"I'm fine, but I'd like to lie down in my room."

Dave nodded and led her past Gwen, who reached out to stop them. "I'm so grateful you're both all right. I heard the gunfire and the breaking glass, and I feared the worst. You saved her life." Gwen kissed the top of Julianne's head.

"We were in front of that window when the first shot hit." Lacy shook her head. "It was a miracle that I dropped to the floor. I think we have God to thank for that."

She pushed past her sister and into the hall with Dave right behind her. He took hold of her elbow and led her to her bedroom door. Lacy stared at the door for a moment and began to shake. What if someone shot out her windows tonight, as well?

Lacy turned to Dave, and he pulled her close. The comfort found in his embrace washed over her. It wasn't the sensation of passion she'd known before; rather this time the embrace offered her safety and protection. Lacy relished the feeling and refused to move for several minutes.

"I'm so glad you're not hurt," Dave whispered against her hair.

Lacy sighed. She couldn't remember a time when she'd felt like this, but the feeling was so wondrous she prayed it would go on forever. If this was love, she very much wanted it to last.

CHAPTER ELEVEN

"I heard about the trouble last night," Patience said as she joined her son just before the Sunday service at Gallatin House.

"It's getting worse," Dave said. "The prospectors are out of control most nights, and it doesn't help that Rafe offers them cheap whiskey and beer."

"What can you do about it?" his mother asked.

"I've been asking the sheriff for more men to help me in this area, but there isn't any money. Rafe has his own group of enforcers to keep law and order in his area, but that doesn't help the rest of us."

His mother nodded and held his arm tight. "I'm worried for you."

He looked at her and smiled. He hadn't meant to cause her fear. "Hank plans a town meeting after services today. Last night he made up his mind about moving."

"Where will they go?"

"The idea is to relocate to property being offered by the railroad. It would be about the same distance for you and Pa to travel, only in the other direction. Hank wants to talk to everyone after church and see who else might want to go."

"I see. Well, that sounds reasonable, but what's to keep this from happening again? I mean, once a town is set up, the rowdies are bound to follow."

Dave considered this for a moment. "I suppose we'll just have to wait and see. I know the railroad officials told Hank they would set up some kind of authority. Maybe they would pay for a better police force."

His mother laughed. "You're the best there is—I've no doubt about that. But you're just one man, son."

He could see the love and pride in his mother's eyes and gave her shoulder a squeeze. "I suppose that's your way of telling me to be careful and to not try to do it all myself."

His mother raised a brow. "Is that such bad advice? After all, you're soon to be a married man. You don't want to make Lacy a widow before you even get her to the altar."

"Well, if we weren't married, she wouldn't exactly be a widow, now, would she?"

"That's beside the point. You need to be careful. You know how I worry about you in this line of work."

"What is your mother worrying about now?" Dave's father asked as he came to join them.

"It would probably be easier to tell you what she's not

worried about," Dave teased. "In this instance, however, she's concerned about my line of work."

"Well, you could always come back to work at the ranch. With the railroad coming through, I've already been approached about providing beef and pork. I've decided to expand again and bring in five hundred head from Texas."

Dave looked at his father in disbelief. "Five hundred? When?"

"They're already on their way. They'll be up here by September."

"When did you decide this?"

The question went unanswered, however, as Pastor Flikkema called out his customary greeting from the Psalms, " 'I was glad when they said unto me, Let us go into the house of the Lord.' "

The Sunday service passed quickly with Pastor Flikkema offering encouragement in wake of the multiple problems facing the small community. A few of the miners had joined them for church in the front room of Gallatin House, but most were still sleeping off the effects of their Saturday night merriments.

After the pastor concluded with prayer, he raised his arms. "If you would all remain seated, Mr. Bishop has asked to say a few words."

There was a rumbling of comments, but no one moved. Lacy watched as Hank made his way to the front of the room. He seemed determined and confident, and she knew he had made up his mind about relocating.

"I wanted to let everyone know that we've decided to re-locate Gallatin House and Bishop's Emporium." There were a few protests, but Hank spoke out above them. "Please hear me out. Last night there were problems, and someone shot out two of my upstairs windows. They narrowly missed shooting my sister-in-law, who was holding my infant daughter at the time. I can't continue to expose my family to such danger."

There were gasps from the women and Mr. Lindquist called out to ask, "Who was the culprit?"

Hank shook his head. "We don't know who was responsible, but we can't ignore that things around here have only gotten worse. Nick and I are planning to ride up to the surveyed area tomorrow. The railroad has already mapped out their route, and we intend to work with them to find a location that will benefit them, as well as the stage company. We believe if we work with these two businesses, we will see great benefit as a town. I just wanted to let you know this so that if you wanted to be a part of it, you could join us."

"What would that involve?" Leon Bradley asked. As the local cheesemonger, he and his wife knew the importance of community.

"The railroad has spoken in the past of offering discounted, even free, land for those who would relocate and settle on the property owned by the railroad. I intend to meet with the offi-cials and see what exactly is available. I would like to be able to go to them with a pledge from as many of you as possible. That pledge would include the promise to set up business and live in the area for, say, five or ten years. If we pledge to remain in place, it will give the railroad adequate facilities to make it worth their trouble to negotiate the land with us."

Lacy listened as other questions were posed and Hank

worked out the details. Though it sounded like a solid plan, for reasons beyond her understanding her heart just wasn't in it. She didn't want to remain here, but neither did she want to trade one problem for another. And how did she and Dave fit into all of this? Frankly, she found herself wishing she could just disappear up into the high country and forget the rest of the world.

She hadn't told anyone else, but all through the night, she'd tossed and turned, worried someone would start shooting again at the house. Sleep only came after she dragged her mattress to the floor and slept on the ground as far from her window as possible.

The formal meeting concluded with everyone gathering for a potluck dinner in the dining room. The conversation about the move continued, but Lacy paid little attention. Instead, she prepared a tray of lunch for Beth and made her way up the back stairs to her sister's room.

"I hope you're hungry," Lacy greeted with a smile. "I brought enough for an army."

Beth closed her Bible and put it aside. "As a matter of fact, I am. I hope you'll sit with me for a while. I get lonely tucked up here away from everyone."

Lacy placed the tray beside Beth on the bed. "I would love to stay." She turned and pulled up a chair. "I find I'm growing weary of crowds. Everyone is always talking at once, and the noise seems to echo in my ears."

"I'm getting all the peace and quiet a body could want," Beth admitted. "I'll be glad when the baby comes and I can get back up and around."

Lacy watched her sister lovingly pat her swollen abdomen.

It amazed her to imagine that a human being—a living baby—resided there. "Are you feeling all right?" she asked.

"As well as I can expect." Beth took up a piece of bread and began to butter it. "I feel completely useless, though."

Lacy laughed. "You don't have to be pregnant to feel that way, I assure you." She offered a blessing on the food and waited until her sister began to eat in earnest before bringing up the idea of the move.

"Has Nick talked to you about Hank's plan to move north?"

Beth nodded. "We discussed it at length last night, after the shooting."

"And what are your thoughts on the matter?" Lacy asked.

Her sister grew thoughtful. "You know that I never wanted to leave Gallatin House. I never wanted to move again."

"That's why I asked."

"The baby changed my heart on the idea, however. I guess when I considered the dangers, it wasn't difficult to agree to the move. I imagined you on the ground with *my* child tucked underneath." She shook her head. "I thought of losing you and baby Julianne. It was more than I could bear to think of, Lacy."

"I hate the mess that's become of our little town. It used to be so peaceful—so perfect. Even Rafe's Friday and Saturday parties weren't so bad—certainly nothing like it is now."

Beth nodded. "It just goes to show how bad company can corrupt. Nick says there is so much trash and destruction that I wouldn't even recognize the river area now. Of course for me, it hasn't seemed the same since our home burned down and Nick lost the livery and smithy."

"So you don't mind the idea of leaving here?"

"Not anymore. I've come to realize that my home is really wherever my husband is—where my family members are. And that needs to be a place where we all will be safe."

"But the new place won't be some utopia," Lacy stated. "The railroad will bring in scoundrels the same as this gold rush. That won't change just because we get away from Rafe. There will be other Rafes, too. We've been fortunate there's only been one saloon to contend with up until now. Most towns have several."

"And this one is soon to have others, as well," Beth said. "At least that's what Nick told me. Rafe is none too happy about it, but apparently the wealth is too good to ignore, and newcomers want a part."

Lacy nibbled on a piece of cold fried chicken. She knew from what she'd heard Hank say that numerous people were arriving daily with hopes of sharing the profits of the gold rush. So far, however, she hadn't seen that much gold changing hands.

"You really seem troubled about all of this," Beth said, breaking through Lacy's thoughts. "What are you and Dave planning to do?"

"I don't know. We haven't talked about it," Lacy confessed. "We haven't had much time to talk about anything."

"What about the wedding? Have you set the date?"

"No. Dave's been much too busy with all the trouble around here. Someone is always getting knifed or shot, or something is being stolen. Rafe has hired people to keep some order on his property, but inevitably, it spills out onto the streets. Dave can't keep up with it, and of course, he hasn't had any time at all to continue looking for Pa's killer."

Beth reached out and took hold of Lacy's hand. "Do

you ever think that maybe it's time to let that go by the wayside?"

"What do you mean?" Lacy asked. "Forget about getting justice for Pa?"

"Don't you think God will see that Pa gets justice?"

"Guilty folks go free all the time—they don't pay for what they've done."

"Don't they? Do you honestly think that God will let them go unpunished?"

Lacy thought about this for a moment. "I have no way of knowing exactly how God will handle it once they're dead and gone, but it doesn't seem to me that there is much justice here on earth unless you demand it."

"It just appears that you're spending a lot of your life focused on the dead instead of the living."

This angered Lacy—partly because it was true but mainly because it made Beth sound as though she thought Lacy foolish. "I suppose you think it was just one of those sad accidents that we will never have answers for. But I know better. Cubby told me that Rafe knows what happened."

Beth looked at her oddly. "Then why hasn't he told Dave or even us?"

Lacy shrugged. "Probably because he had something to do with it. I'm not really sure, but I intend for the truth to come out and the guilty parties to pay. I can hardly do that if I go moving off. The truth must be found right here."

"Oh, Lacy, you can't be responsible for this. Please don't let this keep you from real happiness."

Lacy got to her feet and put her hands on her hips. "I'm not giving up. For once in my life, I'm not going to fail to see this through."

"Is that what this is really all about?" Beth asked.

"What do you mean?" Lacy felt her brows come together as she narrowed her eyes.

"I mean, have you made this about you rather than Pa?"

For a moment Lacy couldn't think of anything to say. Had her focus changed? Was this more about her overcoming failure than honoring her father?

"Lacy, you can't keep doing this. It's too dangerous. If Dave is too busy with everything else that's going on, you'll just have to wait until the time comes when he can work on it. Otherwise, you might pay with your life."

Cubby woke with a horrible headache and wave of nausea that he couldn't hold back. He was glad someone had thought to put a bucket beside his bed. After losing what little contents he had left in his stomach, Cubby moaned and wiped his mouth with the back of his sleeve.

"Well, you sure made a mess of things last night," his father commented from the doorway. "I oughta beat you within an inch of your life for stealing my whiskey, but it seems you've managed to do what I couldn't."

Cubby looked up in his misery to meet his father's self-satisfied expression. "What are you talkin' about?"

"You nearly killed Lacy Gallatin last night. When you shot at Gallatin House, it broke a window where she was standing with the Bishop brat. That put the fear of God into Hank, and now he's making plans to sell out and move north."

"Is she all right?" Cubby asked, struggling to sit up. He felt another wave of nausea but ignored it. "Is Lacy all right?"

Rafe laughed. "They're all just fine. They had a meetin' after church today. I heard about it through one of my men who posed as a good churchgoing miner. Apparently, the civilized people of Gallatin Crossing have had enough of the problems and dangers of living in a mining and gambling town."

Cubby held his head. "You don't have to yell."

His father laughed again. "I'm not yelling. You're sufferin' from over-indulging. I was gonna give you a swift kick in the pants, but like I said, it's hard to be mad at someone who's managed to do what I couldn't."

"I didn't mean to do any of that," Cubby said, feeling sicker by the minute. He'd nearly killed Lacy, and all because he wanted to prove to her that he wasn't like his father. Yet everything he'd done only pointed to that fact more than ever.

"It don't matter what you meant to do," Rafe countered. "Now get out of bed and clean yourself up. I'll go mix you a cure. There's work to do, and I can't have you sleepin' off the entire day. My generosity only extends so far."

Cubby nodded and closed his eyes against the pain. He opened them quickly enough, however, when his father added, "And if you ever think to do something that stupid again, I won't be so forgivin'."

Cubby moaned and fell back against the bed once his father had gone. "What have I done?" Had he aimed for her? Had he meant for it to happen that way? He could barely remember stumbling around in back of the saloon and firing off the gun. Wyman had come and put him to bed, but he'd said nothing about Cubby shooting at Lacy.

The thought of killing someone—especially her—made

Cubby swear off liquor for good. "I'll never take another drink," he promised. Wyman had said he was just like his father. He remembered that much.

"I won't be like Pa. I won't." He opened his eyes and stared at the ceiling. "If I have to leave here tomorrow, I won't be like him."

CHAPTER TWELVE

"I wonder if I might talk with you and Lacy?" Pastor Flikkema questioned as he readied his horse to leave on the circuit. He'd spent the night at Gallatin House as he usually did when he was in the area, but it was clear he was anxious to be on his way to his next congregation.

"I'll see if I can find her," Dave said, glancing at the house, where she'd been in the kitchen just moments before. However, before he could go in search, Lacy appeared as if already summoned. "Lacy," he called. "Pastor Flikkema wants to talk to us."

Lacy, carrying a very contented cat in her arms, put him down before joining the men. "What can I do for you?" she asked.

Dave thought she looked suspicious, as if he had instigated this discussion. He turned back to the pastor and nodded. "Yes, what is this about?"

The preacher smiled. "I know you two are engaged to be married. I'm wondering if you know yet when you'd like to be seeing to the formalities."

Lacy stiffened. "We haven't determined a date just yet."

"I know this may seem strange, but I'm wondering if we could . . . set the date. I've had some family issues come up, and it will unfortunately take me away from the area for at least two months, maybe longer," Pastor Flikkema began. "I thought if you weren't opposed to it, I'd suggest you marry right away. Say, this Friday."

Lacy's eyes widened and her mouth formed a silent O. Dave put his arm around her shoulder for support. "I thought you were leaving for your circuit today," Dave said rather casually.

"I am," Flikkema said, "however, I can return here by Friday if that works for you. You two and your families have come to mean so much to me, and after watching your love blossom, I'd like to be a part of seeing you hitched properly. I can't be sure of how long I'll be gone. My mother has grown ill, and if need be, I might very well remain in the East for some time." He grinned. "I suppose it isn't usual for the preacher to set the date of the wedding, but I do hope you'll understand. If I marry you on Friday, I can catch the Saturday stage."

Dave nodded. "I can see your point, and I have no real objection."

"But Beth is in bed until the baby comes," Lacy protested. "She can't be attending a wedding."

"We could carry her downstairs as we have for other events," Dave offered.

"Why can't we just wait until Pastor Flikkema gets back?"

He recognized the fear in Lacy's eyes. "I wonder if I might speak with Lacy alone for a moment?" he asked, turning back to the pastor.

"Of course. I'm heading back inside to get a lunch Gwen promised me," Pastor Flikkema replied. "I'll return shortly for your answer."

Dave waited until the pastor had gone inside the house before turning Lacy to face him. "I won't make you do this if you don't want to, Lacy. I know you're afraid."

"I'm not afraid," she replied rather indignantly. "Beth is due any day, however. It seems unfair to put this on her."

He grinned. "I don't mind if we marry in her bedroom, if that'll settle matters." Lacy trembled slightly and looked away. Dave reached for her chin and lifted her face to meet his. "I love you, Lacy. It doesn't matter when or where we marry, so long as you know how much I love you."

Lacy looked at him and nodded. "I know you love me."

"But?"

She seemed surprised. "What do you mean?"

"You know that I love you, but it sounds as though you want to add something to that."

"I just feel confused, Dave."

"Why?"

She shook her head, and Dave dropped his hold. "I don't know why."

Dave took pity on her. "Lacy, do you love me?"

She drew a deep breath. "I think so. I'm not entirely sure I

147

understand my feelings for you. You leave me breathless when you kiss me, and I can't help but think about you all the time. My sisters challenged me to imagine my life without you in it . . . and I can't."

He put his hand against her cheek and stroked it gently. "I can't imagine my life without you, either. I promise you, Lacy, I'll be patient and loving. I won't make you marry on Friday if that's not what you want to do. I want you to be sure. This is forever."

Pastor Flikkema appeared in the open doorway of Gallatin House. He was bidding someone good-bye, but Dave couldn't see who it might be. He looked back to Lacy for an answer.

"What shall we tell him?"

Lacy sighed and leaned against Dave as if she'd lost all of her strength. "Tell him yes."

She wasn't entirely sure why she'd said yes to the Friday wedding. There was a part of Lacy's heart that truly wanted this marriage—the sooner, the better. But there was an equally troubled part that felt it was all a mistake.

Did she and Dave really know each other well enough to marry? Pastor Flikkema had spoken of watching their love blossom, but Lacy wasn't sure what he was talking about. She and Dave had known each other for a long while, and it seemed to her they did more bickering than anything else. Well, except for the kissing that had erupted during the last few months.

In a daze, Lacy passed through the house in search of Gwen. She would need to let her sister know of the plan for them to marry on Friday. It still seemed impossible to believe, and Lacy thought momentarily that she'd dreamed the entire thing. What would she wear?

"Are you all right?" Gwen asked. She looked at Lacy with an expression she normally reserved for the sick.

"I . . . well . . . something has happened," Lacy said, taking a seat.

Gwen sat down beside her. "What is it? What's wrong?"

"It's not really wrong. It's just unexpected." She looked up and met Gwen's worried face. "Dave and I are marrying this Friday."

"Friday?" The alarm rang clear in her sister's voice.

"Pastor Flikkema told us he needed to go back East for a couple of months. He wanted to marry us before going."

"And you agreed?"

"It seemed the right thing to do. It was so important to him. I told him my biggest concern was for Beth, but Dave suggested we could carry her downstairs if need be. I . . . well . . . I only wanted a very small wedding anyway."

"Goodness, it gives us even less time than Beth's wedding."

"I know, and I'm sorry," Lacy replied. "I honestly didn't plan for this."

Gwen watched her for several minutes, then covered Lacy's hand with her own. "Are you sure you want to do this? Even if Pastor doesn't come back very soon, you could marry in Bozeman. I know you care about everyone's feelings in this matter, but yours need to come first."

"I know." She looked at her sister and tried to put her thoughts into words. "Gwen, I just want to do the right thing. I don't want to make a mess of things again."

"Lacy, you are much too hard on yourself. You don't make

near the messes that you think you do." Gwen smiled and patted her sister's hand. "Now, tell me how I can help."

"I don't know," Lacy admitted. "I don't know what to do next."

Gwen nodded. "Well, let's plan the wedding. We will need to get the word out and invite the people you want to share in the day."

"I suppose that makes sense," Lacy said, feeling a few of the cobwebs clear from her mind. "We don't have much time."

"True enough. You know, I think you should ride out to see Patience. Tell her about setting the date and have her join us in the plans."

Lacy let out a heavy sigh. "I think she'd like that." Lacy got to her feet.

Gwen rose, as well. "If you have no objections, I'll let Beth know about the wedding, and we can begin working on plans for the day. It will give her something to think about while waiting for the baby to come."

"That sounds fine," Lacy said. She licked her lips and squared her shoulders. "I'll get back as quickly as I can."

"Take your time. There's no stage due in today."

Lacy nodded again and headed for the back door. "I'm getting married," she whispered to herself. "I'm getting married in four days."

"So what do you think of this area?" Hank asked Nick. They sat atop their horses, gazing out across the open landscape. Hank pointed to the west. "The river is just over there."

"Seems like it has good flow. I've noticed a lot of little tributaries," Nick said.

"What about the ground? You don't think it's too rocky?" Hank asked.

"It could be the rock will come in handy for the railroad," Nick said, putting his hand up to shield his eyes from the brilliance of the sun.

Hank studied the map he'd been given of the surveyed route for the railroad. "I think it would suit us well. There's plenty of water and woods. It's a nice distance from Bozeman and yet not too far, especially by rail. Of course, it wouldn't be that bad of a drive over in a wagon, or by horseback, either."

"That's good, because we'll need to bring in plenty of building supplies from there. Not only that, but folks will need feed and seed for farming and ranching. The land looks good for either one."

Hank nodded and once again studied the horizon. He really knew nothing about farming or raising livestock. The fact was, he knew very little about much of anything that related to the frontier. Sometimes his feelings of inadequacy were merely irritating, while other times they threatened to consume him.

"It won't be easy," Nick said, interrupting Hank's thoughts.

"What?"

"Creating a town from nothing."

"Are you thinking of backing out?" Hank asked.

Nick eased back in the saddle and pulled off his hat to wipe the sweat off his brow. "Not really. Simon has written to say that jobs are still readily available out west, but I have to think of what's best for Beth and our children."

"I've considered moving Gwen and Julianne to Boston, but I can't imagine Gwen being happy. Particularly if her sisters remain here in Montana."

Nick repositioned his hat. "I know. I don't think Beth would be happy in Seattle. Still, this change won't be easy. It's going to cost plenty of money and test the stamina and faith of everyone."

"If I can sell the Vanhouten property, there will be plenty of collateral. I'm sure we can encourage others to invest. Plus, I could always cash in some of my stocks and bonds."

Nick frowned. "You can't carry the entire town on your shoulders, Hank. You have too many responsibilities already."

Hank gazed past Nick to the river. "After the windows were shot out, I realized just how unimportant money is. Julianne and Lacy could have been killed. Money can't replace a life."

"Believe me, I feel just as strongly. I guess I'm in a bad place right now. Ever since the fire took my home and business . . . Well, it doesn't do any good to talk about it. Won't change a thing."

"Look, you more than earn your keep. We couldn't have made it without your help, Nick; you have to know that. I won't fight you if you believe it's best for you to move to Seattle, but I hope you won't go. I honestly need for you to be at my side in this move."

Nick straightened in the saddle and cast a glance at Hank. "I appreciate your saying so."

"It's true. I wouldn't tell you otherwise. I know I can trust you, and there will be people who'll come with the railroad intent on taking advantage of folks. We need trustworthy friends in place before that happens."

"Well, I don't plan on going anywhere. Like I said, I don't think Beth would be happy leaving the area. She loves her sisters too much, and now that she's having a baby . . . frankly, I'm glad they're around."

Hank turned his horse toward the west. "If you're in agreement, then, I'll get to work immediately to secure our property."

Nick drew his horse alongside Hank's and extended his hand. "Count me in."

The men shook on the deal and urged the horses forward. "So now we're to have a wedding."

"The last of the Gallatin girls will finally be hitched," Nick said with a grin. "I hope poor Dave Shepard knows what he's getting into."

Hank laughed. "Did we?"

CHAPTER THIRTEEN

Lacy awoke on her wedding day with a sense of dread. *How can I go through with this?* She sat on the edge of her bed, looking across the room at the freshly pressed yellow calico gown. Gwen had offered Lacy the use of her own wedding gown, but Lacy figured if she was to marry, she would do so in her own clothes, and this dress was far and away her best. Still, nothing about it felt right. Did it matter, she wondered, that she was heading into this special occasion without joy?

Dragging herself to her dressing table, Lacy sat down and began to brush her long cinnamon-colored hair. She had prayed so hard about this day. She'd begged God to give her a peace about marrying Dave, yet it hadn't come.

"Why do I feel like this?"

She'd battled all night over whether or not she loved Dave

as much as she should. She knew she cared for him, but she'd never been in love before. How could she be sure? Thoughts of being in Dave's arms caused a shiver to run through her. She liked his kisses and touch. No one had ever made her feel the way Dave did. When she was with him, Lacy felt warm and safe, and if truth be told, there was also an overwhelming desire that couldn't quite be explained.

Lacy put down the brush and studied her reflection in the mirror. "But I can't do it. I'm not ready. It's not fair to Dave or to me."

She felt sick to her stomach. How could she back out of the wedding now? The Shepards had come in to town last night, and while they were the only guests invited outside of her family, Lacy knew she would feel uncomfortable explaining the situation. She and Dave were to be married first thing, and then they would celebrate with a wedding breakfast. How could she disappoint everyone by calling it all off?

"But I have to," she said, shaking her head. "I can't get married with so much doubt running through my head."

Lacy got to her feet and went to her wardrobe. She ignored the yellow calico gown and reached instead for a faded blue blouse and navy skirt. It was hard to think of Dave and how disappointed he would be. He might very well call off the engagement altogether.

"Which could be for the best," Lacy reasoned. "I should never have agreed to marry him. I need to find him and explain how I feel."

But Dave was a good man. Why did the thought of marriage fill her with dread?

"That's just the point," she told herself. "He's a good man, and he deserves a woman who loves him completely—who knows her heart." She gazed up to the ceiling. "God, please help me. I don't know what to do."

A knock on her door interrupted Lacy's contemplation. "Who is it?"

"Gwen. Hurry and come. Beth has gone into labor."

"I'll be right there." Lacy pulled on the navy skirt and tucked the blouse in before fastening the waistband. Stopping abruptly as she reached for her brush again, Lacy suddenly realized she had the perfect reason to stop the wedding.

She smiled and felt a sense of relief wash over her. There wouldn't need to be any arguments or fights about her decision or feelings. Beth had taken care of the matter completely. No one would expect Lacy to marry while her sister labored to give birth to her first child.

Dave knew that with the onset of Beth's labor, the wedding would have to be postponed. His mother gave him a sympathetic smile and offered encouragement.

"Don't worry. Beth won't be in labor forever, and then you two can continue with the wedding."

"But that's just it," he said, shaking his head. "I don't know that we should."

His mother's expression betrayed her shock. "But why?"

Dave looked around cautiously. He was glad the others, including Pastor Flikkema, seemed to be busy elsewhere. "I feel like this was kind of forced on Lacy. Pastor wanted it so much that I did nothing to support her feelings in the decision. I knew she wasn't ready, or else she would have already set the date herself."

"I see." Patience gave him a stern motherly look. "So what will you do to make matters right?"

Dave shrugged. "I'm not sure what to do. Pastor has already approached me about marrying us tomorrow before he leaves. I hate to disappoint him, but I have to put Lacy's feelings first."

"Yes, you do. I know you're anxious to call Lacy your wife, but, Dave, she has to overcome her fears and worries about the past. If she carries those into her marriage, she'll be constantly at odds with herself and with you. That's no way to start life together."

"I know. I suppose I'll just go tell Pastor that we aren't ready."

"Be honest with him, Dave. He'll understand. He wouldn't want you to marry unless you were absolutely sure that it was what God had called you to do."

Dave kissed his mother on the forehead. "Thanks, Ma. I should have talked to you about it in the first place."

Pastor Flikkema was sorry to hear that the wedding wouldn't take place, but he completely agreed with Dave after listening to his explanation. He promised to return to the area as soon as possible but assured Dave that he would understand if they wanted to marry before he came back.

With that resolved, Dave went in search of Lacy. He had never wanted anything more than to marry her—to spend his life with her. He yearned to find a way to help her with her fears.

Lacy was pulling a bucket of water from the hot springs when Dave caught sight of her. She had just placed the bucket in the small cart she used for hauling and was stretching her back. Dave thought her more beautiful than any other woman he'd known. He loved everything about her—well, almost. He smiled at thoughts of her stubborn nature. Truth be told, he could love even that.

Dave watched her reach for another bucket and dip it into the hot springs. He hurried forward to help her, his footsteps crunching loudly on the rocky path.

Lacy straightened rather defensively as she looked to see who might be disturbing her peace. "Is something wrong? Is Beth—" Upon seeing Dave, she seemed to relax.

"Everything is fine," Dave said. "I just saw Gwen, and she said it will be a while still."

Lacy blew out a heavy breath. "Babies have a way of taking their dear sweet time."

He smiled and extended his hand. "Come sit with me a minute. I need to talk to you."

She put down the bucket and took hold of his hand. "What is it?"

Dave led her to a small bench by the fence that quartered off the hot springs pool. "I just spoke with Pastor Flikkema. He had suggested we marry tomorrow morning before he caught the noon stage."

"I see." Lacy seemed to go pale. She bit her lower lip, a nervous habit Dave had come to recognize signaled distress.

"I told him we couldn't."

She looked up in surprise. "You what?"

Dave continued to hold her hand even as they sat. He stroked her soft skin with his thumb. "I told him we couldn't marry tomorrow. I apologized to him but told him that I felt I had unfairly rushed you into agreeing to marry this quickly."

"I see." Lacy looked away, but Dave saw a flicker of gratitude in her eyes.

"Lacy, I don't want to marry you like that. I've been feeling guilty all week. I want to marry you, so don't think I don't. I think about it all the time." She looked back at him, and Dave couldn't help but grin. "I've never wanted anything as much as I want you."

She blushed but held his gaze. Dave reached up and touched her cheek. "But I know we can't marry until you are ready to let go of your fears."

To his surprise, Lacy nodded. "I have been thinking about the same thing."

"So we're in agreement, then. We won't marry tomorrow. We won't even set the date until you feel confident doing so. You'll find me to be a very patient man, Lacy. When I want something as much as I want to marry you, I can wait forever."

Lacy looked at him intently. She seemed to see him with new eyes, and Dave felt a sense of relief and hope. "I promise it won't take that long," she finally said.

He leaned over and kissed her gently on the lips. To his surprise, Lacy wrapped her arms around his neck as he pulled away. She pulled his face close and kissed him again.

Dave felt his heart race and his breathing quicken as he tightened his hold on her. He knew they were making the right decision not to marry on the morrow, but he couldn't help but feel a great sense of disappointment.

"Ah, Lacy," he whispered against her lips.

She pulled away as if sensing the torment. "Dave, there's something else I need to say."

He drew a deep breath to steady his senses. "Go ahead."

"I want to apologize. I know I've been hard on you in regard to my pa's death." She got to her feet and began to pace. "It's not your fault that Pa got shot. It's not your fault that we can't bring his killer to justice just yet. I know I've blamed you, but it's only because you represented the only legal authority in the area."

She frowned and paused. Casting a glance toward the ruckus going on next door and down toward the river, Lacy shook her head. "I'm positive Rafe knows something about all of this, but I know, too, that I can't blame you for not getting it out of him."

"What changed your mind?" Dave asked.

Lacy returned her gaze to his face. "I suppose a little of this and that. Beth talked to me not long ago, and I've been praying on it. Beth told me that she and Nick agreed to sell their land to Rafe. I was angry at first, but she explained that it was her deepest desire to provide for the safety of her child."

She paused and began to wring her hands together. "She said we're all driven to do things we wouldn't normally do— under regular circumstances—when we feel threatened. I guess seeing Pa die like he did made me feel threatened. I always saw this place as so peaceful. It was the first time we were prosperous and the instability of our childhood seemed a thing of the past."

"I'm sorry, Lacy. I didn't know that."

Nodding, Lacy looked again to the constant chaos that churned just beyond their property lines. "Everything here has changed. There is very little peace now. It makes me sad, but it's also made me really think about something."

"And what is that?"

Lacy turned back and stilled her hands. "We can't always make things work out the way we want, no matter how determined we are. It doesn't mean I don't want to find Pa's killer. That's still important to me, but I was wrong to be so angry with you." She put her hands to her head. "I just don't know what to do sometimes. I have all this need inside—desire. Sometimes I feel as though a battle is being fought within me."

Dave got to his feet and came to where she stood. "We all have that battle going on inside. It's a war of a spiritual nature. The old man is fighting with the redeemed man. Your old fears and doubts want control of your life, but you offered that place to God. You promised He could take charge. The devil doesn't like that one bit."

He smiled. "I found a verse the other day that helped me a lot with my own fears."

"You have fears?" Lacy asked in surprise.

Dave chuckled. "Of course I have fears. Losing you has to be right up there at the top, along with failing to be what you need me to be."

She seemed confused by his statement, but he continued. "Lacy, we all have things that make us feel inadequate. We can't let fear control us or overrun the good things we accomplish with God's help." Dave longed to take her in his arms and never let her go, but he held back.

"So what was the verse you found?"

"It was in Isaiah. It says, 'Fear thou not; for I am with thee: be not dismayed; for I am thy God: I will strengthen thee; yea, I will help thee; yea, I will uphold thee with the right hand of my righteousness.' " He grinned. "It gave me a great deal of peace."

She nodded and seemed to consider it for a moment. "It's as if God is promising to take the fear away."

"He is, Lacy. He'll take it away and give strength in return. And He'll never let you go."

"Never?"

The question posed seemed more than just Lacy's concerns about God's faithfulness. She seemed to be challenging his, as well. Dave drew her close, not letting his gaze leave hers. "Never."

Lacy let Dave hold her for a long time. She knew she'd have to draw new water from the springs, as the buckets had no doubt cooled off by now, but it didn't matter. Dave's gentleness was something she so desperately needed. She longed to be loved and cared about in the manner he felt for her. It was easy to let the emotions wash over her.

"I have something else to ask you," he said, stroking her hair.

She was hesitant to disengage from his arms but nevertheless forced herself to do just that. "What?"

"My father was talking to me last night about my future. He wants to expand the ranch by buying the Vanhouten land from Hank. He had hoped to ask him about it after the wedding. He has arranged for five hundred longhorn and Angus to be driven up from Texas."

"I see. Well, that certainly sounds industrious of him, but what does that have to do with me?"

"He'd like me to come in as a partner. It would mean giving up working for the sheriff. Pa would like me to consider moving back to the ranch, despite my having purchased the Vanhouten house."

"I see." Lacy still wasn't entirely sure why he'd brought this up.

As if reading her mind, he continued. "How would you feel about living at the ranch for a while after we marry?"

"I thought we were going to live in the Vanhouten house."

"I figured to," he said with a shrug, "but when Pa put this proposition to me, I knew I wanted to consider it. I won't, however, if you'd rather not be a rancher's wife."

She smiled. He was so concerned about her feelings. She had never known anyone to care so much about what she thought or felt the way he did. It endeared him to her. "A rancher's wife, eh?"

Dave's expression turned serious. "It's a hard life, Lacy."

"It's no harder than anything else I've known." She thought of the ways she'd lived over her nearly twenty-two years. She and her sisters had known great hardship. They had worked, even as children, to keep the household together and food on the table.

"Is that your way of saying you wouldn't mind being married to a cowman?"

"And we'd live with your folks?" she asked.

"At least for a time. That is, if you were in agreement. Pa thought it might be best for all of us. We could save money that way, and I'd be right there to help him and learn what I need to know."

Lacy nodded. "And your mother could teach me how to be a proper lady. Don't think I don't know what you're doing, Dave Shepard."

He looked at her in confusion. "I never . . . I didn't say . . ."

She put her finger to his lips. "I'm teasing you. I love your mother, and I'm sure I could learn a great deal from her."

He kissed her finger tenderly. "You are the perfect lady for me, Lacy Gallatin."

"What about when I wear my trousers and climb up on the roof?"

"Even then," he said, a smile spreading across his face. "Although I'd just as soon you refrain from doing both."

She shook her head. "No. If you're going to marry me, Dave Shepard, you have to take me, faults and all. I won't go changing just because you think to make me into somebody else. If you feel that way, you might as well break the engagement right now."

To her surprise, he laughed and pulled her hard against him. "There's no chance of that, Lacy Gallatin. You need me to keep you out of trouble, and I need you to . . . well . . . I just need you."

And for the first time, Lacy truly believed that marrying Dave was exactly what she was destined to do.

CHAPTER FOURTEEN

"Why did you have to have a boy?" Justin asked Beth. He stared down at the baby in her arms and screwed up his face. "And such an ugly one."

Beth laughed. "He isn't ugly. He's just two days old."

"He's got hardly any hair, no teeth, and he cries all the time," Justin countered.

"He's not crying right now," Beth replied defensively. "Besides, babies aren't born with teeth, and he'll get more hair later."

"I don't like him." He crossed his arms and plopped into a nearby chair just as Nick brought in a wooden cradle.

"It's finished and ready for our new addition," he declared as he put the baby's new bed on the floor.

Beth admired the piece of furniture. She knew Nick had labored over it for several weeks in between his other duties. The pine had been carefully carved with scrolling and stained to bring out the richness of the wood's natural pattern. Nick had even thought to make it quite large so it could be used for some time to come.

"It's beautiful. Thank you so much. I know Max will sleep well in it." She gently stroked the sleeping baby's head.

They'd named the baby Maxwell after Nick's grandfather, but agreed to call him Max for short. He was born on the seventeenth of June after fourteen hours of labor, and Beth had never imagined anything or anyone could make her feel so complete—so happy.

Clearly irritated, Justin asked, "Why didn't you make me a bed?"

"You already have a bed," Nick said, reaching out to gently rock the cradle. "See, it rocks smooth and even. That was the hardest part."

Beth pointed to a stack of bedding. "Gwen made a little pillow for the bottom to cushion it like a mattress. There are also some blankets."

Nick went to retrieve them. "I'll get it all fixed up."

"How come Aunt Gwen didn't make me a pillow?" Justin asked.

Beth could see that the boy was trying to take issue with anything related to the baby. She hoped he would soon settle into the role of big brother and enjoy the new arrival, but for now, he was obviously jealous.

Nick placed the cradle beside their bed and arranged the bedding per Beth's instructions. She then watched as Nick gently placed Max in his new bed. The baby didn't so much as stir.

"I think it meets with his approval," Beth said with a smile. "I know it does mine."

"You love Max more than you do me," Justin suddenly declared. He got up from his chair and threw an accusing glare at his father.

"Son, you know that's not true," Nick said, straightening. He looked at Justin for several seconds before continuing. "I have enough love for the both of you—and any other baby that comes along."

"You made him a bed and never made me anything."

"You're right. I should have done something for you. What do you have in mind?"

Justin was momentarily taken aback. "I . . . uh . . . well . . ." He turned away. "I don't know. You should have thought of something."

Beth rolled her eyes. "Justin Lassiter, are you telling me that you believe love can be proven only by the gifts we give or make? Do you honestly doubt your father's love for you— my love for you?"

Justin looked down at the floor. "You're going to spend all your time with the baby. You won't have time to even teach me my schoolwork or play jokes on folks."

"Ha! That's what you think," Beth came back. "I'll have you know, young man, that I'm already making plans for fall and the things we'll study. Max will be nearly three months old by the time we begin school again, and he won't need me nearly as much. As for playing jokes . . . well, you'll just have to wait and see."

Nick knelt beside Justin. "Are you afraid that we can't love you anymore because Max has come?"

Justin refused to look at his father. "I don't know," he said in a nearly incoherent mutter.

"Well, it seems to me that you believe Max has somehow come to take your place in my heart, and that just won't happen."

Justin looked up at Nick and then to Beth. "But Mama is busy all the time now with the baby, and even before the baby got here, she couldn't play with me like before."

"That's true. Having a baby isn't easy."

"She could have died. Like my first mama."

Nick nodded. "Ah. I never thought about how that must have worried you. She could have died, but she didn't. And she'll get stronger every day, and pretty soon she'll be able to take walks with you and work with you on your schooling."

Beth felt sorry for the young boy and patted the side of her bed. She, too, had never stopped to really consider how the death of Justin's mother might have affected him. "Come here, Justin. Come sit by me."

He hesitated for a moment before joining her. He sat stiffly on the edge of the bed, almost as if he were afraid of hurting her. "Son, you will always be loved," Beth said, gently touching his cheek. "You are the oldest in the family, and that makes you special. Max is special for being second."

"I love you and Max," Nick interjected, "just as I'll love any other child God sees fit to give us. Even if we have another dozen children."

Beth's eyes widened. "A dozen?"

Nick chuckled. "Well, for now two is just fine." He winked at Beth and added, "But I wouldn't mind us having another one in a year or two. Maybe a sweet and angelic little girl—just like her mother."

Grinning, Beth raised a brow. "Sweet and angelic like her mother? Are you intending to get rid of me and find someone else?"

"Silly woman," Nick said. He turned to Justin. "Now, why don't we go downstairs, and you can tell me what I can build for you. What if we made a fort for all your soldiers? We could make something permanent that you could use with those new building blocks you got for your birthday."

"Truly? Could we really build a fort?"

"I don't know why not."

Beth watched them go off together and couldn't help but wonder about the future. Justin had been difficult since they'd announced the pregnancy. Was this just a temporary lull in the storm? She glanced at the baby, marveling that someone so small could stir up such trouble.

Beth still couldn't comprehend that her son was finally here. The pain and joy of his birth made her think of her own mother. "Oh, Mama, I wish you could be with us. I wish you could see your grandchildren," Beth murmured. "I wish I could see you again." A tear slipped down her cheek, and she quickly wiped it away, lest someone come in and see her crying.

Looking down on her son, Beth felt an overwhelming desire to live forever. At least until her children were old, with children of their own. She wanted to see her family grow up, succeed at life, and be happy. She didn't want to say good-bye to them while they were still so very young.

"Oh, God," she prayed, "give me the gift of time."

Rafe watched the miners shuffle in and out of the makeshift restaurant. His girls were busy serving meals during the day and entertaining the men at night. He knew they were worn to pieces, but it didn't matter. He was making good money—better money than he'd ever made before. If they fell over dead from exhaustion, he'd simply get others to replace them.

"Looks like another good day," Jefferson said, coming alongside Rafe. He held a cup of coffee in his hand and motioned with the cup. "We've probably made at least thirty dollars just from breakfast."

"I was thinkin' the same." Rafe scratched his stomach. "It was a good idea to move the place up here on the Lassiter property. Havin' it here, so close to the saloon and the cribs, makes it better for the girls and me."

"Well, hopefully you won't have to burn out our neighbors as you did the Lassiters, and we can obtain Gallatin House and the store. Those buildings are perfect for our needs, and Bishop can't hope to get a better offer than what we can give. When he finally sells, we can move it all over to the Gallatin House. Then the girls can entertain and feed the miners all in one setting. It'll really be worth its weight in gold, especially with the hot springs."

Rafe frowned. "Well, if something doesn't happen soon, we may not find ourselves all that well off. I've seen some folks preparing to leave. They're getting discouraged."

"I heard about it, too. I figured to have one of the men pepper the river with dust tonight. It should be enough to get folks excited again."

"What'll that set us back?" Rafe asked.

"Not that much. Don't you worry. I'm not about to wash my profits away. We'll keep it concentrated mostly in areas where our men are fixed to recover it. It will get folks stirred up, and those that are thinking to head out will reconsider. Some might still go, and that's all right. Others will come."

"You seem mighty confident."

Jefferson smiled. "Truth is, I'm quite confident, and you should be, too. We're making good money here, Rafe. Gambling is supplying a good number of men with a living, and others are earning their keep by working for us. This is how towns develop, my friend. While the money is rolling in, however, we should consider other means of continuing our profits."

Rafe looked at him with interest. "What do you have in mind?"

Jefferson drank the last of the coffee and put his cup on the makeshift counter. "I believe we need to create some form of industry that will provide a much-needed and desired product and employ a great many men."

"But what would that be? This area's a raw, unsettled land."

"There are still possibilities. Lumber, for instance. Folks are going to need it to build cities, and the railroad will need ties and water towers, as well as depots and machine shops. There is plenty of wood to be had in the area, and we could certainly consider milling." He rubbed his chin thoughtfully and grinned. "And I happened to notice on one of my rides to Bozeman that there are several fine crops of barley growing in the area."

"What of it?"

"We could start our own brewery," Jefferson said matter-of-factly. "We could make our own beer and sell it at a huge profit."

"There are several breweries already in place," Rafe stated. "I don't see how we could make that much money or secure the barley for ourselves."

His friend laughed and slapped Rafe on the back. "Old boy, you need to trust me for the details. Have I led you wrong yet?"

Rafe had to admit Jefferson's ideas had only benefited him. He nodded and smiled. "I see your point."

"So that's my proposition," Jerry Shepard told Hank.

Lacy and Dave had joined in on the conversation at Jerry's request. Lacy had known he would make Hank an offer on the Vanhouten land, but Dave had asked her to say nothing to Hank or the others until after his father had a chance to bring it up.

"Having just invested in the additional cattle, I'm short on ready cash," Jerry admitted. "However, if you can trust me for the money until fall, I should be able to make a substantial payment on the land."

"I think it sounds like answered prayer," Hank said. "I'm willing to work this out with you in any manner that will benefit us both."

Jerry looked at Dave and grinned. "Looks like we're in business, son."

Hank cast a glance at Dave and then Lacy. "What's this all about?"

"Pa asked me to partner up with him on the ranch. I'm going to give up being a deputy."

"I hadn't expected that turn of events," Hank said, leaning back in his chair. "So you won't be moving north with the rest of us?"

"No. I plan to live on the ranch with my folks. Then after Lacy and I marry, we'll continue to live there for a time."

"At least through the winter," Jerry added. "As hard as last winter was on everyone, I figure it might be a good idea. And with the railroad coming through and the growing population, I'm also thinking we'll need to start fencing some of the pastures."

"But I thought open range was quite popular here," Hank countered.

Jerry nodded. "It has been, but those days will pass away. More farmers are moving into the area, and they'll want to keep the cattle from getting into their crops. They'll no doubt fence. Then there will be issues with water and rustling as more people move into the area."

"I suppose that makes sense. Tomorrow I'll go into Bozeman and get the proper papers drawn up. That will just leave the small amount of land you don't want, as well as Gallatin House and the store. I'm more than confident that Rafe and his friend will want to buy me out."

"I've always hated the idea of Rafe having Gallatin House," Lacy said. "But I know there's probably no other way. We can't expect any decent person to make a bid on it with all the trouble that's been going on around here. Dave said there were two fights that ended in killings just this week."

"Yeah, I saw the graves being dug at the cemetery," Hank said. "Was anyone arrested?"

Dave shook his head. "No one saw anything, as usual. Rafe's men said both were fair fights but had no idea who else was involved. I had no one to question."

"It's a sorry state of affairs," Jerry said, getting to his feet. "I should be heading back. Patience will worry about me if I don't get home before dark."

Hank followed Jerry to the door. "Thanks for coming."

Lacy contemplated the future as her brother-in-law and soon-to-be father-in-law stepped outside. She looked at Dave and found him watching her. The warmth of the day was fading as the sun moved farther west, but Lacy felt a rush of heat to her cheeks. Sometimes her imagination got the best of her, and she found her thoughts drifting to dangerous places.

"I suppose I should go check on Beth. Nick and Justin are still outside working, and she probably wonders where everyone has gotten off to."

Dave got to his feet and took hold of her just as she started to turn. "I want you to know that I don't plan to quit my work for the sheriff until September. That's when the Texas cattle are due to arrive. In the meantime, I plan to do what I can to find your father's killer and resolve the problems with the highwaymen."

She could see in his expression that this decision was important to him—to them as a couple. Nodding, Lacy murmured her thanks. A tenderness for his considerate nature stirred in her heart.

He really does care, she thought. *He cares about my feelings and knows that this is important to me.* She gave him a hint of a smile and hurried for the front staircase.

These small acts of kindness and attentiveness were Dave's way of courting and wooing her. He was proving his love for her in the only ways he knew would really matter to her, and that touched her deeply.

CHAPTER FIFTEEN

Lacy watched from the kitchen as Hank and Nick signed contracts with the stage company manager. Major, the dog, stood faithfully at Hank's side as if to oversee the entire process. The three men paid him little attention, however. After working out the details over the last few days, they had finally come to an agreement. The stage company was giving them a five-year contract, contingent upon the hotel and livery being in place by October. Given that it was already the middle of July, Lacy wasn't sure how they were going to accomplish everything.

"Have they finished?" Gwen asked, nudging in close behind her sister.

"They're just now signing," Lacy replied.

Gwen shifted Julianne from one hip to the other. The baby

chortled as if she were having a great time. Lacy couldn't help but smile. "Sounds like she approves."

"I'm sure she does," Gwen answered. "She knows how all of this has worn on my peace of mind."

Lacy turned back to check on the cookies she had baking in the oven. "I hope they know what they're doing."

Gwen secured Julianne in the baby chair and then retrieved her apron. "I know Hank already has men and supplies assigned to various building projects. The railroad has deeded him land, and he's quite enthusiastic about seeing this through to completion."

"And what about you?"

Gwen reached for a large mixing bowl. "I'm happy about it. I can't bear this place anymore." Her voice was heavy. "Nothing is the same. The land has been torn up—the peace and quiet is gone. I don't feel comfortable walking about my own yard."

"But who is to say the same thing won't happen in the new town?" Lacy asked.

"Hank and I have discussed that."

"Discussed what?" Hank asked as he strolled into the kitchen. He kissed Gwen on the cheek, then motioned to the stove. "Is the coffee fresh and hot?"

"Of course," Gwen replied. "Would you all like a cup? I can bring some in for everyone."

"That would be wonderful." He looked at Lacy and then back to Gwen. "So, what have we discussed?"

"The fact that corruption could occur in the new town as easily as it has here in Gallatin Crossing," Gwen said, pulling a tray from the far cupboard. She placed three coffee mugs atop it and retrieved the cream and sugar.

"Are you worried about that, Lacy? I didn't think you were going to make the move."

"I'll still need to go to town, and I'll want to know that my family is in a safe place."

"I think things will be different this time around," Hank said, shrugging. "The railroad officials have their own idea of what the town should be. We're working closely with them to position the hotel and livery near the depot. I've also heard some comments that they might pay to build a school."

"Schools and churches always civilize," Gwen said. "I remember Pa saying that." She poured coffee into each of the mugs.

Lacy nodded. "I do, too. I suppose it's true, given that families would be more inclined to move to a place with such facilities available to them. Still, I worry that we are only delaying for a time the misery we've known here."

"Ah, *'plus dolet quam necesse est qui ante dolet quam necesse est,'* " Hank murmured.

Lacy raised a brow. "And that would mean what?"

" 'He suffers more than is necessary who suffers before it is necessary.' There is simply no use working yourself into a lather over something that hasn't happened. Give our dreams a chance."

Lacy considered her own life and all that stretched before her. "I suppose dreams are important."

"Of course they are," Gwen said, smiling. "Dreams give us hope for the future."

Hank reached for the tray as Gwen stepped forward. "Exactly. Oh, and here's a good bit of news: I've heard from Nick's uncle and cousin. They aren't happy in Bozeman. They feel they will be better off joining us and starting over. They've managed to save a small amount of money while working for other folks, but both want to get back to owning their own shop." He secured the tray and turned to go.

"It'll be nice to have Millie close by," Gwen said.

"I thought you'd be pleased to hear the news. Thanks for the coffee." Hank nodded toward the tray.

Lacy pulled the cookies from the oven. "I'll bring you some of these when they cool."

Hank grinned. "I was hoping you would."

Lacy finished serving the men before heading out for the Shepard ranch. Gallatin House was in need of butter and eggs before the stage came in the following day. The countryside, with its gentle swaying grass and wild flowers, revived Lacy's senses. She never tired of the grandeur—the stately beauty of the Rocky Mountains. The rugged peaks had lost their snowy caps, but she knew it wouldn't be for long. Soon enough the high country would once again clothe itself in white. Before she knew it, September would arrive and she would marry Dave. If not sooner.

"Lacy!"

She halted the horse and wagon at the sound of her name. Looking to the right, she saw that Cubby was crossing the field. He carried a rifle in one hand and balanced a long stick on his shoulder with the other. Two dead rabbits dangled from the small stripped branch.

"Hello, Cubby."

He paused and looked at her for a long moment. "I'm sorry I hit you."

He spoke as if the incident had happened only the day before. Lacy met his gaze. "Thank you for apologizing."

Cubby looked away and kicked at the dirt. "Is it true you plan to marry Dave Shepard?"

Lacy nodded. "It is."

He squared his shoulders and seemed to puff up his chest a bit as he fixed her with a hard stare. "I won't help you find your pa's killer if you do."

She narrowed her eyes. "You don't have to help me find him, Cubby. Dave and I are capable of continuing the search. Honestly, why do you think it's acceptable to bully me into calling off my engagement?"

Frowning, Cubby shook his head. "I'm not bullying. I'm just sayin' I know something about it, but I won't tell you if you marry Dave Shepard."

Anger coursed through Lacy. She tightened her grip on the reins. "If you know who killed my father, you need to speak to the sheriff. It's your duty."

"I only have a duty to myself," he snapped back.

"Now you really sound like your father."

His face reddened. "Stop saying that! I'm not like him. You can't see me for who I really am."

"Your actions speak for themselves," Lacy replied. "You bully people and try to force them to do things your way, and when they don't, you strike out to hurt them."

"I told you I was sorry for hitting you," Cubby said, raising his voice.

"I'm not talking about that," Lacy countered. "You are hurting me by suggesting you know who was responsible for my pa's death, yet you won't see the man brought to justice. You say you care about me, but you do nothing but grieve me."

"I could say the same. In fact, I will."

"You just did. Good day, Cubby." She snapped the reins and put the horse in motion.

"I'm not like my pa, Lacy."

The words rang across the open expanse of land. Lacy couldn't be sure, but she thought his voice broke just a bit as he declared it for a second time. She trembled to think he might actually know the name of the murderer. Maybe it was just a game, she reasoned. Cubby might not know the killer, but he knew how important it was to her. Maybe he was simply using it to get her attention.

Well, it had done that, for sure. Lacy could scarcely think of anything else as she continued to the ranch. What if he really did know who killed her father?

"What in the world is that all about?" Beth asked, pointing to a line of wagons as they came around the bend from the south.

Lacy glanced up to see the procession. "I have no idea. It looks like an entire wagon train." She got up from her seat on the porch and handed Max back to Beth. "Where do you suppose they're bound?"

By now the front rider had passed by Rafe's and was headed directly for Gallatin House. "Morning, ladies," the man said, tipping his hat. "I wonder if you might tell me, is this Gallatin Crossing?"

"Yes, it is," Lacy replied.

The man signaled to the first wagon. "This is it!" The wagon came to a halt with the others pulling up tight behind it.

"Can we help you?" Beth asked.

"I sure hope so." The man took off his hat and wiped his forehead with the back of his sleeve.

Lacy thought the man looked to be about fifty. His skin was leathery and weathered, betraying his many hours in the sun. Behind him stood a string of wagons—at least ten that Lacy could count. Women and children were disembarking to stretch and survey the town.

"I'm J. D. Patterson," the man told her, "and this is the group out of Colorado."

"I'm afraid I don't know anything about a group out of Colorado," Lacy told him.

The man frowned. "We have deeds to land around these parts."

Lacy could only imagine that Hank had sold them part of the Vanhouten acreage. She smiled to ease the man's concerns. "You probably need to talk to my brother-in-law, Hank Bishop. He's over there at the store. I'm sure he'll know exactly what's going on. Why don't you come with me."

But Hank knew no more than Lacy. He took a look at the man's papers and then back to the gathering of men. There were thirteen in all, each representing the thirteen families who'd come from Denver to make a new start in Montana.

"I don't know anything about this," Hank told them.

Just then an old miner stumbled up to the counter. "What do you have to ease the miseries of a constipated mule?"

Everyone turned and looked at the man as if he'd lost his mind. He didn't seem to care that they were startled. "My Myrtle has been in a world of hurt for two days, and I need to give her some relief."

Hank nodded and went for a bottle on one of the back

shelves. "This should do the trick. Give her a good-sized dose to start with. The instructions on the back will tell you."

"Cain't read," the man admitted. He pulled some coins from his pants. "But I'll get someone to tell me." He paid Hank and then started toward the door. "Cain't spend time jawin' with ya, either," he told the gathered people. "We can have a good yak after I get Myrtle on her way to happiness."

The wagon train folks watched the miner make his way out the door. The entire event seemed almost surreal, and Hank motioned to Lacy. "Close the door and turn the sign. We don't need to have any more interruptions." She did as he directed, pressing her way through the angry crowd.

Hank continued. "I'm afraid you may have been duped."

"That's impossible. The man was from the railroad," Patterson said firmly. "He had the proper credentials. He told us the railroad was going to run a spur line to Gallatin Crossing, and they could offer us cheap land to encourage town growth."

"But as far as I know there isn't going to be a spur line," Hank countered. "At least none they're talking about for the present." He went to his desk and pulled out the map he'd acquired of the railroad's final survey.

"See here," he said as he spread the map out, "the line runs well to the north of Gallatin Crossing. If a spur was ever to be built, it would be many years down the road. As for land, well, most of the land in this area was previously owned by me." He met the men's expressions. "I hired no agent to act on my behalf and sell any of it."

Lacy could see that the men were upset. She also realized the stage would be in most any time. "We're expecting the noon stage, gentlemen," she interjected amidst their grumblings. "We will need to feed the passengers and change out the horses, but after that, we can certainly revisit this matter." She looked at Hank. "Maybe you could help them locate a place to set up camp and clear the road for the stage."

Hank nodded. "You men can move your wagons to just behind the store. After lunch we can discuss what's to be done."

One by one the men shuffled out the store and back to their waiting women. Lacy didn't envy the worn group. They'd been on the trail since sometime in April and were ready to settle onto their land. Only there was no land.

"I think Justin is stealing some of the baby's things," Beth told Nick as he readied harnesses for the stage team.

He shook his head. "Why do you suppose it's Justin? We've had plenty of other things disappear around here."

"These are things from inside the house," she countered. "And only things that belong to Max are missing."

"Did you ask him? Maybe he just wanted to see them and forgot to return them."

"Yes, I did ask," Beth said, her frustration mounting. "He said he wouldn't touch anything that belonged to Max because he hates him."

Nick looked at her in surprise. "He actually said he hated him?"

"Yes. He said that you are too busy to go fishing with him, and I'm too busy to play tricks with him. He said that it was all Max's fault and that he hated him."

Nick rechecked the harness in his hand and headed for the door. "I have to ready the team for the stage, but I'll talk to Justin about it after the stage goes. It's probably not as bad as you think."

Beth wasn't convinced. She hurried back to the house to help Gwen and Lacy with the meal, her heart heavy with worry for Justin.

"You look upset," Gwen said as Beth entered the kitchen.

"I am." Beth tied on her apron and immediately looked around for what her next task should be. "I tried to talk to Nick about Justin, but he's too busy getting ready for the stage."

Lacy took a stack of plates and headed for the dining room, and Beth lowered her voice to keep her younger sister from hearing. "Justin told me that Lacy loved him more than I did. He said he'd rather she be his mama."

Gwen smiled. "He's just being ornery. He doesn't know how it hurts you." She stirred a thick stew and replaced the lid. "You can't let the antics and comments of a ten-year-old ruin your day."

"I just thought we were closer than that." Beth frowned. "I love him. He's a son to me every bit as much as Max."

"Have you told him that?" Gwen asked.

Beth thought back on the times she'd spoken with Justin about her feelings for him. She thought of all the things they'd done together before the baby had come. True, she hadn't had much time for such fun since Max's arrival, but that would change in time.

"I've tried to. I think he's doubting my words because my actions aren't what they used to be."

"Maybe you should do something with him. Just you and Justin. Lacy and I can watch the baby. Take him fishing and tell him how much you love him—that you miss doing these things with him."

Max began to fuss from the front room, where he and Julianne had been napping. "I suppose I could," Beth said as she moved to retrieve her son.

Still, the idea gave her little comfort. Why couldn't Justin simply understand that people were capable of loving many folks at once? Why couldn't he see that her heart for him was unchanged?

Beth rounded the corner to find Justin bent over Max's basket. "What are you doing?" she asked a little more harshly than she'd intended.

Justin straightened and jumped back as if he'd just touched a hot stove. "He was crying and I didn't like it."

Beth frowned and moved to pick Max up from the basket. "He's just hungry. You make plenty of noise when you're hungry." She soothed the baby even as she studied Justin's expression.

"I don't caterwaul like that," Justin said, starting to leave.

"Wait." Beth watched as the boy turned around hesitantly. "I just wondered if you'd like to go fishing with me sometime."

He narrowed his gaze. "With him?"

Beth cradled Max closer at the look of disapproval in Justin's eyes. "No. Just you and me. Aunt Gwen would take care of Max."

The boy's eyes lit up, but he held his expression in check. "I suppose we could."

"Maybe tomorrow, then. There won't be a stage until evening. We could try to catch a mess of fish for supper."

Suspicion crept into Justin's expression. "And it would just be me and you?"

"Yes," she said with a smile, hoping to alleviate his fears. "Just you and me like we used to do."

He considered this for a moment, then nodded. "I guess that would be all right."

Beth watched him go. She took hold of Max's hand playfully, but then frowned when she noted a red mark on the baby's arm. Max had calmed now, but there were still tears in his eyes.

"What happened to you, darling?" She gently touched the welt and glanced back in the direction Justin had gone. Had he pinched the baby? She let out a heavy sigh. Stealing Max's things was bad enough, but if Justin had actually resorted to harming the child, she would have an entirely different problem with which to deal.

CHAPTER SIXTEEN

"I'm afraid there's little I can do about it," Hank declared to the people of the Denver wagon train. Despite a night of rest, the entire group looked trail weary and worn from their experience. And now Hank had only more bad news to convey.

"The fact is, my land has already been promised to a local rancher, and the hotel and store properties are being sold to the saloon owner, Rafe Reynolds." He pointed in Rafe's direction. "That's him over there."

Rafe stood and nodded to the people. "That's right. I'm buying these businesses to expand my own."

The men and women murmured comments to one another, but Hank hushed them quickly. He'd called this meeting at Gallatin House not only to show the newcomers that he sympathized with their situation but to suggest they might want to join him and some of the others in considering a fresh start elsewhere. He had hopes of telling them about the property available up north, where even now he had arranged to have the new Gallatin Hotel built.

Jefferson Mulholland was also in attendance, and Hank frowned as he whispered something to Rafe. Those two always seemed to be planning something. Ignoring them, however, Hank began again.

"I think you should know that the railroad has no intention of building a line through this area. I spoke personally with the men in charge. It was in our best interests to know if the railroad would come to Gallatin Crossing, after all."

"But gold's been found in the area," one of the men asserted. "That will make the railroad take another look."

"Only if a very large find can be had. So far, there has been only a trickle of color," Hank countered. "Nothing at all to constitute a rush."

"But you do have a rush," the same man replied. "We've seen the men lined up panning the river."

"Yes, but what you haven't seen are any large claims to prove the gold speculation is valid," Hank told him. "However, that's not what I wanted to talk to you about. The fact is that the railroad is going in to the north. I have worked out an arrangement to purchase land from the railroad to start a new town. I want to suggest that you folks consider doing the same. I can take you there tomorrow, if you like, and you can see exactly how the situation is set up. Those of you who want to start new businesses could easily do so there."

"But we already bought land here," a tall man said as he stood. He rubbed a scraggly beard. "We sold our acreage and business in Denver and used all the money to buy the land and get up here. I can't be buying another piece of property to start over."

"Me either" came the cry of most of the men in the room.

"We were assured that the land was ready for us, mister," a tall bearded man announced. "We have lots designated, and the town has already been plotted out. We've come a long, hard way. My Esther, here, is plumb worn to the bone."

Hank saw a woman about six months pregnant. Her eyes were sunken and lined with dark shadows. She looked at him with such hope, almost as if she were willing him to offer them good news. But Hank had nothing good to give. His money was tied up in the hotel and the livery. He had already made arrangements for Jerry Shepard to pay him over time. There was simply very little ready capital that he could invest to help anyone at this point.

"There has to be some mistake," another man declared. He was more portly than the others and held himself as something of an authority. "The paper work was gone over by a lawyer. We know it to be valid."

Hank shook his head. "Then perhaps you should go into Bozeman and secure another lawyer to check it out. Maybe there is another area called Gallatin Crossing. Maybe your instructions and locator marks were misdirected."

Patterson stood at this. "Ladies and gentlemen, we aren't going to get anywhere like this. Mr. Bishop is right. We need to send a couple of men into Bozeman to further check out the land deeds."

Any order that had been maintained quickly dissolved as the men hurried to surround Patterson. They all spoke at once, and Hank dismissed himself. He made his way to the kitchen, feeling as though he'd once again failed to accomplish what he'd set out to do.

Lacy stood by the stove watching him. He met her eyes as she shook her head. "They sure don't like to listen as much as they like to talk."

He forced a smile. "They aren't even really talking. They're rambling—complaining at such a pace that no one can understand a word they're saying."

She glanced beyond him toward the noise. "Well, it's hard to see your dreams crumble. I suppose they are also very frightened."

Hank reached for a coffee cup. "Yes, I'm sure they are. It can't be easy to leave everything you know, sell all you own, and put the money into something that you now realize is nonexistent. They've clearly been robbed, but they cannot accept that at this point."

Lacy poured coffee into Hank's cup. "They have families, and here it is, already the middle of summer. They know their time is limited before the cold weather comes. They've lived around the mountains, so they know how harsh it can be."

"I wish I could do something to help," Hank said, shaking his head. "But I just don't have any answers."

"Well, now we make a new plan," Jefferson Mulholland told Rafe that night after they'd closed the bar.

Rafe looked at his friend and scratched his chin. "What are you talkin' about?"

Jefferson grinned. "The wagon train folks."

"What about them?" Rafe went to work wiping out glasses that had recently been used by some of the miners. He seldom washed them, feeling it was unnecessary. He reasoned that the alcohol was as good a cleaner as water.

Jefferson looked smug as he leaned back in his chair. Rafe stopped what he was doing and looked hard at his friend. "You know something about this, don't you?"

Mulholland laughed. "Of course I do. I don't let anything happen by chance in my life. Every step is carefully calculated."

Putting down the glass and towel, Rafe moved to the table where Jefferson sat. "So you want to fill me in on all of these carefully calculated plans?"

"Of course. Have a seat and I'll explain. I didn't want to say anything too soon. I wanted to make sure that the people actually arrived. I'd hoped there would have been more—twenty families would have been nice. But this is a good start."

"A good start for what?" Rafe asked.

Jefferson fished out a piece of paper from his fine silk vest. "My brother lives in Denver. I received this letter from him back in April. At my suggestion, he enticed several families to purchase tracts of land that they presumed would be prime real estate for businesses along the railroad. He even convinced them that houses were already being built and would be available for their families once they got here."

Rafe looked at the man and realized his friend was twenty times more cunning than he could ever hope to be. "You mean you had him send those folks up here? But why?"

"Why? Because, my friend, we are going to benefit and profit from their arrival. We are going to become their most sympathetic friends."

"I don't understand," Rafe said. "How can we help them? How were they even convinced to come?"

"People believe what they want to believe. My brother rented an office and put up a fancy sign and called himself a lawyer. He dressed the part and then advertised that land transactions could be made through him for purchase of prime real estate in Montana."

Rafe shook his head. "And folks believed him? Just like that?"

Mulholland laughed and snapped his fingers. "Just like that. Like I said, folks love to believe that a bargain is a bargain and good things can be had, just for the taking. They lined up to hear about the incredibly rich Gallatin River valley and all that it had to offer. If we'd had more time, he probably could have sold more tracts. In fact, he may have already done so, for all I know."

"So he convinced the people to put money down for land that they couldn't even lay eyes on. I can't believe folks could be so gullible."

"It happens all the time. I can't tell you the number of swindles that have been made over land. It's really easy. You run an ad in the newspaper, convince folks to commit to buying land at ridiculously cheap prices—or in this case, even tell them that businesses are readily available. My brother convinced three men in this wagon train that there was a livery, bakery, and blacksmith shop to be had, equipment included, for a very reasonable price."

"How did he convince them of that?"

Mulholland yawned as if bored with the entire matter. He glanced at his watch, causing Rafe to do likewise. It was nearly four in the morning. "My brother is a smart man, and frankly, we've done this kind of thing on a few other occasions. He had handbills printed up with descriptions of equipment and their value. He made it look authentic, and people believed what they wanted to believe."

"That's just amazing." Rafe said, looking at the letter Jefferson had laid on the table. "All I can say is, the next time you pull this, I want in. Seems to me you're benefiting quite a bit from my little town."

Jefferson eyed his friend with a raised brow. "Seems we're both benefiting. But if it makes you feel better, you should know that you stand to make a profit from our new arrivals. These people are going to need our help."

"What help can we possibly give them?"

"We're going make them a magnanimous offer. We will take pity upon their situation and suggest they rent from us and work for us. We can even let them know that they will have the opportunity to purchase the land they rent."

"But how are we going to do that? We have a tent city here, and short of the store and hotel, there isn't that much to offer."

"True, but they can labor to build it," Mulholland suggested. He crossed his arms. "You have enough land around here that we can build on. They can cut the trees and glean the lumber for building. They can put their sweat into seeing their families housed before the cruel winter sets in. We can even generously tell them that if they will build houses for their families and stores for the community, we will allow them some months rent free."

Rafe considered this for a few moments. Mulholland's skill at manipulation astounded him. "What if they don't agree?"

Jefferson shrugged. "What if they don't? They can leave on

the same road that brought them here. We won't look any worse for offering so generously, and we certainly won't be out any money. And if they agree, we get our town built for nothing. Oh, we might have to help with nails and such, but that will be nothing compared to having to do it ourselves."

Rafe began to see the truth of it. It was really quite simple. Even if the group sent someone back to Denver, they wouldn't find Jefferson's brother. He would have already moved on to another town and started up another scheme. The wagon train folks were really limited in what they could do to resolve the situation. He smiled.

"Count me in," he said. "I always did favor myself being a landlord."

Dave looked at the man riding next to him. His name was Jonathan Webster, but he went by Big John. He had killed a man the night before in a fight behind Rafe's Saloon. Dave knew Big John as a regular of Rafe's, but little more. The man was at least six feet four and outweighed Dave by seventy pounds. His heavy beard partially hid several rather nasty scars, but it was his dark eyes that made the man look even more menacing.

"You know it was self-defense."

"I know that's your story," Dave said.

"It's the truth. That lowlife threatened to put a knife between my shoulder blades when I won my fifth hand of poker. When I went outside, he followed me and pulled a knife. If you ask around, you'll find out that the knife that killed him was his own."

"I have that information in my report," Dave assured him.

"So do they have good grub at this Bozeman jail?"

Dave shrugged and readjusted his hat. The intensity of the sun made him squint. "I suppose as far as prison food goes, it's decent enough. If you were overly worried about your meals, you should have stayed out of trouble."

The man laughed heartily, as if Dave had told a great joke. They rode in silence for a time and had nearly reached the Bozeman city limits before Big John cleared his throat to speak.

"I'm wondering if we can make a deal."

Dave looked at him and raised a brow. "What kind of deal?"

The sights and sounds of city life rose up to greet the stillness of rural Montana. There was the ever-present smell of pigs and the unbearable dust kicked up from the dirt roads. Dave and John had to ease far to the side of Main Street as a sixteen-mule train loaded to the hilt with supplies came firing down the street like a ball cut loose from a cannon. Bozeman had become quite the busy place in the last couple of years, and pedestrians and horseback riders were starting to fear for their lives. Big John appeared to take in the spectacle for a moment, then turned back to meet Dave's fixed stare.

"Well, I'm wondering if a fella could get out of serving prison time if he had knowledge of crimes even worse than what he was accused of."

"Are you telling me you have information about illegal doings and you want to trade that for a reduced sentence?"

"Or no sentence at all," the man said with a grin. "What I know is worth it, I guarantee you."

"I don't make those decisions," Dave answered. "That would be up to the judge."

"But do you suppose it's possible?"

"I honestly don't know. I believe it would depend on the kind of knowledge you have. You know, whether it's firsthand or hearsay."

"Oh, it's firsthand all right," Big John said with a gruff laugh. "I can vouch for it personally, 'cause I got roped into some of it."

They passed several wagonloads of freight and multiple pedestrians as they made their way to Third Street. Dave considered his next question carefully.

"Big John, how can you possibly expect to be helped by confessing additional crimes?"

"I suppose 'cause I weren't the only one involved. I figure what I got to say will put away some half a dozen fellas. Surely it would be worth having six or seven hardened-criminal types off the street."

"While you go free?" Dave could see that the man was completely serious.

"Why, sure. I'm not such a bad sort. I'd even be willing to move on," Big John stated as if he'd offered some rare and exquisite gift. "My word is good. I might be given to shady dealings from time to time, but I ain't no liar."

"All right, you can start by telling me what information you propose to offer. It would have to be worth the while of the court to even consider it."

Big John nodded and leaned back in the saddle. "Well, for starters, I know who burned down the Lassiter place. Not only that, I know who ordered it and paid for it."

Dave had his suspicions but said nothing. "And what else?"

"I know who held up that little Gallatin gal while she was workin' at the store. Fact is, I know who's been holding up a lot of folks on the road. I can give you not only the names of the highwaymen, but I can lead you to a couple of their hideouts."

A tingle ran up Dave's back. If Big John were telling the truth, it would definitely be worth working out a deal. "And you're confident of your knowledge."

"As confident as can be. I was there. I saw it all."

"You realize you're admitting participation—that you were one of the highwaymen."

Big John shrugged. "Well, I ain't saying I was or I wasn't. I'm just sayin' I was there and saw it all. Anything else, you can only get by supposin'."

Dave drew a deep breath. "I'll speak personally to the sheriff and see if we can get an audience with the judge. I would advise, however, that if you want to make a deal, you be the very model of a perfect prisoner while awaiting the outcome of our talk."

The man shifted his weight and grinned. "I'll be better than a preacher man at Sunday service."

He had his doubts about Big John, but Dave knew this might be the very break he'd been waiting for. He couldn't risk not at least checking into the man's story and seeing what could be done to harvest all of the information possible. Suddenly a thought came to Dave.

"I don't suppose you would know anything about George Gallatin's death?"

The man's grin broadened. "I might. I just might."

CHAPTER SEVENTEEN

Gwen straightened from her work in the garden and dusted her hands. The beans and squash were growing well, and they should harvest twice as much as last year. She mentally calculated how many quarts of vegetables she might put up before they moved in the fall.

"You seem awfully deep in thought," Lacy said. She set down one final bucket of water and asked, "Where do you want this one?"

"Pour it on the first row. I don't think it got nearly enough water the first time around."

Lacy nodded and retrieved the bucket. "Frankly, if we weren't moving, I'd suggest digging an irrigation ditch. It can't be any harder to do that than carry all this water back and forth."

"Hank says the land we have up north is going to have a well right in the back courtyard of the hotel. It will be easily accessible for all of our needs."

Lacy finished watering the beans. "I'm glad you'll have that, but I'm sure you'll miss the hot springs. Heating water all the time is going to get very tiresome."

Gwen pulled her bonnet back and dabbed her forehead with a handkerchief. "Hank says he has an idea for that, as well, although I don't completely understand how it would work. Something about a reservoir on the roof and the sun heating it."

"That will be fine for the three months of spring and summer, but what about the nine months of fall and winter?"

She smiled at her little sister. "He has another plan for that. Hank is full of plans. He wants so much for the town to flourish and be as civilized as anything back East."

Lacy nodded. "I'm going to go see if Beth needs me to bring in more of the laundry."

"Is she still ironing all those sheets?"

"Last I checked, she was."

"Well, you might also check on Hank and Julianne. I hated to leave him to watch over her, but if I didn't take advantage of the cool evening, I would never get this weeding done."

"I'll see if he needs anything."

"Tell him I should be in directly. I have just a few more things to tend."

Gwen turned her attention back to the garden and picked up her hoe. This was definitely a better year for the vegetables.

Even her potatoes were growing well. She smiled. It was satisfying to be able to do something for her family. Most of the time she felt that the stage passengers were the only ones she could give her time and attention to.

Julianne had been rather demanding of late, but Gwen supposed that was perfectly normal. The baby was six months old and actively seeking to make herself mobile. She could already sit by herself and would get up and rock back and forth on her knees when allowed out on a blanket on the floor. Julianne seemed quite advanced for her age, and at this rate, it would only be a matter of time—days, probably—before she started crawling. Gwen imagined Julianne would want to explore everything.

A gunshot rang out down by the river and Gwen startled. The air was already filled with the sounds of men at work, people arguing, and women laughing shrilly to attract interest from the prospectors.

I won't miss the noise, Gwen thought. The gold strike had so completely changed their lives at Gallatin Crossing. Nick and Hank had fenced off her garden, but people still snuck in to steal from them. Clothes and linens had disappeared from the line, and they were reduced to keeping the chickens on the back porch unless someone could watch over them. All because of the underhanded deeds of their new neighbors.

Lacy came out the back door just as Gwen made her way to the house. She frowned at her sister. "Julianne is crying, and Hank can't seem to calm her."

"I'm sure it's nothing. I'll go relieve him as soon as I get cleaned up."

"I don't know. She felt kind of feverish to me," Lacy said.

"It might just be because it's warm today and she's been crying for a while."

This stopped Gwen in her steps. "A fever? Surely not. She was perfectly fine when I came out here." Gwen pulled off her gardening apron and hurried up the stairs to the back porch. She deposited her tools and apron before heading into the house. The moment she opened the inside door, however, she could hear the screams of her daughter.

Forgetting about washing up, Gwen raced up the back stairs and made her way to the bedroom. Hank was pacing back and forth like a sentry at duty, the crying Julianne in his arms. He looked at Gwen as if pleading for salvation.

"What's wrong with her?" Gwen asked, reaching with her dirty hands for the baby.

"I have no idea. She just started fussing, and when I tried to offer her a little water, she wasn't at all interested. I'm no good at caring for her." His voice was gruff.

She put her hand on his arm. "Hank, babies cry. They don't have any other means of communication." She gave him a squeeze, then turned her attention back to the child.

The infant continued to cry despite Gwen's attempts to comfort her. Putting her hand to the baby's head, Gwen realized Lacy was right. Julianne had a fever.

Fear edged up Gwen's spine, and she stiffened. "Have there been any epidemics in the camp?"

Hank met her eyes. "I don't know. I haven't heard of any. Why? Do you think she's sick?"

"I fear she might be. She's quite warm."

"I'll go for the doctor," Hank said. "I honestly didn't know she might be sick."

Julianne calmed just a bit and snuggled her head against

Gwen's neck. She rubbed her head back and forth for several moments and continued to fuss. Gwen had never seen her like this. "Please hurry, Hank. I'm so frightened."

He put his arm around her. "It surely can't be that bad. The doctor should know what to do."

Gwen nodded, but she had little confidence in Hank's statement. Doctors were wrong all the time. Medicine was really little better than a guessing game, as far as Gwen was concerned. After all, a doctor hadn't been able to save her first husband when he contracted measles.

At the thought of the measles, Gwen shivered and clutched Julianne even tighter. This actually seemed to appeal to the child and she calmed momentarily. What if it were measles or whooping cough or diphtheria? Did babies as young as Julianne take on such diseases?

A clutching in Gwen's stomach sent a wave of nausea washing over her. She remembered how hard they had fought to save Harvey. He'd fallen so terribly ill on their wedding day, and by night, he'd been delirious with fever.

Gwen hurried to the crib and laid her daughter in it. Julianne howled in protest as Gwen began to undress her, but Gwen had to assure herself that there were no telltale red spots on the baby's body. She turned the infant several times before convincing herself that there wasn't any sign of measles.

"What do you suppose is wrong?" Beth asked from the door.

"I don't know. I worried that it might be measles, but she doesn't have any spots. She's feverish and fussy, but otherwise I just don't know. She acts as if she's in pain. Look at the way she pulls up her legs when she cries."

Beth came closer and watched for a moment. "I pray it's nothing serious." The fear in her voice was evident as she added, "Nothing contagious."

Worried about her son, Beth made her way back to her bedroom. When she'd gone to see what was wrong with Juli-anne, Max had been peacefully sleeping. Hearing no sound from him, she tiptoed to the cradle and frowned. The blanket had been rearranged to completely cover the baby. Pulling it back, Beth let out a yelp when the cat jumped from the bed and hurried out of the room.

Giggles sounded from behind her bed. Beth turned to find Justin hiding there. "Where is Max? What have you done?"

His smile immediately dissolved. "He's right there under that sheet."

Beth hurried to the still sleeping baby and clutched him close. He seemed no worse for the incident and opened his eyes for a moment, then settled back to sleep.

"That was a terrible thing to do. You might have fallen with him. You might have killed your own brother!" Beth knew she was on the edge of hysteria. "Go to your room. Go there now and wait for your punishment."

"I was just playing a prank," Justin protested. "Just like the ones you taught me. I thought it was funny, and I wanted you to laugh. You never laugh anymore."

"It wasn't funny," Beth countered. "It wasn't funny at all. Now leave—get out of here before I tan your hide."

She settled into her rocking chair, holding Max close to her body, even as Justin ran from the room. Her heart raced within her chest, and Beth found it difficult to draw a breath. She let out a sob. What if something had happened to him?

❦

"I think you have nothing more to worry about than a bit of teething," the doctor told Gwen.

She sighed in relief and sank to the chair. "Are you sure? She seems to be in pain."

The doctor smiled and lifted the baby in his arms. "She probably is. Teething can cause all manner of hurts. Her gums are probably sore, and she might even experience an ear and stomachache." He handed Julianne to Gwen and started to gather his instruments.

"I would suggest just giving her a wet cloth to chew on." He picked up his bag and smiled. "My own mother said nothing works better. They like to have something to chew against to ease the pain. If all else fails, a drop of clove oil can numb the pain, but I caution you: Too much will burn and blister the gums. You must be very careful with it."

Gwen nodded. "I'll try the other ways first." She looked at her daughter and heaved a sigh of relief. Motherhood was such an unpredictable and frightening experience at times.

"Your husband tells me that you'll soon be moving up north."

"We don't feel that it's safe to live in this area anymore. We had no idea what destruction a town could face until gold was discovered. The place hardly seems the same. More lowlife scum move in by the day."

"That's the way of things when you involve gamblers and

those who prey upon them. I'm sure you've heard that the folks from Hamilton are also considering a move north."

"Hank did mention it. Will you relocate with them?"

The doctor shrugged. "I'm not sure. Your husband would like very much for me to consider joining your group."

Gwen thought it considerate that Hank should try to secure a doctor for their community. "I would like that myself. It isn't easy to think of starting over—of setting up a town in the midst of what has only been wide-open land. I would feel so much better knowing that we had some of the basic necessities close at hand, and a doctor such as yourself would be right at the top of my list."

He nodded. "I plan to speak to my wife on the matter when I return to Hamilton. She has a sister in Bozeman, and I'm sure she'd prefer living closer to her than farther away."

Just then Hank returned from tending the store. "How is she?" he asked.

Gwen lifted Julianne up for Hank to see for himself. "She's teething."

"So she's not in danger?" he asked, reaching out to touch his daughter's brow.

"She's just fine," the doctor said. "She'll hurt and cry. It's more annoying than dangerous." He headed for the door. "Well, since I'm here I'd best see if I'm needed elsewhere."

Hank handed the man some money. "I hope this covers everything. And I'm sorry to have dragged you out so late. You're welcome to spend the night if you like."

"This is plenty, Mr. Bishop." The doctor put the money in his vest pocket. "Thanks for the offer of a bed, but I need to check on old Mr. Fraser on the way home. And I'll be in touch about the new town. I must say I'm intrigued."

Nick worked the bellows to build the fire hot enough to work the horseshoes he'd been forming. He longed for the days of his well-organized shop with Simon at his side. He'd heard very little from his brother of late. Ellie had penned a short letter to say they were doing well but that Simon was always busy with work. Having been together for so much of their life, Nick felt Simon's absence in a most keen way.

Of course, Beth and the boys made up for some of that loss. He had to admit should they be taken from his life, he would no doubt feel an even greater void. But sometimes he longed for a talk with Simon. They shared history, understood each other's hopes and dreams. It wasn't that Beth couldn't understand, but she was his wife, and there were things he didn't wish to discuss with her for fear of worrying her.

The metal horseshoe finally glowed red hot, and Nick pulled it from the fire and began pounding it on the anvil. Blacksmithing was a fine art. Too much heat and the metal would become brittle—not enough and it wouldn't be malleable enough to work. Even the amount of pressure applied in each stroke of the hammer had to be just right.

"I see you're hard at work," Dave Shepard announced.

Nick continued working the shoe. "I have to get shoes on two horses, and I've put it off long enough."

"Well, I need to talk to you for a minute if you can spare the time. It's something you're gonna want to hear."

Straightening, Nick plunged the shoe into water. "All right. Let's have it."

Dave drew a deep breath. "I know who set the fire that destroyed your place."

Nick frowned. He had anticipated the day when someone might give him this news, but now that it had come, he found he wasn't as calm as he had hoped he might be. Anger coursed through him as he remembered watching his livelihood go up in flames.

"Who?"

"Now, I don't have all the proof I need just yet, but I have a witness. What I'd prefer is having a confession from the one responsible."

Nick shook his head and tossed the tongs aside. "Who was it?"

"Wyman."

"Are you sure?"

"Well, like I said, I have a witness. I took Big John to jail over in Bozeman yesterday, and he wanted to make a deal in order to get out of prison time. I'm not sure why he was so concerned. He's got witnesses who say it was self-defense, but I'm thinking maybe the man has other crimes to be counted against him and figured those would come out."

Nick was already taking off his leather apron. The only thing he could think of was pounding Wyman's face into pulp. He was headed for the open door of the small shop when Dave reached out to stop him.

"I can't have you going to confront him. Not yet."

Eyeing Dave hard, Nick gritted his teeth. "What do you mean? He's gotta pay."

"I agree."

"Then why not get on with it?" Nick could barely think straight. Rage overtook his reasoning.

"Look, you and I both have known Wyman long enough to be sure of one thing: The man doesn't do anything without Rafe's direction. My guess is that Rafe was the one to start all of this, just as we've always suspected. Rafe is the one who wanted your property."

"And I fell right into his hands," Nick said, his voice filled with disgust.

"The important thing is getting them both to admit their part. I want to put them both behind bars, because I'm fairly confident they were not only responsible for your fire but for most of the criminal activities around these parts. Probably George Gallatin's death, as well."

"Then why wait?"

"Because I need proof. Right now, all I have is the confession and say-so of another criminal. We'd be laughed out of court if we had nothing more than that. Rafe would hire a lawyer to say that the witness held a grudge and was lying."

Nick calmed a bit. He knew Dave was making perfectly good sense, but in his heart he really wanted to take the matter into his own hands. "So what do you suggest?"

"Lacy once told me that Cubby insinuated that he knew a great deal about the death of her father. He's also implied knowing about other things. My guess is that if Rafe is at the center of this, Cubby will have overheard them plotting and planning. He might even be able to get Rafe to confess to it or discuss some of these things while witnesses listen in. If a law official or two could overhear his admission to guilt, and if we could get Cubby to testify, as well, we can see them both without excuse."

Nick drew a deep breath and nodded very slowly. He couldn't stomach living in the same town with men who would risk the lives and welfare of others just to get their own way. He knew evil existed, but he'd hoped Gallatin Crossing would be free of it. Now more than ever, he knew they were making the right decision to leave the area.

Before he could speak, Beth entered the shop with Max in her arms. "Have you seen Justin?" she asked.

Nick shook his head. She appeared worried, but he couldn't imagine what had her so worked up. "He's probably just off fishing. It's getting dark, so I bet he'll be home soon."

"He was supposed to be in his room. I caught him playing a prank with Max and yelled at him. I didn't handle it well at all."

"What kind of prank?"

"He hid Max under a sheet and put Calvin in the cradle and covered him up. When I went to check on Max, Calvin jumped out."

Nick grinned. "You're the one who taught him to play games like that."

Beth's eyes narrowed. "I didn't teach him to risk the life of his brother. Max is only a few weeks old. Justin could have dropped him."

Putting his hand on her arm, Nick tried to soothe her. "Look, I know it wasn't right. I'm sorry if you thought I was making light of the situation. I'll find him and have a talk with him."

"You need to find him and whip his backside." She turned in a huff. "I think we're well past talking."

Nick followed her out but said nothing. He caught sight of his son sneaking around the hot springs pool fence and decided to go confront him instead of trying to talk any more about it with Beth. She needed time to let go of her anger.

CHAPTER EIGHTEEN

"I'm glad for the chance to learn something other than tending bar," Cubby told Hank. "I'm sick of all of that."

Hank spread the ledger open and smiled. "This will be a great opportunity for you. You're a natural at this. I have no doubt you'll own your own store one day. Maybe your pa will even give you this one."

Cubby frowned. "My pa never gave anyone anything—and once he owns it in full, I don't doubt he'll corrupt this like he has everything else."

"Well, be that as it may, I believe you'll be quite successful. You're smart, and folks tend to like you. Keep the friendly attitude, and you'll have customers returning."

"If things work out the way I want, I'll learn well enough

to have my own place and move on. I don't want to live in my father's shadow all my life."

The pain in Cubby's voice was too evident to ignore. "You know, Cubby, you remind me a great deal of myself. My father drank and womanized all the time. It broke my mother's heart until the day he died. In truth, she suffered even after that, because she worried about her sons."

Cubby's eyes widened. "I didn't know your father was like that."

"Not only that, but he was a criminal. That's what he did for a living." Hank grew thoughtful. "The man worked harder at stealing money than he ever would have had to at an honest job."

"Did he kill folks?"

Hank looked at Cubby and shrugged. He'd often wondered that himself. How far did his father's treachery extend? "I don't know. He was hanged for stealing a horse and murdering the man who owned it, but it was wrongfully done. The real culprit was later found out, and everyone realized their mistake. Of course, by then it was too late. My mother said it was probably some strange form of justice—that somewhere along the way, my father had probably deserved it and life was just catching up with him."

The boy's shoulders seemed to sag a bit. "But you're a good man. How did you keep from being like him?"

"Cubby, I guess I decided at an early age that I wanted to be my own man—a man folks could respect. My mother was wise enough to get me away from my father's influence as much as possible. She even took us to Boston after our father died so that we wouldn't have to live under his reputation or the influence of his old friends. It was probably the best thing that ever happened to me. God had a way of working it all out for good, but it was never easy. My pain and bitterness—the hatred I held for my father—nearly destroyed me. Had I not learned to let go of that anger and let God transform it into something better, I would have turned out just like him."

Neither one said anything more for several minutes. Hank could see that his story had deeply affected the boy. He could only hope it would have a positive influence.

Putting his attention back to the ledger, Hank motioned. "Come stand beside me. Now see here, I have listed in this column all of the items I've ordered. This column shows what I already have in stock. It's important to keep an accurate inventory. It's the only way to know for sure what kind of profit you're actually making."

"It also reminds you what you have around to sell," Cubby offered. "I know about inventory because of Pa's liquor."

Hank nodded. "It would be roughly the same." He turned the page. "This is what I've ordered from Bozeman, and this column is what I've ordered from Salt Lake. I post the quantities ordered in this column and the exact amount that gets shipped in this one, and the payment is listed over here."

Rafe had asked Hank to train his son to take over the store so that when the sale was final and the deeds exchanged, business could go on as usual. Cubby was attentive, but Hank could see his expression was troubled.

Hank closed the book and focused on Cubby. "You seem to have something else on your mind."

The boy flushed and looked away. "I'm doing my best."

"It's not that, Cubby. I just wondered if you needed to talk more about your pa."

"It's not just him. It's everyone. No one but you takes me

seriously. Their first thought is that I'm Rafe Reynolds' son and that I'll be just like him."

Hank frowned and nodded at his own painful memory. "But your father takes you seriously enough to give you charge of this store."

"He's just desperate. He wouldn't have me doin' it if he thought he could get someone else to do it for as little as he pays me."

"Why don't we go next door and have some lunch," Hank suggested. "We could talk more about this."

"No. I can't go there. I've made such a mess of things with Miss Lacy that I don't even want to see her."

"What kind of mess?"

Cubby met his gaze. "You mean she didn't tell you?"

"Tell me what?"

"I asked her to marry me a while back, but she told me she didn't think of me in that way. Then I found out she was marryin' Dave Shepard." Cubby pounded his fist on the desk. "It's not fair."

Hank wanted to smile at his boyish indignation but knew it would devastate the young man. "Lacy's a hard woman to understand sometimes. She's been through a great deal, but she has a tender heart."

"I hate myself for how I acted. I hit her," Cubby said, bowing his head. "I'm completely ashamed, and I apologized to her for it, but I can't forget it."

"I certainly can't condone being violent—especially with a woman."

"She told me I was just like my father."

Hank started to speak, but Cubby looked up. "I'm not like him. I got dreams that he can't understand. I want to settle down someday and have a family. I want to have a respectable means of makin' a living. I want a wife, and I want her to be proud of me."

"Cubby, I think most men want those things."

Cubby fidgeted nervously and looked rather embarrassed. "Could you call me Quennell? It's my real name, but no one uses it. Cubby makes me feel like a wet-behind-the-ears boy. Maybe if folks start calling me by my real name, they'll see me as a man."

"Quennell is a fine name, and I will certainly be glad to use it, but you know it takes more than a name to make a man."

The boy straightened and squared his shoulders. "Like what?"

"Well, for one thing, honor." Hank eased back and leaned against the wall. "Keeping your word is one of the most important things a man can do. A man's word is more important than just about anything else. If he doesn't stand by what he promises to do, then folks won't believe him in any other area."

"I keep my word."

"Quennell, I have no doubt you do. Being a man also means enduring the things life sends your way. It means being kind and reasonable when you don't get things the way you want them. And it means never hurting those weaker than yourself."

"Like Lacy," he breathed and shook his head again. "I wish I could take back what I did. She hates me now—hates me for that and for other things."

"I've never known Lacy to truly hate anyone." Hank thought of his feisty sister-in-law and grinned. "She has a temper, that much is true, but I doubt she hates you."

"She told me I was like my pa, but as much as I hate to admit it, my pa is evil—just like you said your pa was. I'm not him, Hank. I'm a good man. I don't do bad things like my father. He cheats people and lies. He doesn't care who he hurts or even if it costs someone their life."

"That may be, I can't say. I do know there is more to life than simply being a good man, though."

Cubby frowned. "What more could there be?"

Hank motioned the young man to take a seat, then did likewise. He pulled open a drawer and found his Bible right where he'd left it after that morning's reading. "Last Sunday the sermon was about the heart of a man. It's kind of like what you and I are talking about."

He opened the Bible to the twelfth chapter of Matthew. "See, here it says, 'O generation of vipers, how can ye, being evil, speak good things? For out of the abundance of the heart the mouth speaketh. A good man out of the good treasure of the heart bringeth forth good things: and an evil man out of the evil treasure bringeth forth evil things.' If there's good in your heart, you'll have more to show for it than simple words. You see the things your pa does, and they trouble you. That's because he's bringing forth evil things. I felt the same way about my father."

"So I have to do good things in order to be a good man?"

"It's more than that. It says that good comes from the good treasure of the heart. Do you know what that good treasure is, Quennell?"

"Gold?"

"You're close. Drop the *l* and you'll have it."

Cubby frowned and shook his head. "What do you mean?"

"God. God is the good treasure in your heart."

"I know you folks are religious. Pa says it's a waste of time—that there is no God."

"And what do you think?" Hank leaned back in his chair. "Do you think he's right?"

Cubby considered the question for a moment. "He's not right about much else." He continued to reason the matter. "I s'pose it would make sense that he's not right about God, either. I know Miss Lacy says that Jesus was a real man and God at the same time, and that He died for our sins. I don't understand why He would do that, though."

"Because He loves us. You and I are a lot alike, just as I've already told you. When I was a boy, I learned about God, but then I walked away from all I knew to be good and true. Thinking about God made me feel bitter and angry. I didn't understand why my father was the way he'd been or why my mother had to struggle and bear such sorrow. I figured God couldn't possibly care about us, and I convinced myself that in order to be happy, a man had to take charge of his own life and make his own decisions. Coming here, I soon saw the foolishness of that way of thinking."

"But why are you tellin' me all this?"

Hank looked intently at the young man. "People without Jesus in their heart are going to do evil things. They won't be able to help but do evil, because that's what exists in abundance in their heart. Evil people are self-centered and care only about satisfying their own needs."

"Like my pa."

Hank didn't want to speak out against the boy's father despite agreeing with his conclusion. "We're all evil and self-centered without Jesus, son."

He stiffened. "What do you mean? I'm not evil. I'm not like my pa. I told you that already."

Forgetting the boy's desire for his given name, Hank tried to find a way to help him understand. "Cubby, we're *all* sinners. Sin makes us evil. It destroys our life and corrupts everything we touch. Jesus did, indeed, come to die for our sins and to save us from that evil. When He rose from the grave, Jesus had victory once and for all over evil."

"But I don't think like my pa, and I don't do bad things. How can I be a sinner?"

"The Bible says we all sin—we all make mistakes. We tell a lie to keep from getting in trouble. We willingly hurt someone. We withhold the truth when we know it needs to be told."

Cubby paled. "Keeping quiet about knowing something is a sin? That makes you evil?"

"There are a lot of things that make us sinners. If you know the truth about something and you don't reveal it when others are trying to hide it, then you're no better."

"But what if the truth will hurt someone you care about?"

Hank felt sorry for the boy. He was certain Cubby was speaking about his father. "Sometimes that happens. I wish there were easy answers, Cubby—Quennell. Being a man isn't easy, and sometimes we have to make hard decisions. I will say this, however." Hank flipped over several pages of the Bible to the book of John. "The Bible says, 'Ye shall know the truth, and the truth shall make you free.' Sometimes it's hard to be honest, but in the long run it's always the best way."

"But this truth will change my life."

Hank smiled. "Truth usually does."

Cubby nodded and got to his feet. "I should get back to the saloon. Pa's expecting a lot of folks tonight, and he'll need my help."

Watching the young man go, Hank felt a burden to pray for him. The odds were against Cubby. He was immersed in a setting of evil and sin, and his father was one of the biggest culprits. It would be different if Cubby could live in a home where God was revered and good was promoted.

Maybe I should talk to Gwen about having Cubby come live with us up north. The thought startled Hank, but just as quickly, it seemed the right thing to consider. He couldn't very well stand by feeling sorry for the boy and not offer to give him a way out of his dilemma.

Lacy found herself restless amid the relentless noise of trees being felled and houses being built. She was saddened that the woods were being torn down without concern to the devastation left behind, all in order to provide housing and new businesses.

But more than the noise and the chaos, Lacy was troubled by the future. The night before, she'd dreamed she'd found her father's killer. The man had been ugly and surly. He had laughed at Lacy's tears and accusations. He had freely admitted to killing her father but said that no one would ever make him pay. In her anger, Lacy had pulled out her rifle and shot the man without giving it another thought. Worse still, she'd felt a sense of rejoicing and satisfaction as the man crumpled to the ground and died.

"You've got your revenge," the man muttered. "Are you happy now?"

The memory of that dream-turned-nightmare haunted her now and kept her from focusing on sorting through the storage sheds and packing things for the move.

Could she kill her father's murderer? If the opportunity presented itself and the killer mocked her in the same manner as the man in her dream, would she be glad to watch him die?

Lacy had never thought of herself as ruthless or lacking compassion. She'd always valued human life, which was why she felt so driven to see her father's killer convicted. At least that was what she'd always told herself.

"I'm not after revenge," she said aloud. She took up a crate of old dishes and considered whether they were worth salvaging. The word echoed in her mind.

Revenge. Revenge.

"Well, what if I do want revenge?" She knelt beside the box and began lifting out dinner plates. "Why does revenge have to be wrong? Wanting someone to pay for what they did isn't a selfish thing." The Bible was full of stories about good winning over evil and justice being served.

Lacy wiped perspiration from her brow with her sleeve. The day had grown quite warm, and Lacy wearied of sorting through the dusty crates. She abandoned the dishes and got to her feet. Walking to the door of the shed, she looked out on the scene behind Rafe's. Tents were lined up, one after the other, to accommodate the newcomers. Children were racing among the narrow walkways, entertaining one another as best they could with made-up games. Weary-looking mothers labored to make a home for their families out of nothing more than the scraps of their former lives.

What a contrast to the peace and tranquillity Lacy had experienced on the Shepard ranch or even in her own home! Of course, living to serve a daily arrival of strangers had never given the Gallatins much peace, but at least she'd known a home and a sense of belonging.

"You look deep in thought," Beth said as she approached with Max tucked protectively in her arms.

Lacy nodded. "I'm glad I'm not them."

Beth glanced in the direction of Lacy's nod. "Yes, me too. I can't imagine how awful it would be to think you had homes waiting for you and then realize you were wrong."

"Hopefully some will move north with you and resettle. I can't imagine them being happy here."

Beth shrugged. "You can never tell what might make a person happy. Each one has to find that for themselves. Satisfaction and happiness come in many ways."

Lacy looked at her sister. "Could you be content staying here?"

"No, I don't think so. With the way things have changed, I'm ready to leave. At least we have a way out." She shifted the sleeping baby and gave Lacy a sad smile. "Remember how we were going to defeat the evils of prostitution? Somehow I got distracted." She smiled and looked down at Max.

"I wish we could have done more. At least we were able to help Ellie get away."

"I'm glad for that, but my heart still hurts for those who remain and the ones who continue to come. Nick says it's impossible to right all the wrongs in the world, but it doesn't stop me from wishing we could."

"But is turning away from the awful truth of what's here the way we should handle it?" Lacy shook her head. "For so long I've wanted justice for Pa. I've longed for evil to be defeated and good to overcome, but as we leave, I can't help but feel that I've given up the fight, that I've failed once again to make things better."

Beth gave Lacy a thoughtful look. "I suppose that could be one way of looking at it, but I just don't see it that way. Nick says sometimes you have to retreat to fight another day. Maybe leaving here will open new doors, new ways to resolve some of these matters. Maybe by being on the outside looking in, we will have the ability to see things clearer. Could be that once we're established in our new town, we'll be so prosperous that we'll be able to work to help these girls get away from Rafe. Right now, though, I think it's right to leave."

"I don't know if I believe that or not."

Her sister smiled. "Well, just remember there were times when even Jesus urged his disciples to walk away. There were times when Jesus did so himself or let others walk away from Him. You can't force right upon the world."

"And if we never find Pa's killer?"

Max stirred and Beth put him to her shoulder and patted his back gently. "It really won't change things for me, Lacy. I'm sorry if that offends you. Pa will still be dead—I can't change that, and neither can you. I hope that if someone did maliciously kill him, they will be caught and punished. But at the same time, if it was the foolish accident that it appears to be, then I would just as soon see it all put to rest. Hopefully that person would have learned his lesson. But since I can't know the truth of Pa's death, I simply pray that God's will be done—in the life of the guilty party . . . but especially in my own."

"And that gives you peace?" Lacy asked, truly wanting to know.

"It does," Beth said. "Because I know that God loves us with an everlasting love, and that no matter what happens, His love will remain."

"And if you came face-to-face with Pa in heaven one day, you would have a clear conscience that you'd done all you could to see his soul rest in peace?"

"Only God gives a body peace in eternal rest, Lacy. What we do or don't do here on earth has nothing to do with it. Once we leave this place, I can't imagine we even care anymore about the wrongs and injustices done us. I can't help but believe when we come face-to-face with Jesus, nothing on Earth will ever matter again."

CHAPTER NINETEEN

"We've got problems," Rafe told his friend.

Jefferson Mulholland looked up from where he'd been play-ing blackjack against himself. "What kinds of problems?"

It was early afternoon and the evening crowds hadn't yet started gathering. There were only two old men sitting at a far table; otherwise the bar was deserted. Rafe could see that the men were occupied with some map, so he took the chance that it was safe enough to speak.

Sitting opposite Jefferson, Rafe glanced around one more time. "Big John is talking too much. Apparently he's decided to make some kind of deal with the law in Bozeman."

Mulholland's eyes narrowed. "What kind of deal?"

"Well, as I hear it, he intends to tell everything he knows. May have already done so."

"But you don't know for sure?"

Rafe shook his head. "No. What I've been told is that he shared information with Dave Shepard on their ride to Bozeman. Now he's keeping quiet until the judge decides what kind of deal they can offer him. He's wanted for murder in Bozeman—something I didn't know. I guess he figured he'd use what he knew about our operation to save his neck from the noose."

Jefferson quietly considered this as he gathered the cards and began to shuffle them. "And Deputy Shepard is the only other one who knows what Big John has said?"

"Well, he's the only one who has heard it firsthand. Big John was too smart to be runnin' his mouth off for everyone until he had some kind of guarantee."

"Good. Then all we need to do is eliminate Big John and Deputy Shepard."

Rafe met Jefferson's hard expression. "Are you serious? How are we supposed to do that? Big John is in jail, and Shepard is no fool."

Jefferson shrugged and smiled. "Accidents happen. Happen all the time. Let me think on this a bit. I'm sure we can see to the matter in short order."

Beth came around the corner of the house just in time to see Justin pull a stick from the trash burning in the bin. The fire had been left unattended for some reason.

Without warning Justin touched the flaming branch to the

ground and watched as the dry grass caught fire. Beth acted without thinking and grabbed Major's pan of water and doused the grass before the fire spread.

"Justin, what in the world is wrong with you? You know you're not to play with fire. You know the dangers of what could happen."

The boy looked up at her, clearly surprised to have been caught red-handed. Beth realized she hadn't managed to put out all of the flames. She began stamping at the ground with her boots, all the while declaring her displeasure with Justin.

"You could get someone killed. I honestly don't know why you've been acting up so much lately, but this is going to stop."

"I hate you! I wish you weren't my ma."

Beth whirled around to look Justin in the eye. "You go to your room and do it right now. I'm going to find your father and—"

"Watch out!" Lacy's voice cried out from across the yard. "Your skirt!"

Looking down, Beth was mesmerized by the sight of her dress catching fire. She froze in place, shocked and uncertain what she should do. Lacy raced for the clothesline and pulled down a blanket. Hurrying to Beth, she beat out the fire, then turned her attention to the grass. Once the flames were extinguished, she returned to her sister.

"What happened?" she asked, inspecting Beth's blackened clothes.

Beth's mind was still muddled by the incident. "It was . . . it was Justin." She looked around to find the boy, but he was gone. Shaking her head as if to clear it, Beth looked at Lacy.

"This has gotten completely out of hand. That boy doesn't listen to anyone anymore, but especially not to me. He's so jealous of Max that he's turning to all manner of trouble to get attention."

Lacy straightened. "Where is he now?"

"I sent him to his room." Beth looked up at the house. "I don't know what to do anymore. Nick doesn't seem to think it's all that important. When I told him about Justin taking some of Max's things, he shrugged it off and said he probably just wanted to better understand what a baby was all about. Then when Justin pinched Max, Nick was quick to believe it was an accident and that his son just got too rough."

"Well, this surely wasn't done on purpose," Lacy said, looking back at the charred ground. "He knew better than to play in the fire, but I can't believe he meant to set the ground ablaze."

"It doesn't matter. He did it nevertheless and has to be punished."

Nick crossed the yard. He seemed surprised to find Beth and Lacy standing by the fire talking. "Seems like too hot a day to be warming yourself at the fire, ladies."

Beth met his grinning expression with anger. "Your son tried to set the place on fire."

Frowning, Nick looked at the ground. "Are you sure it was him? Maybe something blew out of the trash and sparked the grass."

"I was right here. I saw the whole thing. Not only that, but my skirt caught on fire. I could have been killed and the entire town burned down. Justin's disobedience has gone too far, and you must deal with him." Beth knew she was screeching, but she couldn't help herself. Her anger was getting the better of her. "And don't give me some excuse about how he's just a little boy and didn't know better."

"I wasn't going to." It was obvious he was getting mad.

Lacy stepped in at this point. "Look, everything is all right. It was frightening and could have been much worse. I think Justin probably realized how bad the situation was, but he does need to hear from you on it."

Nick fairly growled. "I don't need you to tell me how to raise my son. You haven't got any children of your own, so stay out of it."

Beth was stunned by her husband's harsh words. "You apologize to my sister. She didn't say anything out of line. A person doesn't need to have a child to know when one is out of line."

Nick started for the house. "Seems to me you've been looking for wrongdoings from Justin ever since Max was born. It's no wonder he feels left out and jealous."

Following him to the door, Beth could barely control her anger. "I have done no such thing. I love that boy as much as you do."

Nick stopped abruptly and turned. "You sure have a strange way of showing it. You're always yelling at him, and you never give him the time you used to. Even the other day when you promised to take him fishing, you changed your mind."

"Max was colicky. I couldn't leave him. It had nothing to do with how I feel about Justin."

"Well, I don't think Justin understands that."

Nick drew a deep breath, and Beth could see that he was forcing himself to calm down, but she didn't care. He'd already hurt her feelings by taking the boy's side over hers. He didn't even seem to realize that she could have been killed had the fire gotten out of control.

"Beth . . ."

She turned away. "Leave me alone. You believe the worst of me."

Nick didn't know quite what to do. He realized too late he'd taken up offense for Justin, when he should have comforted Beth. Still, the two were at odds so much these days, and Nick felt caught in between. He loved them both—loved Max, too. Why couldn't they simply be a family and love each other?

He went in search of his son, hoping—praying—that he could help the boy to understand the situation. Justin was old enough to realize the danger of fire. They'd spoken about it many times when Nick was teaching Justin how to tend the fire in the house. They'd talked about it when burning trash and while Nick had been showing Justin how to work the forge.

"Justin?" Nick called as he entered the boy's room.

He wasn't there. Nick turned on his heel and headed back downstairs to see if the boy was in the front room or kitchen. He crossed Gwen's path as she carried a stack of tablecloths to the dining room.

"Have you seen Justin?"

"No. I was watching Max for Beth, but she just came and took him. I haven't seen Justin at all." She put the neatly folded cloths on the table and turned to Nick. "Beth seemed really upset. Is there anything I can do to help?"

Nick shook his head. "I doubt it. Seems Justin was playing in the fire, and one thing led to another and Beth got burned."

"Oh no! She didn't say anything. Is she hurt? Are the burns bad?"

Nick felt the fool for not even knowing the answer to her questions. "I honestly don't know. I know her skirt caught fire and Lacy put it out, but I don't know if she was hurt. She was upset about Justin, and I kind of lost my temper."

Gwen gave him a sympathetic smile. "I'll go tend to Beth, and you take care of finding Justin. I'm sure she's all right."

"But I shouldn't have acted the way I did. I've been on edge ever since Max was born and Justin started acting so rebellious. I don't know what to do about it, but it seems every time Beth brings something to my attention, I feel defensive. Almost like I've done something wrong myself."

"That doesn't sound so strange," Gwen told him. "He's your son and you feel responsible. Time will work these things out. Justin is clearly jealous of his little brother, but with help, maybe he can come to see how important he is in the family—how you'll need him to teach Max important things."

"Could be," Nick said.

Gwen patted his arm. "Don't fret about it, Nick. It'll all work out."

But Nick wasn't convinced. Beth had been angry and hurt, and he'd handled the situation so poorly. Heading outside, he wondered how in the world he could mend the fences and please both his wife and son. He certainly didn't want either one of them mad at him.

By suppertime Nick had exhausted all of Justin's known hiding spots. He was starting to get mad—angry that his son would so blatantly disobey and refuse to face up to what he'd done. Mealtime was oddly silent, and even Gwen and Hank seemed reluctant to speak on the matter. The sisters tried to make small talk at one point, speaking neutrally about the stage that would come in the next day, but even that conversation fell by the wayside after a few awkward exchanges.

When they'd finished supper and Justin had still not made an appearance, Nick began to worry. The long summer days left plenty of light in the sky, but he feared something might have happened to the child. Maybe Justin had run off to avoid the punishment that might await him. Perhaps in being consumed by those thoughts, he hadn't paid attention to his surroundings and gotten hurt.

Nick spied Beth alone at the front door. She was peering outside, and he couldn't help but wonder if she, too, was worried. He approached her hesitantly.

"I'm sorry."

She turned and nodded. "I know. I am, too. I'm worried about him. Where do you suppose he's gone?"

"I don't know, but I guess we'd better get out there looking for him."

"I'll help," Lacy said, coming up from behind them. "I talked to Dave and he's already saddling up."

Nick nodded and turned to Beth. "Are you all right? I realized after losing my temper that I hadn't even concerned myself with whether or not you got burned."

"I have one place that's a little tender, but it's not bad." She looked at him with great emotion. "Nick, I love Justin. You have to know that."

He put his arm around her. "I know. I've let things go for too long. I kept hoping he'd come to see that we're a family and that there was enough love for everyone. When I find him, I'll make sure he knows that—but I'll also make certain he understands that enough is enough and he's got to straighten up."

She hugged him close. Nick breathed in the scent of her hair and held her tighter. Everything would soon be put to order. At least he hoped so.

"Cubby, you seen anything of Justin Lassiter?" Dave Shepard questioned, leading his saddled horse.

The last thing Cubby wanted to do was deal with his rival for Lacy's love. "I haven't seen him."

"Well, he's run off. Been gone several hours and we're going to start a search. You want to help?"

Not if it involved having to be in the company of the two lovebirds. Cubby still couldn't reconcile the fact that Lacy would marry this man. "Can't. Pa has a whole lot of work already lined up for me. He's expecting big business tonight." At least that much was true.

"All right, then." Dave mounted his horse. "I'm heading out southwest toward the Dykstra place if you change your mind. I think Lacy's going to take the road to the Vanhouten house and see if he managed to get that far. Not sure where the others are looking, but I know we need to check the river area."

Cubby nodded and hoisted a case of whiskey to his shoulder. He wanted to say more but battled between a snide remark and his genuine concern for the little boy. Love sure had a way of complicating a fella's relationships with other folks.

He made his way into the saloon and settled the crate on the floor behind the bar. Wyman and several of their rougher customers were holed up in the corner talking in hushed whispers. Jefferson Mulholland was surrounded at one of the card tables by men who wanted nothing more than to win his fortune away.

"You sure took your time gettin' that in here," his father said, joining him at the bar.

Cubby shrugged. "Dave Shepard stopped me to tell me Justin Lassiter's gone missing, and everyone is on the lookout for him. Been gone for several hours now."

"That's hardly your problem or mine," Rafe said, spitting into a nearby spittoon.

"What's that you said about Dave Shepard?" Wyman asked, pulling away from the other men.

Wyman's sudden interest put Cubby on edge. "I said he was looking for Justin Lassiter. The boy's missing."

"Did he say which way he was heading?"

"Toward the Dykstra place. Why?"

"No reason, 'cept if a fella decided to help with the search, he wouldn't want to head the same direction."

The excuse was reasonable, but Cubby got the strange feeling that Wyman's interest had nothing at all to do with Justin and the search. When Wyman motioned Rafe to follow him into the back room, Cubby was convinced. He pretended not to care what his father was up to, but once the two had disappeared and the other men seemed preoccupied with other things, Cubby slipped over to the door to listen to what was being said.

"This looks like the perfect opportunity," Wyman said. The words were muffled and Cubby had to strain to hear. "Reg and Sam said they'd take care of Big John."

"Good. That's one less thing to worry about."

"Hey, how about some whiskey!" a man called from the bar.

Cubby reluctantly turned from the door. He had no idea what his father was up to, but it couldn't be good.

CHAPTER TWENTY

"So we all agree to be back here by nightfall?" Dave questioned.

Lacy nodded, although she felt they were wasting time by going over all these details. Hank and Nick mounted their horses while Beth and Gwen looked on from the porch.

"We'll continue searching around here," Gwen assured.

Lacy was shifting her weight in her saddle when, to her surprise, Cubby sauntered reluctantly over to the group. "Pa is sending me out to look for Justin in our area. I just wanted you to know I'd check out the tent city and down by the river." He cast a glance up at Lacy and quickly looked away.

"Good," Hank replied. "We've all agreed to be back here by nightfall. As best as I can guess, that will give us a couple of hours to search."

Lacy gave a whistle for Major and headed out. She felt there had been more than enough talk and not enough action. Justin could have gone most anywhere by now. The boy was fit and strong, used to walking and playing in the area. He could have all sorts of hiding places.

The trail that led out toward the Vanhoutens' former place was generally well traveled, as it reached beyond to other ranches in the area. Lacy hoped she might even meet someone heading into town to ask if they'd seen the boy, but no one seemed to be out and about.

To the west, dark billowy clouds gathered on the horizon, suggesting some rain for the valley was soon to come. Lacy didn't give it much thought. The weather had been teasing them for days now, and the showers had either gone around them or dissipated to nothing more than a few sprinkles.

"Well, what do you think, Major?" Lacy got down from her horse and examined the road for any sign of tracks. "Did he come this way?"

The dog sniffed around the ground and seemed not the least interested in the reason they were there. He was far too busy enjoying the new scents and keeping watch for a wayward rabbit.

Lacy walked for a ways, leading her horse and paying close attention to details on the ground. This road got very little foot traffic, so if Justin had come this way it should be fairly easy to spot his prints.

"Children certainly seem to be endless sources of trouble," she told the dog. "Maybe I'd be better off not to have any." She wondered how Dave would feel if she told him she didn't want any offspring.

She thought of Dave and wondered what she was going to

do about him and their wedding. He'd been very patient and, in fact, hadn't forced her to contemplate setting a date or even talk about the event since Pastor Flikkema had left. Instead, he'd merely been companionable, sharing her company when time permitted—which was rare these days. So many problems had developed with the gold rush that Dave had been far busier with legal issues than ones that had to do with marriage.

It had been a nice reprieve. She'd been able to think about marrying Dave without the pressure of everyone expecting her decisions on a date, her dress, and who would perform the ceremony. In fact, the peacefulness had allowed Lacy to fall rather comfortably into the idea of wedding Dave Shepard. It seemed especially appealing now that she knew they would live at the ranch with his parents. It made her feel less ill-equipped to face her responsibilities. If she couldn't cook well enough, Patience would be there to show her what to do. And if Lacy couldn't figure out what to say to Dave during dinner conversation, there would be other people with whom she could converse.

Beth had told her she was silly, that most newlyweds would prefer privacy to living with one's parents, but Lacy also knew she wasn't like most folks. She still worried greatly about failing in her role as a wife. Having someone of Patience Shepard's experience seemed a good way for Lacy to avoid hurting a new husband by her own inexperience.

Of course, there would be times when the others weren't around. She tried not to think about what her nights alone with Dave might be like. She knew there was a strong physical attraction between the two of them and didn't figure they would struggle too much in the area of intimacy. Lacy felt her cheeks grow hot just contemplating such a thing.

She blew out a heavy breath. "But do I love him?" Lacy had

asked herself this question at least five hundred times a day. She knew she felt affection for Dave. He was handsome and definitely a good kisser. He was kind to her and gentle most of the time. Why, he'd even given up most of his negative, almost parental, dictating of what she should and shouldn't do. For example, he hadn't suggested she ride with him or anyone else tonight. He'd merely nodded in agreement when she suggested riding out toward what was now his house.

"Someday it will be ours," she said.

Major whined and gave a glance down the road in the direction of home. Lacy shook her head. "No, come on, boy. We aren't done yet."

Lacy had walked another fifteen or twenty feet, leading the horse and paying close attention to the ground, when she caught sight of a small boot print. She'd learned to track at an early age. Her father had been quite good, and Lacy seemed to have a natural talent at picking it up. When she'd been no more than eight, their father had taken in a wounded elderly Crow Indian named Two Elks. The man had been beaten by several local cowboys and left to die. George Gallatin had taken pity on the man and brought him home to be nursed back to health, much to the concern of his family.

Two Elks had healed quickly and as he shared time with them, he had taught Lacy how to pay attention to changes in her surroundings. She had learned to watch the trees for signs of animal activity, as well as to note broken vegetation or tufts of fur left behind on the trail. But her favorite had been the tracking lessons. Not only did she get to increase the knowledge her father had given her, but it was during that time Two Elks told her stories about his boyhood.

She knelt and put her finger to the dusty outline. Surely

it belonged to Justin. It seemed a bit larger than the size she'd remembered him wearing, but it was too far away from town to be just anyone traipsing through. Searching with great patience, Lacy found two more prints mingled with those of horse hooves, all headed in a westerly direction.

"Justin!" she called out, getting to her feet. "Justin!"

"Now that we don't have to worry about your son over-hearing us," Mulholland told the other three men, "we can get down to business."

Rafe nodded and looked to Wyman. "Have you sent out the boys to deal with Big John?"

"About twenty minutes ago. They won't come back until the job is done," Wyman assured him. "It won't be that hard. They'll prob'ly tend to business sometime in the night. I'd expect them back by tomorrow evening."

"And are the others ready to head out and deal with Deputy Shepard?" Mulholland asked.

Rafe felt his gut tighten just a bit at the thought of killing the deputy. Sure, he could be pesky and interfering, but Rafe didn't really want to see the man dead. Still, he most likely knew too much, and he wouldn't hesitate to use it against Rafe.

"They're ready. Do you want him killed straight out?" Wyman asked.

"No," Mulholland stated before Rafe could speak. "It might serve us well to know if he's talked to anyone else. Take him to the Camp Creek hideout and wait for further instructions. Rough him up a bit if you like, but leave him alive."

"I'd be happy to oblige with the roughing up," Wyman

said. "That man's been a bur under my saddle for a long time now. Always snoopin' around, wanting to know who killed George Gallatin or if we have any idea who's ridin' with the highwaymen."

Mulholland nodded and gave a laugh. "Maybe you could share that news with him before you kill him. At least he can die having a few answers."

All the men laughed, with the exception of Rafe. He was feeling a little sick from the events of the evening.

"What if he's found that Lassiter brat?" the man at Wyman's right asked.

Mulholland considered this for a moment. "Well, you had to deal with him once before, as I recall."

The man nodded. "Didn't hurt him none though. I don't particularly care for killing children."

"And I can well understand that, Clarence. You have a soft heart," Mulholland said, smiling. "If you can keep the brat from knowing your identity, leave him behind. Take Shepard and let the boy find his own way home." He looked at Rafe. "Agreed?"

"Agreed." Rafe was already feeling hesitant about killing Dave. There was no chance he wanted to have a child's blood on his hands, as well.

"You're looking a bit green," Wyman said, eyeing Rafe with a raised brow.

Rafe pulled at his waistband and gave a snort. "Nothin' wrong with me. I just want this done with. The sooner we get this resolved, the sooner we can move on with our plans."

"He's right," Mulholland said. "I suggest you boys get to work. Send someone back to let us know when you have

Shepard secured. Then we can deal with getting answers out of him."

Lacy continued calling for her nephew from time to time, but there was no response. As she led the horse farther toward the Vanhouten house, she noted the growing darkness and the approaching storm. Lightning flashed in the mountains to the west, and thunder rumbled as a promise of things to come. If she turned around now, Lacy knew she might make it back to the house before the rain started to fall. But she also knew she would probably lose any hope of picking up Justin's tracks.

"They're expecting everyone back, but I can't just quit," she told Major. "Let's at least get to the house and see if there's any sign of Justin there. Maybe we can hole up until the worst of the storm passes and then get back to tracking."

But she knew this idea was nonsense. Once the storm dissolved any traces of the boy's tracks, she would be at the mercy of her own guesswork and the pitch black of the night. The idea of leaving the boy to weather the storm on his own and then try to get back safely to his family, however, kept Lacy from giving up.

Another mile and Lacy caught sight of the white ranch house and outbuildings that had once belonged to the Vanhoutens. She'd always liked this spread. There were plenty of trees and pretty flower gardens, though the flowers would be in disarray now.

"Someday I might take care of the flowers," she mused aloud. Major gave a whine as if he found that difficult to believe. Lacy laughed. "So I'm not much for flowers, but I could change."

Just then she caught sight a dim light coming from one of the front windows. Maybe Dave had made his way over here after checking with the Dykstras. She shook her head. No, there wasn't time enough for that.

Perhaps Justin had come here to take refuge from the storm. That made more sense. As raindrops started splattering against the ground, Lacy mounted and urged the horse to pick up his speed, Major running alongside. She made it to the largest of the outbuildings just as the rain cut loose and fell in earnest. Thunder cracked nearly atop the flash of lightning as it hit a nearby tree. Lacy fought to control her frightened mount. She hurried to the barn, where she could properly shelter her horse.

Once the horse was unsaddled, Lacy looked around for feed and water. There was a small amount of hay in a feeding trough in one of the stalls at the far end of the barn. She gathered this and carried it back to her horse. "Here you go. It's not much, but then, we hardly planned for this. I'll see you get some water after the storm." Lacy whistled for Major. "Come on, boy, let's get to the house and see if we can find Justin."

Major looked at her and settled down in the straw. Lacy couldn't help but laugh. "Not willing to go out in the rain, eh? Well, have it your way."

She could see it was a short run from the barn to the back porch, but the lightning was fierce and there was always the chance of getting struck. An image of Justin, cowering in terror inside the house, made up Lacy's mind, however. She couldn't just stay there and wait—not if he might be inside and afraid.

Without regard to her safety, Lacy hiked her split skirt and made a dash across the open ground. Blinded by the rain, now whipped into a frenzy by the wind, Lacy made her way as best she could, certain that the distance had somehow doubled from her estimation.

She smacked her hand against the back wall of the porch and made her way to the door. Lacy found it unlocked and hurried to get inside. The kitchen was dark, and the entire house was strangely quiet.

"Justin? Justin, are you here?"

Lacy made her way carefully, not entirely sure of the house's layout. She'd only been to the Vanhoutens' a couple of times and had never spent time in the kitchen. Reaching the hall, she saw the faint glow of light coming from the front of the house.

"Justin?"

There was nothing to indicate the boy's presence, but Lacy knew someone had to be there. "Is anyone there?" she called again. Still nothing.

A shiver went up her spine as the rain and her nerves chilled her to the bone. What if someone was there to rob the place?

But what could they hope to take? There shouldn't be anything of value here. Lacy edged down the hall, wishing that Major had come with her after all.

"I have a gun," she announced, trying to sound braver than she felt. She'd lied about having a weapon. She'd left her rifle in the barn. For a moment Lacy thought about going back to retrieve it. With her next step, however, the floor creaked loudly, causing her to halt. "Did you hear me?" She backed up a step as if to make a dash for the barn.

Silence was her only response. Someone had to be in the house, she reasoned. Someone was responsible for lighting the lamp. Lacy bit her lower lip. What should she do? She touched the hall wall and frowned.

"Give yourself up and come into the hall so I can see you," she called.

She squared her shoulders and crept closer to the front of the house. When she reached the end of the hall, Lacy noted that the front door was open and the wind was blowing rain into the foyer. The lamplight flickered and danced shadows on the wall. Swallowing her fears, Lacy stepped into the open and reached for the door. Closing it, she turned and looked into the front room, where Mrs. Vanhouten had once served tea to the Gallatin girls.

"Oh!" Lacy's hand went to her mouth. She froze in place and wondered at the sight before her.

A man lay facedown on the floor near the parlor table, where a single lamp burned. If that weren't shocking enough, the pool of blood around the man's face was sufficient to leave Lacy feeling light-headed.

CHAPTER TWENTY-ONE

Dave climbed from his horse to better see the tracks in the dirt. The search was proving to be more than a little disappointing. The Dykstras had seen nothing of Justin but promised to keep an eye open for the boy. Dave had wanted to continue searching the area, but with the storm quickly absorbing the remaining light, he knew it was time to turn back.

"Well, maybe one of the others will have had better luck," he muttered, realizing the tracks were too large to belong to Justin.

The wind picked up, and with it a decided scent of rain. Dave was barely back in the saddle when the skies opened up and it began to pour. He drew the edges of his coat together and buttoned the top, hoping to keep as dry as possible.

Pulling his hat low, he encouraged the horse to hurry toward home.

Despite the storm moving in from the west, the winds seemed to pummel Dave from all directions. The horse was less than happy to be in the midst of the summer melee. The gelding snorted and danced to the side as lightning flashed overhead.

"Easy, boy. We'll soon be home," Dave encouraged the mount. But at the same time, he wondered if taking shelter might not be a better idea.

It was hard to imagine Justin out in the storm, but maybe that would serve the boy better than any other punishment. After all, if he had to face harsh elements on his own, maybe he'd think twice before running off again.

Lightning flashed and thunder cracked nearly on top of it. The horse reared up, forcing Dave to fight for his balance. Holding fast to the reins, Dave raised his head as best he could against the wind and rain. Ahead, he could make out four figures on horseback, blocking the road.

He squinted his eyes to see who the men were. Dave figured it might well be part of the search party and called out, "Seen anything of the boy?"

"We found what we were lookin' for," one of the men replied.

As Dave drew closer he realized he was in trouble. All of the men were wearing masks. Three of the men leveled rifles at him, while the fourth brought his horse alongside Dave's and took hold of the reins.

"You're comin' with us."

Lacy did the best she could for the young man. She'd been relieved to find that he was still breathing, but the wound on his head left her little doubt that he'd been shot. She went about the house gathering anything that looked even remotely useful. Grateful for plenty of firewood on the back porch, Lacy hurried to light a fire in the living room hearth.

"We could both use some warmth," she surmised. The additional light was useful, as well. Lacy surveyed the situation.

She knew her sisters would be worried about her, but she couldn't leave the young man to what would be certain death. He needed care, and he needed it now. She might already be too late. Then there was the storm to consider.

"They may worry, but it's probably best I stay here," she decided.

Lacy considered the man. Even though his build was on the small side, she knew she'd never have enough strength to lift him into a bed. The next best thing would be to make a pallet for him near the fire. She could roll him that far.

She stripped away the man's bloody coat and unfastened the buttons of his shirt. Checking him over quickly, she found no wounds other than the head wound. Lacy realized the bullet had ripped a streak of hair from the boy's blond head, leaving behind a nasty gash that threatened to take his life.

"Sure wish I knew who you were and what happened to you." The thought crossed her mind that maybe the person or persons responsible might still be after the young man. Lacy glanced toward the door and frowned. What if they tracked him to this place? What if they came in by force and tried to kill him? She figured she'd need to retrieve the rifle as soon as possible.

She got up and tossed the man's blood-caked coat over the back of a wooden chair. Whether or not folks were coming for this fellow, Lacy knew she had to stay focused or he would certainly die. If someone tried to storm the place, she'd just deal with it when it happened.

It seemed as if hours were passing by, but Lacy knew it was probably nothing more than minutes. She hurried to heat water on the stove and then found some old dish towels the Vanhoutens must have left behind. She tore the towels into strips to clean and dress the man's wounds.

"Man, indeed," she murmured as she began to work. He hardly seemed more than a boy. He was short and skinny without a hint of whiskers on his face. Lacy figured he couldn't be more than sixteen.

"Who would want to shoot a boy?" she questioned as she began to dab the head wound gently. She cleaned away the worst of the dried blood and dirt in order to get a better look at the wound.

"What in the world happened to you?"

The young man stirred and opened his eyes momentarily. Lacy could see there was no understanding of his surroundings. He stared blankly at her for a moment, babbled something incomprehensible, and then he was gone again. The blue eyes closed, leaving Lacy feeling strangely alone.

Once she'd finished cleaning and binding the wound, Lacy decided to see about something to eat. She knew Dave had stayed at the house a few times and hoped that he might have laid in a supply of canned goods. Opening the cupboard, she found several cans of beans and a box of crackers, but nothing else.

"It'll have to do," she said, taking two of the cans in hand.

Hours later, Lacy sat warm and satisfied by the fire. She watched the young man sleep and hoped he was without pain. His bandages revealed some bleeding, but it seemed minimal. Of course, there had been plenty of blood on the floor, so Lacy wasn't entirely sure how much he'd already lost. Once the storm passed and morning came, she could ride out for help. Maybe Dave would realize she hadn't returned and come here looking for her. *Then I'll have the help I need.*

Her last conscious thought was of Justin. She prayed that he would be found safe and unharmed. Yawning, she eased down onto her own pallet and closed her eyes. *Silly little boy,* she thought. *You've certainly led us all on a wild goose chase this night.*

Lacy awoke with a start and immediately found the reason for her strange feeling of discomfort. The young man's eyes were open, and he was watching her quite intently. She tried not to appear as frazzled as she felt.

"Well, I see you made it through the night." She sat up and stretched, wondering what time it was. "How do you feel?"

"Been better."

"I can imagine. Someone took a shot at you. Any idea who it was?"

The young man looked away and closed his eyes. "You're one of them Gallatin girls, aren't you?"

Lacy found his question surprising. "I am. I'm Lacy Gallatin."

He gave the slightest nod. "I figured you were one of 'em."

Lacy smiled. "You figured right, but you have me at a disadvantage. Who are you?"

He shook his head and winced. "You don't know me. Name's Adam."

"Well, Adam, can you tell me what happened to you?"

Lacy wanted to check his wound, but he seemed uncomfortable in her presence. She decided a little more conversation might put the young man at ease.

"I guess I crossed the wrong crowd," he answered, his voice barely audible. He said nothing more, and Lacy decided to let it go for now.

"I'll need to get you some help, but maybe first you'd like a little breakfast. We don't have much, but there are some beans and a few crackers. I can fix some up for you, if you like." He didn't answer, so Lacy got to her feet and tucked her blouse into her waistband. "So you were right, I don't know you. In fact, I don't recall seeing you around at the store or anywhere else. Are your folks from the area?"

He opened his eyes and fixed her with a stare. "I don't have any folks. Been on my own for over four years now."

"Four years? But you hardly seem old enough for that."

"I'm eighteen. Been seein' to myself for most of my life. My folks weren't exactly the kind to fuss over their kin. They got themselves killed and left me and my brothers behind."

"And where are your brothers?"

"Don't know. They went their own way a couple of years ago."

Lacy was stunned at the thought that this boy's brothers could just leave him to make his own way at the age of sixteen.

Why, Cubby was only sixteen and certainly not old enough to care for himself.

"So have you been living in the area long?" She tried to sound lighthearted, but in truth, Lacy felt quite an offense building for the young man.

He continued to look at her, and Lacy thought it was almost like that of a trapped animal considering his captor.

"Long enough."

"Look, Adam, I mean you no harm. You needn't worry about what I'll do or say. I'm here to help you."

He seemed to consider this for a moment. "This is Deputy Shepard's house, isn't it?"

"Yes, but he usually stays in town at Gallatin House. Were you looking for the deputy?"

Adam drew a deep breath and blinked several times as if trying to focus. "Yeah . . . I . . . I thought he would be here."

"I can certainly get him," Lacy replied. "We need to get you a doctor, as well, but Deputy Shepard will be happy to pursue whoever did this to you."

"I . . . don't . . . want a doctor. Don't deserve one, nohow." The boy's words were slightly slurred, and Lacy hurried to his side.

"Adam?" She called his name as his eyes closed.

"You just let me die, Miss Lacy," he whispered. "It's only fair."

"That's nonsense," she said, feeling his reddened cheek. He was feverish. She should have noted that sooner. "You aren't going to die if I have anything to say about it."

He grabbed her hand with surprising strength and forced his eyes open. "Never meant for it to happen. Never wanted him to die."

She shook her head. "What are you talking about?"

"You . . . your pa." He licked his lips and closed his eyes. "I think I killed him."

Dave had never had such a splitting headache in all of his life. Every movement caused him blinding pain, but lying still offered little relief. He moaned and tried to open his eyes, but they refused to obey.

"You hit him pretty hard," someone said in a muffled voice.

Dave tried to figure out who was talking, but the black cloud that surrounded his conscious thoughts blocked out any hope of recognition.

"He was mouthy and deserved it" came the reply. "Look, when are they coming?"

"I can't rightly say. They just said to bring him here and wait. Guess they'll get here when they get here. I sent Jacobs back to let them know we have him. My guess is they'll come as soon as they can get away unseen."

"Probably still looking for that Lassiter brat. Wyman said it would make a good cover."

Dave fought to stay awake and worked even harder to figure out what the men were talking about. He couldn't remember anything that had happened to him, but he had a sense of urgency that extended to something more than his own circumstance.

"Well, if they ain't here by noon, I'm gonna go fetch 'em myself."

Dave heard a snorted laugh. "You just do that. You just

sashay right on up to Rafe and Mulholland and tell them that they're takin' too long to tend to business. I'd pay good money to see that."

"You ain't got good money. You lost it all in that card game last night, same as me. That's why we're here in the first place."

Dave's thoughts blurred, and one voice melded into another. He couldn't fight against the blackness anymore. There was a strange drum beating somewhere, and for the life of him, Dave couldn't figure out what it meant. It was annoying, while at the same time, he somehow knew that it was important that the beat continue. But he knew nothing else.

CHAPTER TWENTY-TWO

A boy? A boy was responsible for killing her father?

Lacy looked at the young man and shook her head. She slid to the chair and continued to stare at him in dumbfounded silence. Of all the times she'd imagined finding her father's killer, never—not even once—had she imagined it like this.

He wouldn't have been more than a child when her father was killed two years ago. Why would he have even had an opportunity to participate in such madness?

This couldn't be true. It couldn't be possible that this boy-man was the one whose bullet had taken her father's life. But why would he lie there—injured as he was, possibly facing death—and suggest that he was the one responsible if he wasn't?

The sky grew light outside, and Lacy heard the unmistakable whining of Major. She went to the door and opened it to admit the dog. He ambled in, sniffing at the air as if to see whether or not breakfast was ready.

Lacy closed the door and leaned against it. She looked back to the pallet where the young man was stirring once again. Major went to the man and licked his face. Adam opened his eyes and struggled to move away.

"Don't . . . let him . . . hurt me."

Lacy pushed away from the door. "He won't hurt you." Her mind reeled with a hundred questions. Walking slowly to where Adam was still struggling to sit up, Lacy bent to touch his shoulders. "You should just lie still."

"Can't. I have to find the deputy."

"You're in no condition to ride. Besides, I didn't see your horse out there anywhere." Lacy felt Adam's head. "Your fever seems to have lessened, but you're still warm."

He fell back against the pallet. "It hurts like nothin' I've ever known." He put a hand to his bandaged head. "Am I gonna die?"

Lacy squatted and leaned her chin against her knees. "I don't think so. The bleeding has stopped, and like I said, your fever seems better." She paused for a moment, then straightened. "Look, we need to talk. I need to know more about what you said earlier."

He turned to look at her. "About your pa?"

"Yes. Why did you say you thought you'd killed him?"

Adam's expression filled with pain. "I was there," he said softly. "It was my first time to a saloon. We were celebrating my sixteenth birthday." He moved his head and moaned against the pain.

"Maybe we should just talk about this later," Lacy said, starting to stand.

"No!" Adam cried out. He closed his eyes and seemed to pant for breath. "Don't you see? You being here . . . it's like . . . like God wants me to confess."

Lacy stiffened. She had always seen her father's killer as some kind of unrepentant monster. A young man in the prime of his life was not at all what she had expected. Much less that he should be seriously repentant.

"Why did you wait so long to say something?" she asked, taking a seat beside Adam. Major did likewise and placed his head on Lacy's lap.

"The boys threatened me. They told me they'd skin me alive if I so much as admitted to being there that night. I was working at the Vanderkamp ranch, and they didn't cotton to drinking. The boys said we'd all lose our jobs if I said we'd been at the saloon. I was still determined to do the right thing, but they just took turns making sure I stayed put."

"Adam, why do you think your bullet was the one that killed my father? There was a lot of shooting going on that night."

"I know, but I was the youngest and most inexperienced. I'd never had beer before then, and that night, I had a lot." He finally opened his eyes. "I remember it all so clearly."

"How could you if you were that drunk?"

He started to shrug, but the action clearly pained him and he stopped. "I don't know, but I see it every time I close my eyes. I have nightmares about it. Your pa looked me square in the eye as he fell. It was like he knew I'd killed him."

Lacy felt her chest tighten at the memory of that night. She remembered her father lying in the dirt, blood staining his shirt, his eyes going glassy. Gwen had wanted to get him to the house, but their father had known he was dying.

"I'm done for," he'd said with such finality that it sent a shiver up Lacy's spine.

"I never meant for it to happen—you have to believe me," Adam said.

Lacy wanted to declare that believing him wouldn't change anything, but seeing the overwhelming sorrow in his expression, she couldn't.

"I wanted to turn myself in the very next day, but the boys wouldn't let me. They said I was being stupid, that I hadn't killed anyone—at least I couldn't be sure. They said so long as we all stuck together, we'd be fine.

"None of them seemed to have any trouble forgetting what happened, but I couldn't. I don't think I'll have any peace at all until I pay for what happened."

The image of the skinny boy hanging from a gallows sickened Lacy. She shook her head. "Adam, you . . . you need to rest." Getting to her feet, Lacy longed only to distance herself from the entire matter. "I'll see about getting you something to eat."

"No. Wait."

The longing in his voice caused Lacy to turn. She felt as if her feet were nailed to the floor as she waited to see what Adam would say next.

"Please forgive me." Tears ran down his cheeks. "I know I can't do anything to bring him back—I know that nothing I do can make it better, but I need your forgiveness. I can face my punishment if I know you and your sisters will forgive me. I can even face death."

Lacy said nothing. Forgive him? She'd never expected this.

"Please, Miss Lacy. I know I don't deserve it, but please . . . can't you just think about it?"

She felt her brows knit together as she looked at the boy in confusion. He wanted her forgiveness? He was just a young man, barely a man at all, who had made a horrible mistake and now found it impossible to live with the deed. How could she not forgive him?

Her stomach clenched, and Lacy knew without a doubt she was going to be sick. "I . . . I'm sorry." She ran for the front door.

"Justin just seems to have disappeared," Nick said, pacing the floor at Gallatin House.

"So have Lacy and Dave," Gwen said, worry edging her tone. "They didn't come back last night." She wiped her hands on a flour-sack towel and looked at Beth. "Do you suppose we should go looking for them, too?"

"I don't know. Maybe they changed their minds and decided to look all night," Beth said, giving her sleeping son's head a gentle touch. She cradled him close but found little comfort in the action.

"They didn't show up at all?" Nick asked. "It was Dave's suggestion that we all be back here for the night. I figured they came in after Hank and I got back."

Gwen shook her head. "No."

"I'm sure they're fine," Beth said. "We really have to keep our attention on Justin." She grimaced at the thought of all the bad things that could have happened to the boy. *If only I hadn't yelled at him. If I hadn't been so angry, he might still be here.* She felt tears come again to her eyes.

Nick nodded in agreement. "I guess Hank and I will go out and search for Justin. He's out getting the horses ready. If you hear anything from the others, tell them I've gone north. Hank said he'd ride out to the Shepards' place and see if Justin showed up there." Nick took up his hat.

"I'm going to look, as well. I can at least walk around the immediate area," Beth said, getting to her feet. "Gwen, would you watch Max for me?"

"Of course." Gwen took the baby.

Nick secured his hat and turned back to Beth. "It would be better—"

She held up her hand. "Don't. It's my fault he ran off. I have to at least try to make this right. I feel so useless sitting here while everyone else is searching. He's my son, too." Her voice cracked. "I couldn't bear it if something happened to him."

Nick came and took her in his arms. "It's not your fault, Beth. Justin has been defying us since he found out we were going to give him a brother or sister. I didn't take it all that seriously until now. So if anyone is to blame . . . well, it's probably best left at my door."

Beth took strength in his caress and embrace. She was grateful that Nick didn't blame her, but it did little to assuage her guilt.

"You ready?" Hank asked from the doorway.

Nick pulled back. "I'm coming." He looked back to Beth. "Don't go too far. There are a lot of unsavory characters in the area. I don't want harm to come to you."

She bit her lip to keep from saying something about the

danger Justin must surely be facing, and instead nodded. She waited until Nick had gone before turning to her sister. "I'll try to be back for his next feeding."

"Do be careful," Gwen said.

Beth was grateful that Gwen wasn't attempting to stop her. "I will." She started to leave but halted when Gwen called out.

"You know, Nick is right. This isn't your fault. Justin was wrong to play with fire, and he was wrong to run away. He knew what he did was dangerous—it could have resulted in you getting seriously injured or even dying. He ran off because he feels guilty for what he did."

Beth met Gwen's sympathetic expression. "Seems we've all dealt with our guilt over the years. It certainly has a way of making a person do foolish things."

Gwen smiled. "Hopefully we can learn from our mistakes."

Nodding, Beth headed for the back door. "And maybe practice more compassion for the mistakes of others."

Cubby spied Hank standing at the back of Gallatin House. He looked disheveled and tired. A wide-mouthed yawn seemed only to confirm his assessment.

"You look spent, Hank. You get any sleep last night?"

"A little. We're heading out again," Hank told him. "We still haven't found the boy. You're welcome to join us."

"He's still missing? That's not good, is it?"

"No, it's sure not. He's too young to be out there by himself. I'm just hoping maybe he found his way to someone's house and took shelter for the night."

"I asked all around the river. No one had seen him. I even talked with the wagon train folks, but they hadn't seen him, either."

Nick bounded down the back porch stairs. "We're on our own this morning," he commented as he joined Hank and Cubby. "I guess Dave and Lacy didn't make it back last night."

Hank frowned. "Not at all?"

"No one's seen them."

"It's not like Dave to break with his own rule, though I could see Lacy ignoring it." He grinned and shook his head. "I'd even expect it, but not from Dave."

Cubby instantly had an image of Lacy in Dave's arms. "They're probably just spoonin' somewhere."

Hank looked at him oddly. "Neither one would put Justin's safety aside to do any such thing. They probably teamed up to keep searching through the night. Could be they found his trail. They'll come back as soon as they've exhausted all possibilities."

"You still riding out to Shepards'?" Nick asked.

Hank positioned his hat. "Yeah. I'll head out there and ask if they've seen him. If not, I'll check the other area farms and ranches on the way back."

"All right. Let's meet back here by noon," Nick said. "Cubby, if you get a chance to look around the area again, I'd appreciate it."

"Will do, Nick. I'll have some time while Pa is sleeping. It won't be much, but I'll do what I can."

"Thanks. I appreciate the help."

Cubby watched the two men head off to the corral for their mounts. He stalked back to the saloon and the freshly cleaned spittoons he'd left drying in the early morning sun. Collecting his work, Cubby headed inside to return the spittoons to the saloon. He was about to head out to look for Justin when he heard voices coming from his father's office.

In all his life, Cubby had never known his father to conduct business at this hour. Easing to the door, Cubby clearly heard Jefferson Mulholland's voice.

"Killing him is the only way. Shepard knows too much."

"He's right, Rafe." Cubby recognized Wyman's deep voice.

"And how are we going to avoid catching the blame?"

"Why would anyone suspect us?" Wyman asked. "There are highwaymen still at large. We'll just make it look like he was caught unawares by them."

Cubby felt the hairs on his neck prickle. They were going to murder Deputy Shepard, just like they'd murdered George Gallatin.

Lacy had been on her knees in prayer since Adam's request for forgiveness. To her surprise, she not only wanted to forgive the young man, but she found that she needed to in order to be free of the past.

"Oh, Father, I'm so tired." She buried her face in her hands and prayed silently. *If Adam truly killed Pa, then I know it wasn't on purpose—it was an accident. I know he feels horrible about what happened—he was just a child.*

Her emotions churned and whirled like a summer storm about to strike. Tears dampened her cheeks as she lifted her face. "That's right, isn't it, Pa? I won't be failing you if I forgive him, will I?" She could almost hear her father's laughter. He would think her silly to hold anyone a grudge—even the person responsible for his death. George Gallatin had never withheld forgiveness, and he'd expected no less of his girls.

"There are too many sorrowful things in life," she remembered him saying. *"You girls must never add to them. Never be the cause of anyone's pain, and if you have the ability to ease their suffering, then do so quickly."*

"I will, Pa," Lacy whispered. Suddenly she knew what she had to do.

Getting to her feet, Lacy wiped her face with the back of her hand. She drew a deep breath and headed back to the front room, where she'd left Adam.

He looked up at her from where he sat slouched against the wall. Lacy could see the unasked question in his eyes. "I forgive you, Adam," she said in a barely audible voice. For a moment, she wondered if he'd heard her, but when she spied the tears rolling down his cheeks, Lacy had no further doubt.

She sat on a nearby chair and folded her hands together. "I've been looking since that night to find my father's killer. I was sure that whoever had done such a heartless thing must have no conscience. I was convinced they couldn't possibly have suffered or even given it a second thought, otherwise they surely would have come forward to confess. Now I know I was wrong."

Lacy struggled to keep her voice even. "Adam, we have no way of knowing whose bullet killed my father. My sisters have been trying to tell me this for the last two years, but I tend to be a little stubborn." She smiled. "A lot stubborn."

He smiled in return, then grimaced against the pain. Lacy frowned and got to her feet. "We need to get you to Gallatin

House so we can send for the doctor. I'll saddle my horse and bring him around front."

She left without waiting for Adam to comment. Lacy felt freer than she had in years. Forgiveness wouldn't bring her father back to life, but neither would her bitterness and anger. Nothing could undo the events of the past, but she had the power to change her future by simply yielding her failings to God.

With a great sigh, Lacy opened her heart to the possibilities before her. The feeling of failure—her constant companion since childhood—faded just a bit as she determined to give at least this one thing to God. It might not make things right immediately, but she had the hope that in time, it would.

CHAPTER TWENTY-THREE

Nick sat perched atop his gelding, studying the trail up and down the river's edge. To the south, the tiny town of Gallatin Crossing had exploded into a tent city of several hundred, maybe even as many as a thousand, people. To the north lay open prairie grass and cottonwoods in the same unspoiled fashion it had always known.

In this part of the country, the water ran in a northern direction, rushing over rocks while twisting and snaking its way to where the Gallatin would join up with the Madison and Jefferson to form the Missouri River. The river had always run clean and clear, but since the miners had come, this had changed and sediment now clouded the waters.

He checked the shore for any sign of his son. While the water wasn't all that deep at this time of year, it still moved with a strong current. If the boy had tried to cross, he might have lost his footing and been swept away. Nick didn't like to think of that as a possibility, but then, he didn't like to face the fact that his son had spent the night away from home, either.

Nick urged his mount down the small embankment and into the water. Glancing again to the south, Nick saw man after man working in the stream. There had been no major strike of gold, but still, people pursued the possibility. He thought them all crazy for the time and effort they spent.

"They'd be more productive if they'd trade their pans for fishing poles," he mused.

The thought of fishing stirred a memory. Nick remembered a place well downstream that he'd taken Justin on one of their many fishing ventures. The place was secluded, and the river bowed in toward land to form a small, calm pool away from the main flow of the water. Justin had told him how it reminded him of a fishing hole his grandfather had taken him to in Kansas.

Nick turned the horse and came back up the bank. Giving the mount a bit of heel, Nick urged him north on the river path. His heart raced with every inch that passed. Justin just had to be there. It was the one place Nick hadn't thought to search, and it was the only place that made sense.

Trepidation welled up as Nick finally approached the area. A grove of trees sheltered the area near the river, causing the path to go up and around. Nick dismounted, tied his horse to a sapling, and then continued on foot.

"Justin! Justin, are you here?"

Nick pressed through the vegetation, frightening a rabbit

from its hiding place. When he reached the clearing, he saw his wide-eyed son standing to face him.

Justin broke into tears. "I didn't mean to set Mama on fire, Pa. I didn't mean it to happen."

Opening his arms, Nick could barely hold back his own tears of joy. "I know you didn't, son. I know."

Justin ran to him and wrapped his arms around Nick. "Please don't hate me."

Nick lifted his son and carried him to a log where they could sit. "I could never hate you, Justin. You've scared ten years out of me, but I could never hate you."

"What about Mama? Is she . . . is she dead?"

"No. She's just fine. She's been out looking for you. She's been worrying something fierce. I don't think she even slept last night. This morning she left your brother with Aunt Gwen and set out to find you."

Justin looked at his father oddly. "She left Max to look for me?"

"She did. She loves you, Justin—so do I. You are just as important to us as Max."

"But I thought you loved him more. He belongs to just you and Mama. I don't."

Nick shook his head and cupped his son's chin. "That's not true. You belong to both of us. Maybe Beth wasn't your mama by birth, but she is your mama by choice. Justin, she has enough love to give both you and Max."

"But I did a lot of bad things. I made her sad and angry. She yelled at me."

"I know. The choices we make, however, can sometimes do more harm than we ever thought possible. If your fire had spread to the house or if Aunt Lacy hadn't been there to put out the fire on your mama's skirts, someone could have died. I know you realize this because you were afraid your ma was dead."

The boy bit his lip and nodded slowly again. "I won't ever do it again, Pa. You can even send me away."

"No. I could never do that. I love you, and you're my son. If I could have been a father to you from the time of your birth, I would have been. I'll never send you away from me." Nick drew him close once again. "Jesus tells a story in the Bible about how this man had a hundred sheep. He loved all of his sheep and only wanted to keep them safe, but one of the animals ran off."

"Like me?" Justin interjected.

"Exactly like you. Now, the man still had ninety-nine sheep, and some folks might have thought, 'I still have most of the sheep; so what if I lose one?' But not this man. He loved all of the sheep and didn't want to lose any of them."

Justin's eyes grew wide. "What did he do?"

"He left the ninety-nine sheep safe and sound in their pen and went out to look for the one lost sheep. All he could think about was finding that one little sheep because that sheep could have been in danger. He knew the others would be all right, because they were safe at home. He went to find the one lost sheep, Justin, because he loved him and didn't want to leave him in danger—even if the sheep had put himself there of his own free will. Do you understand?"

"I'm like that sheep."

"We all are at one time or another. God comes looking for us and brings us home, away from the danger we got ourselves into. He loves us so much that He doesn't want to lose even one of us. I feel the same way about you. I love Max, and I'll love any other babies that come to your mama and me. But it won't change the fact that I love you—that your mama loves you."

Justin lunged forward and wrapped his arms around Nick's neck. "Can we go home? I'm so hungry."

Nick laughed. "We sure can." He stood and led his son through the heavy thicket of brush. When they reached the horse, Nick swung Justin into the saddle before grabbing the reins and sitting behind him.

"Pa, do you think Mama knows the sheep story?"

Nick turned the horse and headed for home. "I'm pretty sure she does, but why don't you tell her about it when we get back? I'm sure she'd love to hear it from you."

Justin settled down against Nick. "I'm sure glad I don't have to sleep outside again. It got mighty cold last night."

Chuckling, Nick held the boy close, "I'll bet it did, son."

Lacy started back toward Gallatin House with Major plodding faithfully at her heels. Adam was clearly in pain atop her horse, but he held tight to the saddle horn and didn't complain. She noticed the sweat on his brow and thought perhaps she had pushed him too hard.

"Would you like to rest?"

"No. We need to keep moving. Will Deputy Shepard be at the house when we get there?"

She looked back over her shoulder. "He could be. But if they haven't found my nephew yet, he'll probably be out looking for him."

"We have to find him."

Lacy stopped the horse. "Look, I appreciate that you want

to confess to the deputy that you think you might have killed my father, but it's not important anymore. You can't know for sure that you did the deed."

Adam shook his head and barely suppressed a moan. "It's not that."

"Then what? What's got you tied up in knots now?" She hadn't meant to sound insensitive and softened her tone. "You're still badly hurt and in need of a doctor, you know."

"It can wait, but this can't. Deputy Shepard may be in danger."

Lacy felt her heart skip a beat. "What?"

Adam closed his eyes. "Someone wants to hurt him."

"But why?"

"He's causing trouble for a lot of folks. One of the fellas I worked with, well . . . his brother runs with some of the local outlaws. I heard them talkin' that Dave Shepard was stirring up trouble. The deputy had gotten one of the highwaymen to confess, and they were afraid the man was going to have the law coming after them."

"What do they plan to do?"

Adam shrugged. "I don't know all the details, but I think they mean to kill him. When I told them I couldn't be part of that, well, they shot me and left me for dead."

Lacy couldn't waste any more time. She motioned Adam to free his foot from the stirrup. "I'll ride with you. The horse can take us both. We're neither one that big."

She hurried up behind him and secured the reins with one hand and wrapped her other arm around Adam's waist. Kicking the gelding hard on the side, Lacy tightened her grip. "Hold on. Come on, Major—let's go!"

They'd gone no more than a mile or so, however, when she

saw a rider rounding the bend ahead of them. Lacy shifted and felt for the rifle. Just then, she recognized Cubby and brought the horse to a stop barely a foot away from the boy's mount.

"I sure am glad to have found you," Cubby said. "There's trouble, Lacy. They're going to kill Dave."

Lacy felt her throat tighten. "Who is going to kill him?"

"Wyman and Pa. They say he can cause them too much trouble. He knows things about them."

"We have to hurry and warn Dave."

"It's too late for that. I heard some men talking with Mr. Mulholland this morning. They captured Dave last night on the road to the Dykstra ranch and took him to a hideout close by. I heard that much, but I don't know where they went after that."

"Where is this hideout?"

"I'm not sure, though it sounded like it would be right off that same road. At one point Wyman said it was easy to get him to the place without anyone else noticing because they didn't even need to come back to town."

Lacy slid off her mount. "Cubby, this is Adam. Help me get him down. I need you to put him on your horse and get him back to Gallatin House so Gwen can send for the doctor. He's got a bullet wound on his head, and he's pretty weak from loss of blood. My sisters will know what to do."

"What are you going to do?" Cubby asked even as he followed her orders.

Lacy was already back in the saddle. She pulled out her rifle and checked to make sure it was loaded. "I'll take the shortcut through the woods to find Dave. You take Major with you and see that he gets home, all right?"

Cubby frowned. "What if you're too late?"

"Then only God can help the ones responsible, because I'll put a bullet in every last one of them."

∞

Beth wearily made her way to the house, fighting back tears and offering prayers on Justin's behalf. No one had seen the boy. He had disappeared without a trace—without a word to anyone.

"Oh, please, God . . . please keep him safe. I don't know what I'll do if he's—" She couldn't bring herself to finish the sentence.

Stepping onto the front porch, Beth took a seat and tried to gain control of her emotions. She sniffed and wiped her eyes. "Lord, I know you know exactly where he is. I just pray that you'll keep him safely in your care so that we can find him. Oh, God, please help him. He's just a little boy." She sobbed uncontrollably and buried her face in her hands.

"Mama!"

At first Beth feared her mind was playing tricks on her. She listened and caught the sound again.

"Mama! It's me!"

She looked up and saw Justin running toward the house. Nick sat atop his horse near the road and gave her a wave. Beth ran down the few stairs and hurried to take Justin in her arms. Kneeling on the ground, she pulled him close and cried.

"I thought I'd lost you forever. I was so afraid."

Justin held fast to her. "I'm sorry, Mama." He began to cry and pressed his face into her hair. "I'm very sorry."

For several minutes, Beth just held him and let her tears flow freely. The thought of how close she'd come to losing someone she loved so dearly was more frightening to her than she could have imagined.

"Oh, thank you, Father. Thank you for bringing him home," she whispered.

They both calmed at this short prayer of thanksgiving. Justin pulled back and Beth looked deep into his eyes. "Please don't ever run away again. It just about broke my heart."

Justin nodded, his eyes wide. "It 'bout broke mine, too."

Beth couldn't help but smile at this. "We can always talk things out. You know that now, don't you?" She thought of how harsh she'd been with him. "I'm sorry for the way I acted, Justin."

"Pa told me about how you love me just like Max. That you can love us both. Pa said I'm a sheep and when I ran off, you came to find me."

She looked at him oddly, not having any idea what he was talking about. "Sheep?"

Justin took hold of her hand. "Like in the Bible. There was this man who had one hundred sheep. . . ."

Beth listened as Justin retold the story his father had shared. She thought back to a time when she'd worried that Nick wasn't saved—didn't have any interest in Christian matters. Time and the man himself had changed her heart on that, but perhaps it was never so clear as now.

"So I'm like the sheep, Mama."

Beth nodded and hugged him close. "That you are, and I'm so glad to have you safely back in the fold. Are you hungry?"

"I sure am."

"Then let's get you something to eat, my little lamb." She got to her feet and pulled him along to the house. She'd never seen him so filthy, but she wasn't even going to suggest cleaning up first. Sometimes it was all right to be dirty.

"Mama?"

"What, Justin."

"Do sheep eat berries?"

She smiled down at him. "I wouldn't doubt it. I can't be sure, though."

He laughed. "Do you think they'd eat berry pie?"

It was Beth's turn to chuckle. "I'm sure if your Aunt Gwen made them a berry pie, they would happily partake."

"Good," he said, picking up the pace. " 'Cause that's what this sheep wants to eat."

Nick watched his wife and son disappear into the house. It did his heart good to see things put back to right. All of his life, he'd known the importance of family, but perhaps this moment served to remind him of the delicate balance it entailed. He heard traffic on the road behind him and turned to find Hank racing down the road on his black gelding.

"Any sign of him?" he called.

"I just found him," Nick announced.

Hank brought his horse to a stop in a cloud of dust. "Did I hear you right? You found him?"

Nick nodded. "He was at that fishing hole to the north—the one where the river pools off to the side. He thought he'd killed Beth and broke into tears."

Hank dismounted and slapped the dust from his shirt. "Is he all right?"

"Hungry and scared, but also contrite and ready to start anew." Nick remembered times when he'd grieved his parents something fierce. "Guess I'm getting some payback for those less-than-thoughtful moments that went unpunished when I was a boy. My mother always said nine times out of ten, I could charm my way out of a whoopin'."

"And what about that tenth time?" Hank asked with a grin.

"Made up for the other nine."

They both laughed at this, then walked their mounts to the corral. "I hope I won't have the same thing in store with Julianne. Surely a little girl will be less trouble."

Nick rolled his eyes. "I'll bet they said the same thing about Lacy."

Hank feigned a shudder and blew out a long breath. "I'm gonna forget you said that."

Nick grinned. "Forgetting won't change the fact that your little daughter is related to that whirlwind."

CHAPTER TWENTY-FOUR

Cubby helped Adam up the steps to Gallatin House. Twice the young man caught his boot and started to fall forward. "We're almost there. Miss Gwen will know how to help you best. She's done a lot of nursing around these parts."

The wounded man panted for breath. "I don't want to be a bother."

Adam barely made the last few feet across the porch, and Cubby struggled to support the man while knocking on the door. "Miss Gwen won't think it's a bother. She likes helping." He knocked again, this time a little harder.

When Gwen finally appeared, Cubby shifted Adam and smiled. "Miss Lacy asked me to bring this fella here for some doctoring."

Gwen nodded and motioned Cubby to bring Adam upstairs. Cubby strained against the man's weight but pressed on. Once he'd reached the first spare bedroom, Gwen already had the covers pulled down ready for her patient.

"Bring him over here." She helped Adam to sit on the bed, then bent to pull off his boots. "Where is Lacy? We've been worried about her and Dave."

Cubby took Adam's boots from Gwen, and then they helped him to lie back on the bed. Adam moaned and put a hand to his head. Cubby straightened, anxious to leave.

"Lacy is just fine, but she's gone to look for Dave." Cubby guarded his words so that he wouldn't reveal too much. He didn't want to unduly worry Gwen. "This here is Adam. He's got a bullet wound on his head. Lacy did what she could for him."

"Goodness," Gwen said, finally getting a good look at Adam. "What happened?"

"He can tell you all about it, but I need to go. Say, did you find Justin?"

"Just a little bit ago," Gwen replied. "He's safe and sound. Thanks for looking for him."

"Sure, Miss Gwen." Cubby hurried to the door. "Is Hank around?"

"He's at the store right now."

Cubby nodded. "Then I'll go there. I need to talk to him." He darted out and ran down the porch stairs. He didn't want to give Gwen a chance to ask him more questions or assign him other duties. He was still uncertain as to what he should do. A part of him wanted to get back on his horse and go after Lacy, while a more sensible part told him to get help.

"Hank?" he called out as he entered Bishop's Emporium. "Hank!"

"You don't have to shout. I'm right here," Hank declared, rising from behind the counter. "What's the problem?"

"It's . . . well . . ." Cubby looked at the man for a moment. How much should he reveal? If he told Hank everything, his father would be sent to jail or even hanged. Of course, Dave and Lacy would know the truth and send Rafe there anyway. Cubby shifted nervously. "I need to tell you something."

Hank seemed to understand that the matter was grave. "Do you want to sit down?"

Cubby shook his head. "There isn't time." He met Hank's calm expression. "I need your help. Actually, Lacy and Dave do."

"What's happened? Do you know where they are?" Hank came from around the counter. "We've been worried about them. They never returned."

"There's been some trouble." Cubby began to pace. "Look, I've known something was going on for a long time, but I didn't know the full extent. I've overheard so many things that I couldn't be sure what was truth and what wasn't."

"Son, calm down and tell me what this is all about."

Cubby took off his hat and twisted the rim nervously. "It's just that my pa is involved, and I don't want to get him in trouble. I keep thinkin', though, about what you said. Good men face up to the truth even when it involves folks they love." He looked at Hank in desperation. "I know he's a bad man—he's done bad things—but he's still my pa."

"Of course he is, but what does this have to do with him?"

Cubby slammed his fist against the door. The impact rattled the window something fierce. "It's that Wyman and Mr. Mulholland. They've been bad for Pa. They've had all sorts of underhanded stuff going on."

"Like what?" Hank asked, crossing his arms.

"There isn't time to explain it all. But Lacy and Dave are in trouble. My pa was talking this morning with Wyman and Mr. Mulholland. I stopped to listen because it wasn't like him to be up so early. They said they had taken Dave and were planning to kill him. They want to get him out of the way just like they did Lacy's pa."

Hank shocked Cubby by crossing to him in two long strides. He took hold of the boy's shoulders, and Cubby found it impossible to look away. "Your father killed George Gallatin?"

"No . . . but . . . well . . . Wyman did." Cubby hung his head. "Pa ordered it."

"But why? And why do they want to kill Dave?"

"He knows too much about them. Apparently, they killed Big John for talking to Dave and telling him about the operation. At least Wyman said his men had gone to Bozeman to do the job. Pa and Wyman are behind the highwaymen and a lot of the other trouble going on around here. They did it to drive the good folks away so that they could take over the town. It's why they killed Mr. Gallatin. They wanted to buy the hotel, and now they have."

Hank shook his head. "The deal's not final. We have ownership until September. But that's hardly important now. Tell me where they have Dave."

"I don't know for sure. I heard them talking about having surprised him on the road to the Dykstra ranch and that they took him to a hideout nearby. I'm figurin' it has to be somewhere off the same road Dave was on. Lacy's gone to track them."

"Lacy? She's out there alone?" Hank let go of Cubby.

"She made me bring in an injured man. When I rode out to find her this morning, I caught up with them as she was making her way back from the Vanhouten place. Lacy didn't say a whole lot, but she had me bring the man and Major back to the house. The man's name is Adam Barnes. He told me on the way that he got himself shot and that Lacy helped him. He knew, too, that Dave was in trouble. Apparently Lacy decided to take shelter at the Vanhouten house when the storm hit and found Adam there bleeding and unconscious. That's about all I know." Cubby frowned as he remembered leaving Lacy to ride off in the opposite direction. "I wanted to stay with her, but she insisted I bring the man here."

"That sounds like Lacy." Hank muttered something else that Cubby couldn't understand.

"She has a rifle and told me if they hurt Dave, she'd shoot every one of the men responsible."

Hank looked at Cubby as if considering the possibility of something so outlandish. "I'm sure she would. You wait here while I go get Nick. Did you say anything to Gwen when you dropped the man off?"

Cubby shook his head. "I didn't say any more than I had to. I didn't want to have to tell her that Lacy was in danger."

"That's probably for the best, but I don't see how we can keep it from her now. If Nick and I go out with you, she'll know something isn't right." Hank sighed. "I'll be back as quick as I can. You wait here, and we'll head to the Dykstra road together."

Cubby plopped down on a barrel marked *Molasses* as the truth washed over him. Pa was evil. He had to be. How else could he have done all those bad things—especially arranging murder?

He thought back on how much he'd liked George Gallatin. The man had been kind. He always had a story to tell; he always treated other folks like they were important. Mr. Gallatin was probably one of the best men Cubby had ever known.

"And Pa had him killed, all so he could buy Gallatin House." The news had been hard to hear but even harder to understand. Why would his father stoop to such dealings? It had to be the bad influence of Wyman Jenkins.

Cubby felt a burning anger toward Wyman. Mulholland, too. Neither one of the men had been of a good cut, and his father had been easily taken in by both of them. But even as Cubby tried to convince himself of this, he knew it wasn't true. His father wasn't any better. For as long as Cubby could remember, Rafe Reynolds had swindled and cheated people in whatever manner best served his needs. That's why it bothered Cubby so much to think he might be anything like him.

The minutes ticked by, and Cubby grew anxious. He got up from the barrel and glanced outside to see if there was any sign of Hank and Nick. He only saw a handful of the miners and other rowdies milling around. A couple of them looked to be headed to the store. Cubby didn't want to have to deal with them and quickly slid the lock in place and pulled down the shade.

He crossed the room to Hank's office and searched out a piece of paper and a pencil. Quickly, he jotted a short note to Hank to let him know that he couldn't wait any longer to go in search of Lacy. He would leave them a marker on the road to Dykstras' if he found the place where Lacy and the others had gone. Otherwise, he would see them when Hank and Nick caught up to him.

Positioning the note in plain view on the front counter, Cubby ignored the knocking of the miners and slipped out the back of the store. He came around the building to retrieve his horse and shook his head as the men gave him a glance. "There's no one in there. Guess Hank closed down for a spell."

The men muttered their disapproval as Cubby mounted his horse and headed back down the road. As he passed his father's saloon, Cubby couldn't help but feel a sense of sorrow. Everything was about to change—that much he knew.

"But there should be something we can do to help," Beth protested. "That's our sister out there."

"Look, we're wasting time arguing with you," Nick said as he strapped on his gun belt. "Hank is right. You two need to stay put. Send someone for the sheriff if you know they can be trusted. Otherwise, remain here."

Gwen came alongside Beth and took hold of her arm. "You know they're right. We can't help out there, but we can pray."

"It seems so little," Beth said, shaking her head. "I know it's not, but it seems like nothing at all."

"I know," Gwen admitted. "But we have to think of the children. It's dangerous enough for the men. But if we found someone to watch the babies and something happened to us, they might well become orphans."

That thought silenced Beth. Justin came up and took hold of her other arm. He seemed to want to reassure her at the same time he needed assurance. Beth pulled him close. "We'll stay."

Nick nodded. He gave her a quick kiss, then turned to Hank. "Let's go."

Hank drew Gwen into his arms. Beth thought she saw tears

in her sister's eyes and looked away. What a horrible thing to happen, and just when things had seemed so much better! Justin had come home unhurt, and Beth had felt there was finally hope that they could be happy as a family.

"Don't worry, Mama. Remember God doesn't want to lose any of His sheep. He's already going after Dave and Aunt Lacy."

Beth looked down at her son. "You're right, Justin. He has already taken care of them. We have to remember that." She met Nick's eyes and saw his nod of agreement. It wasn't much, but it gave her enough courage to stand strong.

Lacy noted the multiple sets of tracks and jumped down from her horse. The imprints were fresh and veered off onto a rocky slope and disappeared. Lacy studied the terrain and traced every inch of the area. Catching sight of something in the brush, Lacy made her way on foot to check deeper in the vegetation. A few feet in, broken branches littered a beaten-down path in the grass. This had to be it.

She strained to listen for any sound of men or horses. Nothing. Even the birds had fallen silent at her arrival. A chill slid down her spine. This was no game of hide-and-seek. The men she sought were killers. They intended to hurt the man she loved.

The man I love. She mulled the thought over in her mind. *I love him.* The revelation seemed natural and easy. *How silly I've been to even wonder it.* Sure, Dave Shepard had been like a thorn in her side, but that was only because she longed for his approval and companionship. Every time he scolded her or took her to task, she was angry—but more at herself than Dave.

"And you wait until now to figure all this out," she muttered.

She thought of Dave being hurt and felt sick. How could she have doubted her love for him? Why had she fought her feelings for so long?

Dave had once commented that she was making this hard on herself. "He certainly had that right," Lacy said, shaking her head again.

She went back for her horse but didn't bother to remount. Instead, she led the animal through the brush and along the small path. There in the distance, hidden quite well by the woods, she saw a small cabin. She snuck forward a bit more and realized there were a couple of even smaller buildings near it—perhaps outhouses—and several horses grazing nearby. Hopefully she would be able to sneak up on the hideaway without being heard or seen, but in case she couldn't, she knew it was best to be prepared. Pausing only long enough to pull her rifle from its scabbard, Lacy squared her shoulders and pressed on.

Rafe sat at his desk and stared blankly at the wall. His life just seemed to go from bad to worse. All he'd wanted was to expand his saloon and take over the hotel. He'd never figured on the gold rush deception or Mulholland's wagon train people. Now Mulholland and Wyman were determined to kill Dave Shepard, and Rafe was tied into it like a spring calf ready for branding.

He'd never bargained for all of this. Mulholland had a way of manipulating Rafe and the people around him. Men who had once called Rafe *Boss* now looked to Mulholland for instruction. Oh, they didn't come right out and say as much, but Rafe saw the looks they exchanged. Even Wyman, who had hated Mulholland at first, seemed to have a newfound respect for him.

"They're both bloodthirsty," Rafe muttered. "That's what makes them good companions."

"Here's your supper, Rafe," Marie said from the door. She brought in a bowl and placed it in front of him.

He stared at the stew for a moment, then shook his head. "Take it away. I ain't hungry."

"What's wrong with you? You've been in a bad way all day. You sick?"

He looked at the woman as if seeing her for the first time. Marie wasn't so very old, but she looked at least twenty years his senior. Life had been hard on her.

"I ain't sick," he muttered. "Just take this and get out. Leave me be."

Marie didn't say another word. She picked up the bowl and hurried from the room. Rafe looked back at the wall. Now was a poor time to go getting a rush of conscience.

He didn't know why the idea of killing Dave Shepard bothered him so much. He supposed it might be because Dave had always treated him fairly. He really didn't have anything against the man. Of all the lawmen Rafe had known in his day—and he'd known plenty—Shepard had impressed him with his honesty. There had been many times when Rafe had hinted at putting Dave under his hire, but the man had stood fast.

Reaching into his drawer, Rafe took out a bottle of whiskey. He didn't even bother with a glass, just lifted the bottle to his lips and took a generous swallow. The amber liquid burned for a moment, then warmed and soothed the empty feeling Rafe held within.

He thought of Dave's mother and how he'd often traded with her for eggs and butter. She would be beyond grief when she learned that her son was dead. And for what? Because he knew more than he was supposed to? Because he did his job well?

Imagined pictures of Dave's funeral ran through his mind and melded into all-too-real images of George Gallatin's burial. George was the first person Rafe had ever arranged to have killed. He was also the last. It didn't set well with Rafe to kill. For all his bravado about being willing to take the life of any man who crossed him, Rafe found murder difficult to live with.

Maybe that's why he was in this state of mind. He hadn't been able to think clearly since the early-morning talk he'd had with Wyman and Mulholland. They had dictated how things would be, and Rafe really had no choice but to let the pieces fall into place.

"What a waste," he muttered.

Sometimes Rafe couldn't help but wonder what his life might have been like if Cubby's mother would have just settled down and married him. If they could have been a family with a home of their own, maybe things would never have gotten this crazy.

Rafe took another drink and wondered if Wyman had done the deed yet. Had he killed Dave Shepard? Would he leave his body in the nearest canyon ravine like they planned to do with Big John's? A thought of Lacy Gallatin came, unbidden. He remembered the night her father had been killed. She'd knelt in the dirt beside him, staring at the men around her with a burning accusation that had shaken Rafe to his boots. She had never stopped looking for her father's killer—never stopped seeking justice. Somehow she had known George Gallatin's life had not been claimed by a simple accident.

"Just like she'll know it was no accident that took her fiancé."

His thoughts turned to Cubby. "I've failed that boy for sure." He was what? Sixteen, seventeen by now? Rafe had lost track of the years but not the memories.

Cubby might have known an entirely different life had Maryland lived and cared for them both. He would have had a mother's love and comfort. He would have known the tenderness that Rafe had never been able to give him. Of course, if Maryland had stayed, perhaps Rafe would have been able to show his son kindness and love. After all, didn't a person have to experience those things in order to pass them on?

"It's all her fault," Rafe declared. "She was nothing but a no-good, cheatin'. . ." He didn't bother to finish the statement. It was clear what she was. Why validate it by speaking it aloud? Maryland had been the beginning of all his troubles, even if he'd thought otherwise at the time. They were better off without her—especially Cubby. He didn't need that kind of a woman in his life. She would have only hurt him more had she stayed.

Rafe shook his head and stared at the whiskey. What would happen to the boy now? What would Cubby think of him once the truth was revealed? He was more like those Gallatins every day. Cubby's strange sense of values only served to remind Rafe of his own rotten, hard heart.

"Well, he can be a do-gooder if he wants. He ain't no use to me." Rafe pulled the bottle close. This was the only real friend he'd ever had. The only faithful companion.

Rafe looked around the room. The saloon and land were all he had to show for his years of swindling and cheating. Mulholland had grandiose schemes for the future, but Rafe realized he had no desire to be a part of them. Especially if he had to play a subservient role to Mulholland.

It was odd, Rafe thought. He'd always believed himself far more cunning than most. He'd seen himself as a leader among men. But Mulholland's arrival seemed to reveal all of his flaws. Where Mulholland was suave and sophisticated, Rafe was blundering and unpolished. Jefferson Mulholland could smoothtalk his way out of trouble and into success in a way that Rafe could never hope to accomplish.

"Well, who cares?" Rafe muttered. "I'm not gonna stick around to be anyone's lackey." He finished off the bottle and tossed it to the floor. The glass shattered at his feet, but Rafe ignored it.

Opening the drawer of his desk, Rafe pulled out a revolver and smiled. "No one's gonna tell me how to run my life. I'm the boss here. I'm the one who decides what will be."

CHAPTER TWENTY-FIVE

Gwen and Beth heard the gunfire and exchanged a glance. "I won't miss that when we move. The people around here seem determined to kill each other off."

Beth shook her head and looked at the now-sleeping Adam. "I wish the doctor would hurry up and come. You don't suppose that fellow we paid to fetch him has run off without doing the deed?"

"No, of course not. You promised him another coin when he returned with the doctor. He looked bad off. I think he'll do the job in order to get his pay."

Beth folded another dish towel and nodded. "Let's pray the other man you found went straightaway to Bozeman for the sheriff and not to the saloon."

"Well, I suppose we won't know for some time. I hate to think of our men without additional support from the law." Gwen looked out the window. "I know they had to go, but I can't help wishing they had a few more to ride with them."

"I know. I feel the same way."

Gwen turned back and glanced at the clock. "The stage will be here in less than two hours."

"The rooms are ready. If the stage is full, we'll have to put some of them in the addition since Adam needs a room to himself," Beth said, getting to her feet with a stack of folded towels.

"That's what the addition is for," Gwen said. "Still, I hope there won't be any complaints. I'm not in the mood to deal with surly folks tonight."

"At least there shouldn't be any complaints about your baked chicken and sponge cake."

A knock sounded at the front door, and Gwen immediately went to see who it might be. She sighed with relief when she saw Dr. DuPont standing on the other side, along with the miner who had gone to get him.

The older man smiled. "I heard I was needed."

Gwen stepped back. "Yes. We have a young man who was shot in the head. It's a graze wound, but he's in a lot of pain."

The doctor nodded and stepped into the house. "Used to be the only wounds I dealt with were gorings and falls; now it seems guns are involved all the time. Show me the way."

Beth joined them and smiled at the miner. "I have the rest of your pay," she told the man. Depositing the towels on the hall table, she reached into her apron pocket and pulled out the coin. "Thank you so much for your help."

The man grinned proudly, revealing several blackened teeth. "No problem, ma'am. Glad to help. You just call on old Jasper anytime you need."

"I'll do that, thank you."

Beth watched him head down the porch steps and toward Rafe's before she closed the door.

"I hope he doesn't drink away his pay. But I suppose it's his business what he does with his money." She was heading to the kitchen when pounding sounded on the back door. This was followed by a woman's shrieks for help.

Beth put the towels aside once again and opened the back door. It was Regina, the youngest of Rafe's prostitutes. Tears were streaking down her ashen face.

"You've got to come quick, Miss Beth."

"What in the world is wrong?"

"It's . . . it's Rafe. He's shot himself."

"Shot himself?" Beth asked. "Are you sure?"

"Yes. There's blood everywhere. I think . . . he's . . . I think he's dead."

Dave took another blow to the face. Wyman seemed to enjoy inflicting pain. He only laughed as Dave's head bobbed back and forth.

"Sooner you cooperate," he told Dave, "the sooner we can be done with this."

Licking his sore lips, Dave shook his head. This man meant to kill him, and Dave knew it was just a matter of when. So far at least, Dave had managed to ward off the more debilitating blows by ducking his chin against his chest. Weakening, however, he'd caught Wyman's fist twice to his mouth and nose. He desperately needed to figure a way out before the attack knocked him unconscious.

"I'm going to ask you one more time: What did Big John tell you and who did you share the information with?"

Dave looked up through swollen eyes. "I'm not telling you anything, Wyman. It's enough that you know I have the facts I need to see you and your associates put away for life."

Wyman got down in his face. "You ain't in a position to do nothin'. Big John is dead and can't testify against us. What do you say to that?"

He had already suspected as much. Pity that the man had been killed, but they had his signed statement. He had privately testified before the judge shortly after his arrival in Bozeman.

"I say you'd do well to stop this now, before anyone else gets killed. You're already facing murder charges for Big John. Why kill anyone else and make matters worse for yourself?"

"Big John ain't the first man I've killed," Wyman said, sounding proud of the fact. "In fact, I find killing pretty easy. It's the askin' and answerin' questions that annoys me." He pulled out his revolver and waved it in front of Dave's face. "Now tell me, who all did Big John talk to and what did he say?"

Dave returned his stare as best he could. He could feel his nose starting to swell. Wyman put the revolver against Dave's knee.

"I'll shoot you, just as sure as sin. You'll suffer a lot before I'm through with you. It won't be a quick and easy death, like your friend George Gallatin had."

The words hit Dave harder than one of Wyman's punches. "What did you say?"

Wyman's laugh was cold and calculating. "Don't tell me I wasn't a suspect. You'll hurt my feelings, Shepard." He delivered an unexpected punch to the side of Dave's head.

Dave felt blinding pain as stars danced in his vision. Much more of that and he would be unconscious. Unconscious. Dave thought for a moment and pretended to be worse off than he really was. "I knew you . . . and . . . Rafe . . . that you . . . had the responsibility. Didn't . . . know . . . who pulled the trigger."

"Rafe doesn't do his own dirty work if he can get someone else to do it—just like now. He wants you dead, but he doesn't wanna have to do it himself. 'Course, given the fact that I rather enjoy these things, I woulda done it for free."

"And . . . George?"

"What about him?" Wyman laughed. "He was a stupid old man, and Rafe wanted the hotel. You know that. He wanted to expand and have a big place for the cowboys to spend their money. We were set to make a fortune together. Me dealing cards, and him selling cheap whiskey. When Gallatin wouldn't even consider Rafe's offer, I suggested we take matters into our own hands."

Wyman seemed so pleased with himself that Dave figured to buy time by keeping the man talking. The more Dave pretended to slur and struggle with his speech, the more Wyman seemed to relax and share his story. "When did . . . you . . . decide . . . to kill him?"

Wyman gave a little shrug. "Well, we thought about takin' one of the girls. We knew that would get the old man's attention, and we could threaten to hurt them or kill them unless he signed over the property."

"But you . . . didn't," Dave gasped out.

"Rafe wasn't keen on the idea. He figured it would bode bad

for us and that the law would catch up eventually." Wyman waved the gun. "He was right—I could see that for myself. That's when we figured if we killed the old man, the girls would pack up and leave."

"How were you going to keep the law from figuring out that you killed George?" Dave hadn't meant to ask the question so clearly. He moaned and let his head bob again from side to side.

Wyman looked at him as if he'd lost his mind. "Well, you didn't know I did it until just now, did you? We knew there'd be a night when it all came together—we just watched for an opening. That night when the boys were good and drunk and startin' to get out of hand, I knew it would be the perfect cover. The only thing I needed was an excuse to get George in the same vicinity." He sneered and gave a huff. "But fate smiled on me as she's always good to do. I was gettin' ready to send Cubby to fetch George when he came walkin' across the road just as the boys began firing off their guns in celebration. I just grabbed my gun and joined in."

Dave let his head fall back. He stared at Wyman from barely opened eyes. "Just like that?"

Wyman shrugged. "Why not? It took care of the problem. Well, in part. We didn't count on the Gallatin sisters wanting to stick around after that. Rafe tried about everything he could to get 'em out of there. They're such a stubborn lot."

Then, as if realizing he'd somehow been duped, Wyman's eyes narrowed. "This ain't about Gallatin or his girls."

He hit Dave with the butt of the gun. Dave pulled back to avoid the impact, but he wasn't fast enough. The wooden grip struck his jaw. Suppressing a moan of pain, Dave forced himself to keep staring at Wyman. He wasn't about to give the man any satisfaction.

"Now, tell me what I want to know or I swear I'll put a bullet in your knee."

"I already told you," Dave said, barely able to make his mouth work. "I know enough . . . to see you put behind bars for good."

Wyman hit him with the gun again—this time making a jabbing punch into Dave's nose. Stars danced in the deputy's eyes as a burning sensation ran up his face and spread. Knowing he couldn't withstand much more, Dave pretended to black out. He slumped forward and would have toppled over had he not been bound to a chair.

Cursing, Wyman called for one of his men. "Get some water and get him awake. This ain't over yet."

"Sure thing, boss."

"Are you telling me you still haven't gotten the information?"

Dave recognized the voice as that of Jefferson Mulholland. Wyman sounded surprised to see the man.

"When'd you get here?"

"Just now. I figured it was best to come check on things myself. I left Rafe to tend to business at the bar. He doesn't seem to have the stomach for this kind of thing."

Wyman laughed. "Yeah, he's braver with girls than guys. He don't mind at all cuttin' on his girls, but he'd rather hire his dirty work done when it comes to men."

"That's why we work well together, Mr. Jenkins."

"I s'pose so," Wyman replied. "Didn't care much for your ways at first, but I'm startin' to have a newfound respect."

Chuckling, Mulholland stood beside Dave's chair. Dave

could just make out his highly polished boots and the finely creased trousers. "Is he too far gone?" Mulholland asked.

"Nah," Wyman answered. "I can still get the information out of him. Don't you worry 'bout it."

Dave heard someone else come into the room as Mulholland and Wyman continued to talk. He knew he had to keep his wits about him, and that wasn't going to happen if he kept getting hit. He'd been constantly testing the ropes that held him and knew there was no chance of getting out of them quickly. He was hopeful, however, that if Wyman would just give up on him for a time and leave him be, Dave could work them loose.

"Just pour it on him," Wyman ordered.

All at once cold water covered Dave's head. The shock instantly caused him to start. There was no denying he'd rallied, but Dave knew he had to keep Wyman from questioning him. Blurry-eyed, Dave looked up.

"Pa? Is that you?"

Wyman frowned and Jefferson Mulholland rolled his eyes. "You've scrambled his brains. You'll have to leave him be until he comes to his senses."

"Or I can just kill him now," Wyman suggested.

"Don't be ridiculous. We don't know who all he's talked to. We can't just suppose that he and Big John kept the information to themselves. Once we know exactly who else has been involved, we can either pay them off or silence them in some other manner." Mulholland looked at Dave and leaned in. "Deputy Shepard, you have been a most unpleasant bur under my saddle."

"I swear, Pa, I cleaned out the stall just like you asked. You can see for yourself." Dave slurred his words for impact.

Mulholland shook his head and turned back to Wyman. "Look, kill him as soon as he tells you what we need to know. Then meet us back at the saloon. We've got plenty to do."

"I'll be there. Shouldn't take much longer." Wyman followed Mulholland and the other man outside, leaving Dave alone.

With Wyman gone, Dave immediately pulled against the ropes. It seemed to him they were a bit looser than before. He wriggled to the left and felt the rope that held his shoulder slip up over the back of the chair. With any luck he'd be able to get free before Wyman returned.

Lacy watched in the dimming forest light while Wyman and Jefferson Mulholland emerged from the shack, discussing something as the latter made his way to his horse, which was grazing alongside several other horses in a makeshift corral outside the cabin. She was also keeping a close eye on the other group of men that seemed to be waiting nearby. Ten minutes earlier, she'd barely managed to slip out of sight when she'd heard the horse and rider coming up behind her. Lacy had been surprised to see Mulholland. She'd half expected Rafe, but not his friend. She couldn't help but wonder just how much Mulholland had to do with all the problems that were afflicting their little town. Seemed things had gotten much worse after his arrival.

Hiding in the shadows, she gently stroked the horse's muzzle to reassure him. Lacy watched as Mulholland and Wyman continued to talk. What were they doing? She longed to overhear the conversation but knew she couldn't risk getting closer. All at once, the discussion ended.

Mulholland mounted his horse, said something else, then turned the animal back down the trail he'd come in on. Lacy watched as Wyman crossed to where the other men stood. He seemed upset about something and waved his arms as if to emphasize his displeasure. He spoke for several minutes to the men. Again, Lacy wished she could hear what he was saying.

Wyman stepped back, signaling an end to his instruction. One by one, the men nodded. They quickly went to retrieve their horses, and before Lacy knew it, they'd mounted and followed after Mulholland. She couldn't help but wonder if Wyman planned to have the man killed. Surely Rafe would never stand for that.

Once the men were gone, she waited to see what Wyman would do next. If she'd kept accurate track of the situation, everyone was gone except Wyman and Dave. Of course, she hadn't actually seen Dave, but his horse was standing in the makeshift corral.

She leaned back against a tree and drew a deep breath as Wyman made his way back to the cabin. What if he'd already killed Dave? She uttered a silent prayer for wisdom and help. This wasn't going to be easy, no matter how much she wanted to protect Dave. Wyman was a mean-spirited, evil man who wouldn't care a bit if she got hurt. In fact, he'd probably relish it.

Lacy bit her lower lip and tried to form a plan. *If I can get to Dave and he's alive, then everything will be all right.* She checked her rifle and felt a small reassurance that the odds were in her favor. She wouldn't have a problem shooting Wyman if he was threatening Dave's life. At least she didn't think she would. She frowned at her own nagging doubts. This was a situation that called for her utmost confidence. She couldn't fail in this. She just couldn't.

⚬⚬

Nick studied the way ahead. "I haven't seen any sign of a marker. We've been up and down this road three times now, and there isn't anything."

"I know. I'm thinking maybe Cubby didn't have time or maybe somebody caught him snooping around," Hank answered.

"I wonder if he had the wrong road. I see plenty of tracks, but there's also been quite a few riders and wagons passing through."

"Maybe we haven't gone far enough. Cubby never said where along the trail they took Dave, or where he thought the hideout might be located. I say we keep going west and see if we happen upon something."

Nick surveyed the terrain. "We can't go home without Lacy and Dave."

"I know." The statement was brief, but the tone told Nick everything he needed to know. He and Hank would be at this for as long as it took. There was no sense considering any other possibility.

"Come on, then. We best get to it." Nick urged the horse forward.

They'd only gone a few yards, however, when Nick held up his hand and halted the mount. He strained to listen, certain that he'd heard something up around the bend. Hank appeared to have heard it, too.

Nick motioned to the trees and turned his horse to head into the cover of the forest. He and Hank were barely out of sight when a man rode past, headed back toward Gallatin Crossing. It was Jefferson Mulholland.

Neither Hank nor Nick spoke, but the look they exchanged left little doubt that each was encouraged by this new development. If Mulholland was in the area, then they were, no doubt, on the right path. Rafe's friend would have no other reason to be there.

Waiting until the man was well down the road, Nick finally turned to Hank. "He has to be involved."

"I was thinking the same thing. I imagine he's coming from the hideout."

Nick nodded. "We'll trace his tracks. They'll be the freshest, and Mulholland probably didn't bother trying to cover them up."

"That's a—"

"Quiet!" Nick whispered harshly at the sound of other riders approaching. There were several men talking amongst themselves. He couldn't make out what was being said, but he certainly didn't want them to realize he and Hank were hiding nearby.

The riders moved quickly after Mulholland, as if trying to catch up with him. Nick couldn't help but wonder if they were the men who'd taken Dave to begin with. Once they were gone, Nick sat in silence for several minutes.

"What do you think?" Hank asked, taking out a handkerchief to wipe sweat from his neck.

"I don't know," Nick answered honestly. There were at least a dozen different scenarios running through his head, and he didn't like any of them. "I wish we had a few more men on our side. I can't help but think those men are a part of Rafe and Mulholland's boys."

Hank replaced the cloth in his pocket. "I figure the same thing."

"One good thing: With that many men traveling, we ought to be able to catch some sign of the trail they've come down. Let's get at it while there's still light enough to see what we're doing."

CHAPTER TWENTY-SIX

Lacy knew she had to get closer to the cabin. She needed to see for herself that Dave was still alive. If she could just know that much, it would give her the strength to figure out what to do next.

She tied her horse to a sapling and crept around the back of him. The ground sloped just a bit toward the cabin; Lacy had chosen this vantage point in order to better survey what was going on. To the left of the corral was what she had now determined was an outhouse and a small loafing shed, and then the cabin. All of the buildings looked slapped together, as if the owner had needed them in a hurry.

Slipping through the trees, Lacy tried to position herself so that she could see the back of the cabin. She needed to know if there was a second entryway into the house. No other door existed, but there was a solitary window. Well, at least there was a hole where a window might have gone. It looked like someone had tacked up a sheet or piece of oilcloth to block out the elements. That could prove easy enough to get through.

A plan began to form. If she could just get into the house unnoticed, she could get the drop on Wyman and force him to turn Dave loose. Once that happened, they could tie Wyman up and make their way home. The plan required just a couple of very important things: getting into the house without Wyman catching her, and Dave being alive.

Lacy made her way back to the horse for her knife, knowing that she'd need it in order to cut the material blocking the window. She was nearly to her mount when someone clamped a hand over her mouth and knocked her to the ground. Determination to live welled in Lacy. She fought for all she was worth.

I'm Dave's only hope. I can't fail him!

"Stop fighting. It's just me, Cubby."

Lacy finally hesitated a moment, then went still. Cubby rolled off of her and turned to face the angry young woman. He tried to help her up, but she slapped his hand away.

"Why did you do that? You didn't have to throw me to the ground." She barely whispered the words, but Cubby could clearly hear the anger in her tone.

"I didn't know how to get your attention without risking the noise. I've come to help you."

She looked at him in disbelief. "By accosting me?"

"I told you why I did what I did. Now tell me what's going on. What do you know?"

"Wyman is down there. I don't know if anyone else is. Mulholland and about four other men were here earlier. Mulholland and Wyman seemed to argue about something; then Wyman backed down, and Mulholland left. The others followed after Wyman talked to them."

"I saw that much. I was over there across the way for a while. I've been looking for you, but you hide real good." He smiled.

Lacy dusted off her clothes. "Such skills have saved me more than once." She pulled a small twig from her hair. "What do you suppose Wyman's up to with Mulholland? At first he acted like he was Mulholland's best friend. Then he seemed pretty upset when he was talking to his boys."

Cubby considered this for a moment. "I heard them talking over by the corral, but I couldn't get close enough to really understand what was being said. Wyman's never liked Mulholland. He was jealous of the way the man just showed up one day and kind of took his place. Fact is, I think he plans to eliminate Mulholland first chance he gets. Wyman's probably just makin' him think they're friends for now so Mulholland doesn't get suspicious. Maybe he's told his boys to go kill him."

Lacy nodded. "I thought of that, too."

"Have you . . . did you see Dave?"

"No, but his horse is in the corral." Lacy pointed. "It's just over there."

Cubby got up and walked to where he had a better view. Dave's gelding was clearly visible. "All right, so we know he's here."

Lacy had followed him. "But we don't know if he's dead or alive."

"Well, we need to rectify that matter. Wyman won't put

it off for long. I know they wanted to get information out of Dave, so maybe he's still alive. I'll go down and pretend my pa has sent me."

"No!" Lacy put her hand on Cubby's arm. "You might get hurt. Why don't you go back and get some men to help us. Hank and Nick will come to Dave's aid if you let them know what's going on."

Cubby jerked away from her. "I told Hank all about it." He frowned and muttered to himself, "I'm not a child."

Why couldn't she see him for who he truly was? "I can do a man's work, Lacy Gallatin, even if you don't believe it."

"I didn't mean to offend you, Cubby. It's just that Wyman is an evil man, and he won't care if he kills you."

"He won't have a chance, if I take care of him first."

Shaking her head, Lacy pulled him back deeper into the woods. "Cubby, I don't want anything to happen to you. I may not be able to love you the way you'd like, but I do care about you. You're like a little brother to me, and I feel responsible for your being here, caught up in this mess. Wyman's going to know you shouldn't know about this place. He'll suspect something right away."

There was an element of truth in what she said. Wyman was always suspicious, but Cubby couldn't let Lacy discredit his abilities. "I can just tell him that my pa decided I needed to know—that I needed to tell him to come back to the saloon. If I tell him something important has happened, and that he's not to hurt Dave, then maybe he'll leave."

"It's too much of a risk. Just go get Hank and Nick, and then we can—"

"Maybe I should just go home," Cubby interrupted. "You think me so incapable."

"That's not what I said, but you . . . well . . ." Lacy seemed to be considering her words carefully.

"I've had enough. You can take care of this matter yourself."

Cubby felt guilty for leaving Lacy, but he couldn't bear that she saw him as a child. He was a man—same as Dave Shepard. He'd come to accept that she didn't love him, but the fact that she couldn't see him for who he was left Cubby frustrated.

Fine. Let her figure it all out for herself.

"And that's why I need you to forgive me," Adam told Gwen and Beth.

Beth looked at her sister as if to confirm she'd really heard right. Gwen shook her head and centered her gaze on Adam. "Why do you believe you killed our father?"

"I already told you. I was there, firin' off my gun. I suppose I can't be sure, but I can't help but think God's kept it on my conscience all this time because it was my bullet that killed him."

"Maybe he's just babbling because of the head wound," Beth said. Then reaching for his forehead, she added, "Or maybe he has a fever."

"I'm not babbling. I told your sister Lacy the same thing. I was trying to find the deputy to tell him first, and that's why Lacy found me at his house."

Across the hall, Beth could hear one of the stage travelers retiring to his room. There had only been three passengers and the driver, which had been a relief to both sisters. With Adam's wound and the situation with Lacy and Dave, Beth had difficulty focusing on anything else. She and Gwen were so preoccupied with their sister's safety that they'd barely been able to act as proper hostesses. Thankfully, the babies had fallen asleep early.

Gwen took hold of the young man's hand. "Of course we can forgive you for any guilt, real or imagined."

Beth nodded. "Yes. You certainly didn't mean to kill Pa, and it appears you've definitely learned your lesson."

"I have. I'm ready to face my punishment, too. If I have to hang for my offense, I will. I'm willing to die for what I've done."

"Well, I'm not willing for you to die," Beth said.

"Me neither. You made a mistake, and if you are correct and your bullet took our father's life, then it was a costly mistake, indeed. But, Adam, you never set out to kill him. It wasn't murder. It was an accident."

Adam seemed to relax a bit. "Miss Lacy told me the same thing."

Gwen and Beth exchanged a look. "If Lacy told you that, then you are truly forgiven. She's been the one who has demanded justice for our father's death. If Lacy is willing to let it go, then you must realize that the matter is closed."

The young man sighed a long breath of relief. "I can die in peace, then."

"Not here, you can't," Beth said. "We don't have time for a funeral. If I catch you trying to die on us . . . well, just be forewarned, I won't go easy on you."

Adam grinned. "You know, the local hands are always talking about how feisty you Gallatin gals can be. I guess they're right."

Gwen laughed out loud and got to her feet. "Adam, you don't know the half of it."

Later, as the sisters worked to clean up after the evening meal, Beth couldn't help but reflect on Adam's confession and Rafe's suicide. "You know, it took a great deal of courage for Adam to take responsibility for Pa's death."

Gwen finished putting away a stack of plates. "I know. I was thinking the same thing."

"It's hard to be honest and face up to the wrong you've done. I mean, look at Rafe. He obviously couldn't deal with his sins, or he wouldn't have killed himself. It's like Judas in the Bible."

"Or he was just purely selfish," Gwen countered. "I keep thinking of poor Cubby. Rafe obviously never gave his feelings a single thought."

"What do you suppose he'll do now?" Beth wondered aloud.

"Hank has been talking about taking him with us when we move. I guess that will be a real possibility now. The biggest obstacle we saw was Rafe, and now . . ." She left the rest unsaid.

"What will happen to the girls? We've long wanted to see an end to the prostitution at Rafe's place, but what will they do now? They have no money of their own and no place to go. Most don't even have families."

"I hadn't really thought of that," Gwen said, "but you're right. Seems there ought to be something we could do."

"I was thinking maybe we could gather them over here and discuss the situation. We could give them each a few dollars and let them decide what they want to do. Maybe we could find some way to take them north with us, as well."

"We can't save everyone," Gwen countered. She went to the stove and checked the coffeepot.

"I know we can't save everyone, but we also can't turn our backs on them. With Rafe dead, I don't know what the legalities are. I would guess Cubby would own his property, though. We could talk to Cubby about selling out. Maybe Mr. Mulholland would buy the place."

In an odd coincidence the man appeared at the kitchen entryway, as if they had summoned him by their discussion. "I hope I'm not interrupting. One of the stage passengers was returning from a walk, and I thought to simply follow him in. I heard you two talking."

Beth startled and nearly dropped the coffee cup she'd been drying. "What . . . what do you want?"

He smiled in his charming manner. "I came to inquire as to what was going on at the saloon. There seems to be no one around. There are no lights, and the place is locked up tighter than a bank on Sunday."

Beth looked to Gwen, realizing that Mulholland didn't know about Rafe. Gwen took charge and came to where he stood.

"Would you like to sit down and have a cup of coffee? I'm afraid I have some bad news."

Mulholland frowned and his brown eyes narrowed. "No, thank you. Tell me what's going on."

His tone was brusque, and Gwen licked her lips as if stalling for time. "There's been . . . well . . . I'm afraid something has happened. Rafe . . . he. . . ." She looked at Beth, unable to finish her sentence.

"He's dead," Beth said, stepping forward.

Mulholland's expression changed from one of suspicion

to shock. He looked at Beth as if she'd suddenly pulled a gun on him. She stepped forward and apologized. "I'm so sorry to be so blunt."

"What happened?"

"He shot himself. He didn't leave a note or say anything to anyone that would suggest he meant to die," Gwen replied.

"Then how do you know he did the deed? Maybe one of his customers—or one of the women—lost their temper with him." Mulholland shook his head. "This is impossible."

"I'm so sorry, Mr. Mulholland. I know he was your friend," Gwen continued. "Apparently, there were things that Rafe couldn't bear. The doctor tended him. He said it was clearly . . . suicide." She practically whispered the word.

Beth shuddered. "He's never been a very happy person." She knew the comment sounded lame but felt it somehow justified the situation.

"Where's Cubby?" Mulholland asked.

"Uh, he was on an errand for Hank," Gwen replied. "He's not come back yet. He doesn't know."

Jefferson Mulholland considered this news for a moment. He brushed back his reddish brown hair with one hand while reaching into his vest pocket with the other. He pulled out his pocket watch. "It's nearly nine. It'll be dark soon. My things are in one of the back rooms at the saloon."

"Marie is there cleaning up. She can let you in. The doctor suggested she keep everyone out until the sheriff arrives to look things over. But since you've been staying there, it shouldn't be a problem."

"The sheriff is coming?" Mulholland asked, sounding more disturbed than when Beth had shared the news of Rafe's death. "But why?"

"Because a man is dead," Gwen answered quickly. "Now, if you'll excuse us, Mr. Mulholland, we need to finish our work here. The stage will pull out quite early, and we need to get our sleep."

He nodded and gave a slight bow. "Thank you for your help, ladies. If one must hear bad news, it is always easier to receive it from such kind souls."

Beth waited until he was gone before turning to Gwen. "What if he's caught up in all of this? What if he has something to do with Dave being taken and the plan to kill him? What if he somehow threatened Rafe and left him without hope to go on? Maybe he's responsible for Rafe's killing himself."

"We can't let our imaginations run wild. Look, I think I'm going to go talk to Ralph. He's been driving stages long enough that we know him well. I feel nervous enough about Hank and the others being out there, but if Mulholland gets it in his mind to come back, I want a man to deal with him." Gwen headed for the stairs.

Beth thought back to when she'd been caught up in one romantic adventure novel after another. In those books, men were always facing death and their ladies fair were always in some kind of jeopardy. Funny, she'd always thought she'd welcome such things into the boredom of her life at Gallatin House. *Goodness, but I was quite a silly goose.*

She went to the cupboard and pulled over a small stool Nick had made for her. Stepping up, she reached for the highest shelf and what they'd hidden there. Pulling the revolver from its hiding place, Beth checked to make sure it was loaded. It was.

Clenching her teeth so tightly her jaw ached, Beth stepped down and slipped the gun into her apron pocket. She didn't know if she could use it when the time came, but she felt better just knowing they would have some recourse.

"I may be silly," she murmured, "but I'm not stupid."

"Any sign of Cubby or Lacy?" Hank asked as Nick eased back through the brush.

"No. There's some light coming from the cabin, though, and Dave's horse is in the corral. I don't know how many people are inside, but some riders just came in. Might be the same ones who took out earlier—the ones following Mulholland."

Hank nodded. "What do you think we should do?"

"I don't know. If I knew where the others were, I'd feel better. I don't know if Wyman has them or if they're out here in the woods somewhere."

At the sound of shouting, Nick and Hank made their way to the edge of the trees nearest the corral, where several men seemed to be in a heated argument. Wyman Jenkins appeared to be at the center of it.

"Why didn't you do like I ordered?"

"I'm telling you, there was no way to get a clean shot. Mulholland was already well down the trail, and when we caught up with him, there were too many witnesses around to just kill him."

"I sent you boys out to do a simple job. You couldn't even kill one man?" He swore a steady stream of obscenities, then turned to head back to the shack. "I've had all I'm gonna take from you. I'm gonna kill Shepard, and then we'll go deal with Mulholland. Seems like I've always got to do everything myself."

"Wait, boss. There's more."

Wyman turned and headed back to the men. "It better be worth my time, or I'm gonna kill you, too."

CHAPTER TWENTY-SEVEN

As soon as Lacy saw Wyman head for the corral, she knew she had to make her move. She pressed through the brush, wincing as the branches clawed at her face. Tripping over tree roots, Lacy righted herself and steadied her nerves. She couldn't help but wonder if Cubby was still somewhere near. She wished he would have stayed to help but at the same time was just as glad he'd gone. The last thing she wanted on her conscience was that boy's injury or death.

The darkness swallowed her up as Lacy made her way to the clearing just behind the cabin. She prayed that no one would see her movements or come to investigate her noisy steps. Hurrying to the back of the structure, she took out her knife and cut away the oilcloth that covered the only window. The ripping sound seemed to echo in the air, and Lacy grimaced. Despite the volume of the men arguing from the front, she couldn't help but worry that they might somehow hear her actions.

Her hands trembled as she replaced the knife in her boot. Fear gripped her like nothing she'd ever known. She had to make this work. She had to reach Dave and save him. If she couldn't do this simple thing, she didn't even want to live. The thought of going on without Dave filled her with anguish. This had to work.

She thought of the verse from Isaiah that Dave had once shared with her. Lacy had never told him how much it meant to her. She'd cherished it so much, in fact, that she'd memorized it to give her strength for just such times. *Fear thou not; for I am with thee: be not dismayed; for I am thy God: I will strengthen thee; yea, I will help thee; yea, I will uphold thee with the right hand of my righteousness.*

Lacy glance heavenward. "I'm trying, Lord."

She looked into the house cautiously and realized this was a small bedroom. It was dark, except for the light that filtered in from the open door to the rest of the cabin. Lacy climbed into the room and crouched down beside the bed. She listened for the sound of Wyman returning but heard nothing except a strange scraping sound.

Edging toward the door, Lacy held her rifle ready for action. She peered into the room and immediately saw Dave, struggling against his bonds. Relief washed over her. She could see well enough by the light of the two lanterns to see that he was bloodied and battered, but he was alive. She threw caution to the wind and hurried into the room. Rushing to his side, she smiled at his look of amazement. She fought back tears as she saw just how much damage had been inflicted on him.

Don't think about his pain, Lacy. You have to set him free. Think only about getting him out of here.

"You seem to always get yourself into these awkward messes, Deputy Shepard." She shifted the rifle, then bent and pulled the knife from her boot. Sawing at the ropes, she continued, "You look awful."

"You need to get out of here. Wyman will be back any minute."

"Let him come. Let them all come. I have plenty of bullets for everyone."

Dave seemed to choke a bit, and Lacy wasn't sure if it was laughter or a cry that caused such a sound. "Get out, Lacy."

"No, we can argue about how unladylike this is later," she said, frustrated that the rope didn't cut easier. "I love you."

"Well, it took you long enough to figure it out."

She shrugged as the last bit of rope gave way. "Sometimes a girl has to be careful."

He smiled, but it only served to cause his split lip to start bleeding. As she began to wipe away the blood, the door flew open with a resounding bang. Wyman stalked in, muttering. He stopped midstep, however, when he caught sight of Lacy. For a moment he seemed too surprised to move. This gave Lacy time to reposition her rifle, but Wyman wasn't deterred. He pulled out his revolver nearly as fast.

"So you've come to die with your fiancé?"

"No," Lacy countered. "I've come to free him. You need to put down your gun, Wyman."

He laughed. "Or what? You gonna shoot me, little girl?" He sneered and took a step forward.

Lacy felt Dave stiffen at her side. She longed to pass him the rifle but knew there wasn't time. "I'll do what I have to do, Wyman. You know me well enough to understand that much."

"You know, that's the trouble with you Gallatins. You just don't know when to leave well enough alone. Still, I don't think you got it in you to kill."

"Unlike you, Wyman," Dave interjected. "You've killed plenty and seem quite proud of it. Why don't you tell Lacy about how you killed her father?"

Lacy looked at Dave for a moment, then quickly returned her focus to Wyman. She felt her grip tighten on the rifle. "You?"

His dark eyes narrowed as he smiled. "I s'pose there's no harm in admittin' it. After all, you're both gonna die."

Lacy thought of poor Adam, bearing the guilt of killing a man by accident, when all the time it had been Wyman's doing. What if she had chosen not to forgive Adam? *I could have told him he didn't deserve forgiveness—then let him die.* The very thought pierced her to the core.

"So now you know. I killed your pa." He laughed. "It wasn't like it was all that hard to do." He seemed almost pleased to share this with her.

Lacy shook away her confused jumble of thoughts. "Why?" She couldn't say another word. This was the murdering fiend who'd killed her father. This was the man she'd searched to find for over two years, while everyone around her condemned her for believing the death to be more than an accident.

"Why? Because I was paid to do it. Rafe wanted to buy your pa out, and he wouldn't budge." Wyman motioned at her with the gun. "Now put that rifle down, or I'll put a bullet in the good deputy's head. You might shoot me if you have the courage to actually pull the trigger, but I'll kill him first." His face contorted and took on an expression of pure evil. "And I'll enjoy every minute of watchin' him die."

Lacy frowned. She'd never considered this possibility. The rifle grew heavy in her hands.

"Don't listen to him, Lacy. He'll kill us both anyway. At least this way, you have a chance."

"He's wrong about that. My boys are back, and as soon as they hear this ruckus, they'll come running." Wyman cocked back the hammer. "Time to die, Deputy."

Lacy couldn't bear it. She threw herself between Dave and Wyman just as the sound of a shot fired. Lacy waited for a burning pain but felt nothing but Dave's hands holding tight to her arms. He pulled her against him.

Oh, God, she prayed, *please don't let him die. Don't let Dave be hit.*

He breathed her name almost mournfully. "Don't die, Lacy." He held her with more strength than she'd imagined him capable of in his injured state.

She pushed against him and straightened. "I'm not hurt. Are you?"

They turned to see Wyman fall to his knees. He looked at Lacy with dark, lifeless eyes and crumpled to the ground. To her surprise, Cubby entered the door, his revolver still aimed at the dead man.

His expression was pained. "I told you I could take care of him," he whispered. Cubby looked back at Wyman's body. "He's dead, isn't he?"

Dave assisted Lacy to her feet then stood. "He is, thanks to you."

Cubby blew out a breath and looked at his gun as if seeing it there in his hands for the first time. "Guess I'll be going to prison for murder." He looked at the revolver for a moment more, then handed it toward Dave.

"Hardly," Dave said, wincing. "You saved our lives. Keep your gun. You're a hero."

This seemed to surprise Cubby. He looked to Lacy. "I know how you feel about me—how you can't love me—but I just want you to know . . . I did this for you." He slowly put the revolver back in his holster.

Lacy went to him and took hold of his hand. Drawing it to her cheek, she smiled. "I know you did, and I thank you from the bottom of my heart."

"Is everyone all right in here?" Hank asked. Nick followed him into the room.

"We're all in one piece—except for Wyman," Dave said, kneeling beside the dead man. "Cubby saved Lacy and me."

"We saw. We were at the corral tying up the others."

"You got them all, then?" Dave asked.

Nick gave a nod of satisfaction. "Yeah. They're not going anywhere."

Lacy stepped away from Cubby and watched as Dave checked for any sign of life in Wyman. It was clear the man was gone, but Dave was doing his duty.

Hank came to Lacy and took hold of her. "Are you hurt?"

"No. Tired. And I was pretty scared, but I guess that has passed."

Chuckling, Hank pulled her into an embrace and kissed the top of her head. "You ought to be terrified still. Your sisters are going to have plenty to say about this escapade. You'll be lucky if they let you out of your room for a month."

Lacy pulled away. "They know about all this?"

"Most of it, anyway."

She rolled her eyes and shook her head. "Maybe I should just get on my horse and keep riding."

The men laughed, but it was Nick who took hold of Lacy's arm. "Oh no. You are going back to face the music. That way, we won't have to. With Beth and Gwen focused on their little sister, we men can slip off to bed and get a good night's sleep." He pulled her into his arms, then threw her over his shoulder. "Hank, we'd better tie her up, too."

Lacy looked over Nick's back at Dave. "Are you just going to let them take me away?"

Just a hint of a smile lingered on Dave's face. "Only until I recover from this beating. I'm too tired and sore to hunt you down."

After Marie let him in the saloon, Mulholland poured himself a drink and considered the turn of events. He was glad Marie had left him alone. He needed time to think without her tears and questions. With Rafe out of the picture, he could take over Gallatin Crossing. Wyman wouldn't be any problem. He'd see to that. He already had it figured how he would pin Wyman with Dave Shepard's death. The men who worked for Rafe could easily be paid off to testify against Wyman. Mulholland would offer them enough money to swear the entire thing was Wyman and Rafe's plan.

Smiling, Jefferson Mulholland began to plan for the future. He and Rafe had made a small fortune swindling the good folks of Gallatin Crossing. The Gallatin gals and their men would be out of his hair by September, and the entire place would be left in his care. But then another thought came to mind. What if Big John had already talked to the authorities? What if he'd incriminated Jefferson in all that had taken place? After all, he knew about the fake gold rush. What else did he know?

Mulholland toyed with his glass. That could prove to be a worrisome problem. Wyman might not be able to get Dave Shepard to talk—or if he talked, he might not be completely honest. He thought about this for several minutes. The only way to ensure his safety was to move on. Pity, when there was such a great opportunity right here.

"But I can't take a chance," he said aloud. He put the glass aside and got to his feet. He would have to pack quickly and leave. He wasn't at all sure where he should go, however. He could ride his horse south, maybe go to Virginia City and farther on to catch the train to California. His brother had often talked of how they should venture west.

Heading to his room, Jefferson was surprised when Marie stepped out of the shadows. "Where are you going?" she asked.

He gave a shrug. "I figure with Rafe gone, there's nothing to hold me here."

"I thought you were his friend."

"I was."

She put her hands on her hips. "So you'll leave, just like that. You won't even wait for his burial?"

Jefferson laughed and pushed her aside. He went into his small room and took the saddlebags from under the bed. Tossing them atop the quilt, he opened them and turned to the small dresser. "Rafe was never one for standing on ceremony," he told Marie, who was now standing in the doorway. "He's not going to care whether I'm there or not. All that mattered to Rafe was whether a person was there for him in life."

"But what about his boy? What about us?"

He looked at her oddly. "What about you?"

"What's going to happen to the business?"

Shrugging, Jefferson threw all of his worldly goods into the saddlebags. "How should I know? I tried to get Rafe to make me a full partner, but he had no desire to let me in on everything. Said he needed to keep some things private." Mulholland laughed. "Guess they're good and private now. By law, I suppose Cubby will inherit Rafe's properties. Unless Rafe had some other agreement—maybe sold Wyman a percentage of the place. Hard to say."

"But that doesn't help me at all." Marie's expression was one of pure confusion. "I still don't know what's to become of me."

Mulholland had no time or patience for the woman's concerns. "You're just another piece of property, as far as I'm concerned, Marie. You'll probably be sold with the place."

She spit, and it barely missed Jefferson's highly polished shoes. He narrowed his eyes. "I'd be careful if I were you."

"You don't care about Rafe. You never did. You just used him."

"We used each other mutually." Mulholland crossed to the far side of the room and knelt. Marie watched as he pried open a floorboard and took out several bags. "Makes a pretty good vault, wouldn't you say?"

"Is that Rafe's money?"

"No. This is mine, fair and square. We divided it up. I have no idea where Rafe kept his fortune, nor do I care."

"You're a heartless man." A tear spilled down her cheek.

Jefferson shoved his bags of money into the saddlebags and buckled the straps. He turned to face Marie. "That I am."

CHAPTER TWENTY-EIGHT

"Well, that takes care of Wyman," Nick said as he secured the body to a horse. Hank and Nick had already tied the other outlaws to their horses. "Dave, we'll help you get this bunch back to Gallatin House so you can figure out what's to be done. The girls were going to send for the sheriff, so hopefully he'll be there by now."

"I'll help, too," Cubby declared, adjusting a lantern.

Dave nodded and licked his swollen lips. "I appreciate all of the help tonight. It sure looked grim there for a time." He put his arm around Lacy and pulled her close. "Cubby, you definitely earned your spurs."

"We didn't have nothin' to do with wantin' you dead, Deputy Shepard," one of Wyman's men called out. They were all tied securely to their horses and each horse had been tied to the other, with Hank in charge of them all.

"You shouldn't have allowed yourself to be caught up in this," Nick told the man.

"Wyman sent us to kill Mulholland, and we didn't do it," one of the other men said. "Doesn't that count for good behavior?"

"You'll have to take it up with the judge," Dave replied. "But I think if you boys will cooperate and testify against Rafe and Mulholland, it could go better for you."

"Ain't no need to testify against Rafe—he's dead," the first man declared.

Cubby turned on his heel, nearly dropping the lantern. "What?"

Hank came alongside him and put his arm around the boy's shoulders. "We didn't have a chance to tell you, but it seems your father . . . well . . . he shot himself. The men here were telling me that when they rode back after Mulholland, they arrived in time to see something of a ruckus going on at the saloon. Marie told them Rafe had taken his life."

The glow of lantern light revealed Cubby's stunned expression. "My pa is dead?"

Lacy pulled away from Dave and came to stand beside Cubby. She gently took hold of his arm. "I'm so sorry."

The boy shook his head back and forth. "But why? Why would he have done such a thing? He had all these plans—he told me so."

Dave rubbed his tender face. "Maybe your father realized that his bad deeds were about to be exposed. He might have feared prison would be worse than death—or that because he hired George Gallatin killed, he'd face the gallows anyway. Some men don't like other folks having control of their life."

Cubby drew a deep breath. "Pa never wanted them to kill you, Dave. I heard him arguing with Wyman and Mulholland. They said it was the only way, but Pa wasn't happy about it. They gave him a real bad time about it."

Dave felt sorry for the boy. "I believe you." He didn't bother to comment on the fact that Rafe did nothing to stop the others from trying to do him in. It would only hurt Cubby, and in time, he'd probably reason it through for himself.

"It might seem like poor timing," Hank began, "but we'd like you to come stay with us for as long as you like, Cubby. Gwen and I've been talking about asking you to come north with us, but we weren't sure your father would allow it. We'd like to give you an opportunity to start fresh—go to school if you like."

"So I wouldn't have to stay at the saloon tonight?" Cubby asked, as if not understanding the full impact of Hank's comment.

Lacy patted his arm, and Dave's heart swelled at her gentleness. "You don't ever have to stay there again if you don't want to. Come home with us and rest. It's been a hard night for everyone."

Dave watched as Cubby nodded, then went to mount his horse. He set out ahead of the others, and they let him go. No doubt he needed some time to think about all that had happened. Dave knew it couldn't be easy for him to face having killed a man, even if that man was a ruthless no-good like Wyman Jenkins. Added to that was the loss of his father. Cubby would do a lot of growing up tonight.

Hank and Nick led Wyman's men out and followed after

Cubby, leaving Dave and Lacy behind to bring Wyman. Dave reached out and touched Lacy's wild hair. Somewhere along the way, the mass of cinnamon waves had come loose, spilling around her shoulders.

"I love your hair." It seemed a silly thing to say, but Dave couldn't help himself.

Lacy smiled. "You sound terrible. Your lips are so swollen that your words come out in a cross between slurs and growls. I think we'd better get you back to Gallatin House, where you can have a nice long soak in the hot springs and put some ice to your face."

Dave pulled her close. "My lips aren't so swollen that I can't kiss you."

"Oh no, you don't," Lacy said, pushing him back. "You let Nick haul me off like a sack of potatoes. It'll be a while before you get any kisses."

He grinned. "We'll see about that."

Her expression grew serious. "Dave, before we join the others, I have to say how sorry I am that we didn't marry sooner. I feel like a fool now for having kept you waiting."

"I don't. I wanted you to be sure. You were right. Just because we felt a physical attraction—"

"A *strong* physical attraction," she amended.

He laughed, and spikes of pain rushed across his face. "All right, a strong physical attraction. Either way, it wasn't enough to make a marriage. I . . . well . . . I needed for you to want to be my wife in every way. Through the good and bad."

Lacy wrapped her arms around his waist, and Dave couldn't suppress a groan. She pulled back in alarm and looked at him questioningly.

"I might have a few busted ribs."

"How do you intend to sit a horse? You should have said something sooner."

"Come on. It doesn't change anything. I'll be in as much pain whether I ride, walk, or sit." He led her to her horse. "I sure hope you won't be given to seeking out this much danger and excitement in the future."

Lacy climbed into the saddle and looked down at him. She grinned. "I have it on the best authority that I am to become an old rancher's wife. Boring, predictable, and oh . . . ladylike. If I can learn how."

Dave chuckled and gave her leg a pat. "Lacy, you will never be boring or predictable. I'd almost wager on that. As for lady-like—well, honey, you're doing just fine in that area, too."

She threw him an enticing grin. "Come along. I have a wedding to plan, and I've put it off for much too long."

Jefferson Mulholland gathered his things and headed for the entrance of the saloon. To his surprise, however, the sheriff and several men stood just outside the door.

"Mr. Mulholland?" the sheriff questioned.

"Yes." He tried not to appear surprised or concerned. "I'm sorry, gentlemen, but the bar is closed. My dear friend Rafe Reynolds ended his life earlier. We're in mourning."

"We know all about it," the sheriff countered. "Mr. Mulholland, I'd like to ask you some questions."

"By all means." Jefferson stepped back and put his saddle-bags aside. He said nothing more as the sheriff and five rather large men entered the establishment, watching him intently. He would have to give the performance of his life to get out of this unscathed. He couldn't exactly say why, but he had the strangest sense of being trapped.

Once all of the men had gathered, Mulholland motioned toward the nearest table. "Won't you have a seat?"

The sheriff shook his head. "What do you know about Dave Shepard's disappearance?"

"Nothing, really," Mulholland replied. "I was asked if I'd seen him, but frankly, I've been far too caught up in the death of my friend. Even now, I was preparing to go to Bozeman to arrange for his funeral."

"Were you, now," the sheriff stated more than asked.

He continued with his game. "I believe Rafe Reynolds was a man worthy of a decent burial, whether anyone else feels that way or not. His son hasn't even been told of his death, at least not to my knowledge. I haven't seen the boy all day." He paused and pretended to have a great thought. "Isn't it possible that Dave and Cubby might be together? I thought them to be good friends."

"So you're telling me that you know nothing about Dave's whereabouts?" the sheriff countered.

Jefferson folded his arms against his chest. "No. I really couldn't say where anyone has taken themselves. I've been too consumed in my grief."

"What do you know about the murder of Jonathan Webster, otherwise known as Big John?"

Mulholland shrugged. "Nothing. Should I know something?"

"You did know the man, didn't you?"

"I believe there was a man going by that name who frequented Rafe's Saloon, but otherwise, no. We weren't associates." An uneasiness came over him. What was the sheriff really trying to learn? Had they come at the behest of the Gallatins to aid in searching for Dave Shepard, or were they here for an entirely different reason? Jefferson wasn't about to stand by and be taken if he could fight his way out. He moved back toward his things.

"If you'll excuse me, gentlemen, I need to be on my way."

The sheriff stepped toward him. "Why not wait until morning, Mulholland?"

Catching sight of movement behind the sheriff, Jefferson was only too aware of the deputies reaching for their revolvers. "I don't understand what this is about."

"Well, it's like this: I have a signed statement that suggests you were responsible for a great many problems in this community," the sheriff started. "Not only that, but until we locate Deputy Shepard, I'm going to hold you on suspicion of his disappearance, as well."

"I've done nothing to merit this action," Jefferson said, moving a few steps closer to his things. If he could get to his saddlebags, he might be able to retrieve his derringer.

"You need to stop right where you are. These boys are gonna take you into custody."

Two of the deputies moved toward him. Jefferson thought to make a dash for his gun but instead stood in wait. "You have the wrong man, Sheriff. I assure you I know nothing about Dave Shepard."

"That's funny," a bruised and bloodied Dave said as he stepped into the dimly lit saloon. "I distinctly recall that you instructed Wyman Jenkins to kill me. It couldn't have been more than a couple of hours ago."

Jefferson couldn't contain his surprise. He fought to keep

a cool exterior, but it was like watching a ghost rise from the grave. Wyman should have killed Shepard by then.

"Dave! You look like you tangled with a wildcat," the sheriff said. "What in the world happened to you?"

"It seems our Mr. Mulholland conspired with Rafe and Wyman to see me dead. I have witnesses, in the form of prisoners, just outside the door. You'll want to talk to them, but they'll confirm that Mulholland also worked with Wyman to see to the death of Big John."

"What about Wyman?" the sheriff asked.

"He's dead," Dave replied. "When he tried to kill Lacy and me, Cubby shot him and saved our lives. Body is outside, tied to the back of a horse."

Jefferson glanced to one side. If he left his things, he might be able to reach the back door. He could push the sheriff aside and send him into the path of the deputies. Then no one could even attempt to shoot at him without the risk of hitting their boss.

"I wouldn't, Mulholland," Dave said, coming closer. "I can almost read your mind. You think you're gonna get out of this, but you're not. You've caused enough trouble to last a lifetime, which is probably what your crimes are going to cost you."

Narrowing his eyes, Mulholland fought back his rage. "I've done nothing wrong. I don't care how many people you have to speak against me. I'm innocent."

"Hardly. I think we've got a pretty solid case against you, what with Big John's confession to the judge and the willingness of the men outside to turn over evidence to see you found guilty."

Dave turned to the sheriff as the two deputies moved to take hold of Jefferson. "There's a couple of decent storage rooms inside the addition at Gallatin House. We can put him in one room and the others in the second. Post a couple of men at each door and they should be secure until morning."

The sheriff nodded. "Sounds good to me."

Lacy allowed Nick to take her horse, along with the others, back to the corral. She wanted to see what was happening at the saloon but knew it was probably just as well that she let Dave do his job.

Coming up the steps to Gallatin House, she was surprised to find Cubby sitting on the porch. The shadowy darkness kept her from seeing his face, but she knew it was him.

"Are you all right?" she asked.

Cubby said nothing for a few moments. He got to his feet and went to the rail. "I guess so. It seems so strange to realize my father is dead. I never thought about Pa dying before."

"I know. I never thought about my pa dying, either."

He turned to her, and the soft glow from the front room window gave her just enough light to discern the outline of his face. "I can't tell you how sorry I am that my pa was responsible, Lacy. I knew he had something to do with it. I have known for a while now; I just couldn't prove it and didn't know exactly what it was."

"I know."

"I wanted to help you. I wanted to make you love me and see me as a man who was strong enough to take care of you."

Lacy nodded. "You are an incredible man, Quennell." She hoped that by using his given name, he might understand that she truly saw him as grown up.

"You don't have to call me that." He turned back to the porch railing and leaned out to look above to the skies. "Hank helped me to see that a name wasn't going to make me a man—only my actions would do that."

"And you more than proved yourself tonight." She put her hand on his arm. "Cubby, my inability to fall in love with you had nothing to do with you. It had everything to do with the fact that I was already in love. I just didn't know it."

"How could you not? Love is such a powerful thing. I couldn't stop thinking about you. If you were really in love with Dave Shepard, how could you not know it?"

Lacy laughed softly. "I've been asking myself that, too. I think my crusade to find Pa's killer tainted everything else in me. It wouldn't let me consider any other feeling except revenge." She paused and sighed. "I certainly never meant to hurt you."

He said nothing for several moments. "Hank asked me to come live with them."

"I know. I think it's a good idea."

Cubby nodded. "He wants to help me get some schooling."

"You have a quick mind, Cubby. An education would be a marvelous thing. Think of all you could do with a little more book learning."

Pushing back from the porch rail, he walked to the bench where he'd been sitting. "I don't know. What if I'm no good at it? I haven't been to school in a long time."

"Cubby, I know without a doubt that you will accomplish anything you set your mind to. Just like tonight."

"I never wanted to kill anyone."

Lacy came to sit beside him. "I know. But you saved our

lives, and I'm so very grateful. Wyman really didn't give any of us a choice."

"Pa was just . . . well . . . he was a bad person." Cubby's voice broke, and Lacy slipped her arm around his shoulder as he fought to continue talking. "He . . . and Wyman . . . they didn't care about folks. He didn't care . . . about me." He shook as an uncontrolled sob consumed him.

Lacy pulled him against her and let him cry. "Some people are damaged so much they don't know how to care for folks or to love. I think your pa loved you, or you wouldn't still have been with him. You know as well as I do that he was perfectly able to get rid of anyone he didn't want to be bothered with."

Cubby stilled and then straightened. "You're right." He sniffed back tears but didn't even attempt to move away from Lacy. "He could have gotten rid of me."

"He could have, but he didn't. I think he loved you, Cubby. I just think he didn't know how to show it."

"Pa never told me he loved me. Not even once."

"I'm really sorry about that. It makes me sadder than I can say."

A gentle breeze blew across them, chilling Lacy. She didn't move, however. It seemed important to stay right where she was. Cubby needed to talk, and he needed to know that someone cared enough to listen.

"I was so afraid tonight—afraid that you'd get hurt," Cubby admitted. "I'm glad you didn't. When I saw Wyman pointing that gun at you, I couldn't think of anything but to keep him from killing you."

"It was truly a selfless act, Cubby."

"So was throwing yourself in front of Dave. I guess that's when I knew how much you really loved him."

"Lacy? Is that you?"

Cubby pulled away at the sound of the door opening. It was Beth. Lacy got to her feet. "Yes, it's me."

"She's here!" Beth called over her shoulder. "Get in here. You've worried us half to death. Are you all right? Are you hurt?" She came out to the porch and half dragged Lacy into the house.

Squinting, Lacy could see Gwen's worried expression as Beth pushed her forward. "Lacy, we were so scared."

"I'm no worse for the wear," Lacy assured them. She looked back to see if Cubby had followed her into the house. He hadn't. "Things got pretty ugly, and Dave was beaten within an inch of his life. But we're both safe now. Thanks to Hank and Nick, but especially to Cubby."

"Cubby?" Gwen asked. "Is he all right, too? Have you heard that Rafe is dead?"

Lacy nodded solemnly. "Yes. Cubby knows, too."

CHAPTER TWENTY-NINE

OCTOBER 1, 1881, SHEPARD RANCH

Cubby shifted nervously. "I don't much care for dressing up. Don't know why I have to be in the wedding, anyway."

Hank laughed and tossed him a hat. "Sometimes dressing up is necessary. Besides, you're the best man."

"I still can't believe Dave actually asked me to stand up with him."

"You saved his life. A man doesn't forget a thing like that. Besides, I think Dave admires the way you've handled yourself these last weeks. You were good to the wagon train folks, seeing to it that they got their money back."

"Didn't seem right to do much else. I know it's not what Pa would have done, but I'm not my pa."

Hank smiled. "No. You aren't. You're a good, upstanding young man, even if you don't like dressing up."

Cubby pulled at the neck of his shirt. "This collar is too tight."

Laughing, Hank helped Cubby into his suit coat. "Besides, if you go back East to school, you'll have to get used to it."

"I don't know about that. Seems to me a lot of fuss and nonsense," Cubby admitted. "I like learnin' and all, and you've been a good teacher, but I don't think I want to go away."

"You don't have to if you don't want to," Hank told him. "I just don't want you to make a decision based solely on hating to dress up." He brushed a thread off Cubby's shoulder. "There's a lot the world has to offer a smart young man like you. I'd hate to see you pass it up."

Cubby crossed the room to look at himself in the mirror. He pulled on the lapels of the coat and turned first one way and then another. Hank could see he was pleased with the outcome.

"Don't break your neck trying to see yourself," Hank teased.

"I just can't believe it's me," Cubby said. "I haven't ever been this gussied up."

A knock sounded on the door, and Hank opened it to admit Nick and Justin. They both looked equally uncomfortable in their Sunday best.

"Beth and Gwen are fussing over Lacy. You can hear them clear at the other end of the hall. I'm afraid if they don't calm down, there's going to be a fight between the Gallatin girls," Nick declared.

"What are they fussing about?" Hank asked, certain he'd be sorry to even know.

"Well, as best I could tell," Nick began, "Lacy just wanted to leave her hair down, and Beth insisted she had to pin it up. Then Gwen got in on the conversation and said it should be fixed a certain way. Then, just when that whole thing started to calm down, the issue of some gloves came up. That's when Justin and I decided it would be best to stay as far away as possible."

"What about the gloves?" Cubby aked.

Nick shrugged. "I don't know. Seems Gwen thinks Lacy needs them, but Lacy disagrees."

"They ought to be glad they even got her to wear a wedding gown," Hank said, laughing. "Knowing Lacy, she would have been just as happy to marry in britches."

"Nobody your age wears their hair down," Beth insisted. "Goodness, but you'd think you were still wearing short dresses."

"I wouldn't be wearing dresses at all if I could get away with it, and you know that full well," Lacy protested. "Honestly, I feel like I did when we were little and you two would clean me up for church."

Gwen came forward with a hairbrush. "Well, this has been nearly as difficult. This is your wedding day, Lacy. Don't you want to be beautiful for your groom?"

"I really don't think Dave is going to notice whether I wear gloves or not," Lacy replied with a giggle. "In fact, years from now I'll bet he won't even remember the gown."

"He'd better. We put a lot of work into it," Beth countered.

"And it's lovely." Lacy held out her hand to stop Gwen and

Beth from their fretting. "Both of you just need to calm down. This is a simple family wedding. No one will care whether my hair is up or down."

Gwen and Beth exchanged a look that suggested Lacy had gone quite mad.

"I'll go find the gloves," Beth said. "You fix her hair."

"Where are the hairpins?" Gwen asked, beginning her own search.

"Oh, I think I left them in the other room," Beth replied. "Come. I'll show you where."

Lacy stood in bewildered amazement. It was as if she weren't even in the room. Her sisters were determined to continue with their primping as if she had no say in the matter whatsoever.

"Well, they can't fuss over me if I'm not here," she stated.

Lacy made a mad dash out of the bedroom and down the back stairs. The Shepards' ranch had been busy all day in preparation for the wedding, and Lacy was relieved to see that no one was working in the kitchen when she made her escape.

Exiting out the back door, she gathered her wedding silk in hand and ran at full speed across the barnyard. She wasn't sure what she was doing or where she was going, but Lacy knew one thing—she had to get away from her sisters and their demanding ways.

She hurried into the barn and closed the door behind her. Light shone in from the other open end, but at least she couldn't be seen by anyone in the yard or house. Breathing a sigh of relief, she let the silk gown fall into place and prayed it wouldn't get too dirty. She was really quite fond of the gown—impressed by the way it made her look all grown up, with its bustled skirt and lace-edged bodice. Her sisters had copied it out of *Harper's Bazaar* and were proud of the way it had come together.

"You aren't running away again, are you?"

She looked up to find Dave stepping out of the shadows. "The thought crossed my mind, but I wouldn't have gone without you."

He stepped forward, and Lacy smiled at the dashing figure he cut in his new suit. He made her heart skip a beat and her knees grow weak. Dave grinned as if reading her mind. "And just where was it you were planning to go?"

"Anywhere my sisters couldn't follow. They're treating me like a doll to be dressed up and played with."

"Well, I have to admit they did a fine job. I've never seen you lookin' more beautiful, unless it was that night in the cabin when you saved my life."

Lacy felt her breath catch in her throat as he continued to advance on her. "Beth wants my hair pinned up one way, and Gwen wants it another. Then Gwen wants me wearing gloves, but Beth misplaced them."

Dave stopped inches away and touched her face. "And what do you want?"

Lacy could barely breathe. "Just you."

He kissed her passionately and pulled her close. Lacy wanted to melt into the floor. Goodness, but this man had some kind of special power over her. She wrapped her arms around his neck and encouraged him to never let go.

"I heard it was bad luck to see each other before the ceremony," Dave whispered, trailing kisses to her earlobe.

"I don't believe in luck—bad or good."

He chuckled low and kissed her neck before pulling away from her. "Well, I think we're going to be in trouble anyway if we don't behave ourselves."

She felt the loss of his arms intensely. "Are you sure we can't just elope?"

"It would break my mother's heart. Then there'd be your sisters to contend with, not to mention Pastor Flikkema. He hurried back from out East just to perform the ceremony." Dave gave her a sultry wink. "Besides, it would take hours to reach another preacher, and I'm not waiting that long to marry you."

"I guess I'd better go back, then, and let them finish me," she said with a sigh.

"I have a better idea," Dave said, reaching out to take hold of her arm. "Let's just march in there and tell them to get on with the ceremony."

Lacy smiled. "Do you mean it?"

"I certainly do. The sooner we get in there, the sooner this will be over."

"Where did she go?" Beth asked, casting a glance around the room.

Gwen shook her head and looked behind the dressing screen. "She's not here. She's gone."

"Obviously if she's not here, she's gone," Beth declared. "Honestly, you are making no sense today."

"I'm making as much sense as you are," Gwen countered. "You're the one who lost the gloves."

"I didn't lose them. I simply misplaced them. Besides, many people marry without gloves." Beth put her hands on her hips and surveyed the room once again. "I guess we'll have to go look for her. You don't suppose she's run away? If she's done that—"

"Who's done what?" Patience asked, entering the room. She held up a pair of gloves. "I found them."

Gwen stepped forward and took the gloves from Patience. "Well, now all we have to do is find the bride."

"What?" The color seemed to drain from the older woman's face. "Lacy's gone?"

"We left her for just a few minutes," Beth said, "and when we came back she wasn't here."

"Maybe she went to the outhouse."

Gwen and Beth looked at Patience in horror and replied in unison, "In her wedding dress?"

"Well, even brides must visit the necessary from time to time," Patience answered. "Or she could have simply gone downstairs to see if things were ready. I didn't see her there, but maybe she was in the kitchen."

Beth went to the window and glanced out. The sky was crystal clear blue, without a hint of clouds, and the landscape was a mottle of golds, greens, and oranges.

"There she is!" Beth called out. "Oh no! She's with Dave!"

"Well, they are getting married," Patience said with a shrug.

"But he's not supposed to see her yet. He's supposed to wait until the ceremony," Beth protested.

Gwen became the voice of reason. "I think we're fortunate she didn't run away. I'm afraid we haven't made things very easy on her."

"If you're gonna be a part of this wedding," Dave bellowed from below, "you'd best come join us now."

Patience's eyes widened. "Oh my! We'd better hurry. He sounds serious."

"But she hasn't fixed her hair," Beth said.

"And she doesn't have her gloves," Gwen said, holding them up.

Patience began to laugh. "I don't think she cares about either one. She's got Dave, and that's really all she came here for."

"I must say this has been the nicest wedding I've attended in a long while," Pastor Flikkema said, polishing off a second piece of cake.

"It was a very nice ceremony," Gwen agreed.

Beth sighed. "And Lacy made such a beautiful bride. She was positively elegant."

"It's probably the last time you'll see her that way," Hank mused.

"Hank, that wasn't kind," Gwen reprimanded.

"Maybe not, but it was true," Nick said with a laugh.

"I thought her perfectly radiant," Beth said dreamily. "She was just like a princess in a story, and Dave made a very handsome prince."

Cubby scratched his neck. "I'm just glad to be out of that suit."

"Me too," Dave announced from the stairs. He had changed into more comfortable clothes, as had Lacy. She now wore a split skirt, cream-colored blouse, and brown riding jacket.

Everyone laughed and got to their feet. "Are you sure you don't want to spend the night at Gallatin House?" Hank asked. "We could make it a most memorable night of song and revelry."

Dave shook his head. "I prefer to make it memorable in other ways."

"Are you sure you don't want to tell us where you're heading?" Hank asked. "That way if something happens, we can find you."

Laughing, Dave shook his head again. "We don't want to be found."

Lacy blushed, and Gwen and Beth only laughed all the more. Jerry Shepard stepped forward and motioned to his son.

"I'd like a word alone with you—outside, if you can spare it."

Dave looked at Lacy and nodded. "I guess a few more minutes won't matter."

Gwen took Lacy by the arm. She had wanted to speak to her younger sister earlier—before the wedding, but Lacy had disappeared and given her no chance. "I want to talk to you, as well."

"Me too," Beth said, following them into the kitchen.

Gwen embraced Lacy as soon as they were away from the others. "I can't tell you how happy I am for you."

Lacy smiled as she glanced from Gwen to Beth and back again. "I'm happier than I've ever been. Thank you for this wonderful day and all that you did to make it so perfect."

"We're going to miss you," Beth said, her eyes welling with tears. "We've never lived apart. Not really. Even before Nick's house burned down, we weren't that far away."

"We still won't be," Lacy assured them. "The ranch is only four miles from town. Besides, I have a feeling we'll all be too busy to even worry about missing one another."

"And we'll see each other at Sunday services," Gwen said, wiping her own wet cheeks.

"You two are being silly. We'll probably see each other all the time. I'll be bringing you eggs, milk, and butter throughout the week," Lacy said, shaking her head.

"It's just that for so long, it was the three of us," Gwen said. "We'd have never made it if not for each other."

Lacy sobered. "I know that, too. It's like God knew we would need each other more than anyone else in the world."

"And He knew we would always work through our differences," Beth said, sniffing back tears.

"It hasn't always been easy," Lacy said, reaching out to Gwen, "but you were a mother to us both, as well as a sister. You sacrificed so much to take care of us. Don't think I don't know it. I might have been the youngest, but I always knew that you were giving more of yourself than you should have had to."

Gwen bit her lip and told herself to be strong. Lacy turned to take hold of Beth with her other hand. "And you taught me the blessing of laughter and seeing the lighter side of even the worst problem. I couldn't have asked for better sisters or friends."

The trio embraced, and Gwen knew that even though things would change forever after this, the three would always remain close. They had been, and would always be, an intricate part of each other's lives.

"You'd better go on now," Gwen said, pulling back. She wiped at her tears again and smiled. "I'm sure Dave is anxious to go."

Lacy nodded and headed for the door. She glanced back

over her shoulder. "Good-bye for now, Mrs. Bishop, Mrs. Lassiter."

They smiled and waved. "Good-bye, Mrs. Shepard."

∽

"I'm going to kill her!" Lacy came bounding out of the bedroom at the small mountain cabin Dave had secured. She held up her nightgown. "Look what Beth has done."

Dave had been busy stoking the fire for the night when Lacy left to change clothes. He turned to see what the problem was.

"Just look at this. She cut it off." Lacy held the damaged gown against her. "Why, it doesn't even reach to the knee!"

Grinning, Dave dusted off his hands and stood. "I like your sister Beth. Did I ever tell you that?"

Lacy's eyes widened. "She ruined a perfectly good nightgown just to play a prank."

Dave shook his head and came to where she stood. He pulled the piece from her hand and tossed it to one side. "If it's ruined, we might as well throw it away." He took her into his arms without giving her a chance to protest. "I'm sure we can get by without it."

Smiling, Lacy met his gaze and began to laugh. "Your mother warned me about you, Mr. Shepard. She said you were ornery. She told me you were her most troublesome child, and she never had a moment's peace when you were young."

"Did she, now?"

Lacy nodded. "She said you were headstrong and used to having your own way."

"What else did she say?" he asked, nibbling on her earlobe.

Sighing, Lacy continued. "She said that you were also the most loyal of her children—the most trustworthy . . . hmmm, the most loving."

He laughed and lifted her into his arms. "I won't tell you what your sisters said about you."

"You can't believe everything you hear," Lacy said with a look of innocence.

"Where you're concerned, Mrs. Shepard, I'm inclined to believe only half of what I hear. I'm more encouraged to rely on what I see."

She grinned. "And what do you see, Mr. Shepard?"

"That's easy. I see a woman whom I love very much. I see a dream to call my own."

EPILOGUE

NEW YEAR'S EVE 1886

"To Belgrade, Montana! The best town in the territory!" a well-dressed man declared. People all around the room held up glasses in a toast or else cheered their approval.

"I've never seen so many people gathered in one place," Lacy told her sisters. "There must be over three hundred."

"I heard it was over four," Beth countered. "Mrs. Lindquist told me that at least two hundred invitations had gone out." The music started up again and couples abandoned their toasting glasses and hurried to dance.

Gwen shook her head. "Thomas Quaw certainly knows how to throw a grand party. We'll be talking about this for years to come. Imagine hiring fifteen different bands and setting up separate places for dancing. Why, a person could be here and never even know who all had attended!"

Beth smoothed out the brown-and-blue plaid material of her skirt. "I can't figure out where in the world he found enough musicians."

Lacy spied Dave standing in the corner, talking to Hank. She was glad he'd been willing to take time away from the ranch to come celebrate. "Looks like our husbands are plotting and planning."

Following her gaze, Gwen nodded. "I heard Hank say that he and Nick were going to talk to Dave about some investment. Hank's become very good friends with Mr. Quaw, and the two of them have been discussing all manner of improvements for the town."

Lacy could well imagine. Hank had come into his element. The small town had grown rapidly, benefited by a natural gravel bed that ran between the East Gallatin and West Gallatin rivers. It made a much better foundation for buildings, and it also provided a great industry for those who didn't mind the hard quarry work. Beyond that, multiple farms had gone into the area—great news for some and a point of frustration for others. Ranchers were no longer able to be quite as free with their grazing land, but open range still prevailed.

Farmers found the area quite good for growing wheat, and this, in turn, brought a great deal of attention from Bozeman's founding fathers.

"Did you hear that we're going to get a telephone installed at Gallatin Hotel?" Gwen asked. "Hank says telephones will soon be the only way to communicate, all over the country. Every house will have one."

"I can't even begin to imagine," Lacy said. "Just a few years ago, we had to send someone riding for the doctor. Now you'll be able to simply call him as if he were in the next room."

"Oh look! There's Cubby," Beth said, pointing to the door.

"Who's the young lady at his side?" Lacy asked. The woman was quite lovely, with pale blond hair and finely arched brows.

"That's Betsy McCollum. She's the eldest daughter of a family that moved here just a few weeks ago. They stayed a couple of days at the hotel until they could make arrangements for their house. Her father is a dentist."

"Cubby certainly seems taken with her," Lacy mused. The boy had grown into a handsome man.

"He is," Gwen agreed, "but she's just as taken with him. If I believed in love at first sight, I'd say that we have a bona fide case of it here."

Lacy laughed. "Love at first sight, eh? As I recall, love had to beat each one of us over the head and hog-tie us before we'd see it for what it was."

Beth laughed and began to sway as the music started up once again. "I don't know about you ladies, but I want to dance." She threw her sisters a smile before heading off in search of her husband. "Happy New Year, by the way."

"Happy New Year!"

Lacy had never cared for large gatherings, and this party seemed to be expanding by the hour. The plan had been to furnish food and dancing all night. Rumor had it that Quaw had made it clear the party wouldn't break up until everyone tired of the festivities and headed home.

She stepped outside and took a deep breath of the cold air. Lights blazed all over town in celebration of the new year. Hugging her arms around her body, Lacy marveled at the changes she'd seen in the last few years. Nothing had remained the same. Hamilton had moved their small town to intercept the railroad tracks, some eight miles to the west, and renamed their community Moreland. Farther west, the small community of Canyon House burst to life and called itself Logan after the railroad set up business with a roundhouse and homes for their company officials. It seemed with growth and innovation, a fresh naming was required. It was rather like being born anew.

"I thought I saw you slip out here."

Lacy turned to face Dave. "Too many people to suit me."

He smiled. "I know where there's a quiet room, just for two."

She looked back at the building as someone struck up "Cotton-Eyed Joe" and several people let out yells. Rolling her eyes, she nodded. "I don't suppose we'll be missed."

Dave took hold of her arm and pulled her in step beside him. She liked the way they fit together. "So how do you suppose your folks are doing?"

Patience had volunteered to take on Gwen and Hank's three children, Beth and Nick's four boys, and Lacy and Dave's two-year-old son while everyone went to the celebration and stayed overnight in town.

"Hopefully they're all sleeping at this hour. I've never known my folks to stay up this late unless they were dealing with calves being born. I can't say I've ever really been given to it, either."

"I just hope that Thomas didn't give her any trouble. This is the first time we've been away from him for any length of time."

Dave gave her shoulders a squeeze. "Missing him, are you?"

She looked up and met his eyes. "Yes, but . . . I'm glad to have you to myself."

"I see. Does that mean you have plans for me?" He gave her a wicked grin.

"I do indeed, Mr. Shepard. I have plans for you that involve the rest of your life."

He let out a wild yell and pulled her into his arms, whirling her around in a circle. Lacy felt dizzy when he finally stopped and set her feet on the ground, but even dizzier when his mouth captured hers in a kiss.

Lacy shivered. She didn't know how she could have ever doubted loving this man.

"Are you cold?" he asked, pulling back. He started to take off his coat.

She grinned and shook her head. "Not in the least."

He looked at her in mock surprise and pretended to be exasperated. "You are quite a handful, Lacene Gallatin Shepard. I honestly don't know what I'm going to do with you."

Laughing, she let go of him and headed across the street. She looked back over her shoulder. "I'm sure you'll figure it out, Mr. Shepard."